'What I'm tr

made a pact
any relation:
a man.'

'Ever?' Travis asked, astounded.

Cori's eyes darted over his entire face before she said, 'Well, someday. After a wedding ceremony. On the honeymoon.'

'The honeymoon?' he bellowed.

'Believe me,' she said quickly, 'this in no way means I'm trying to force anyone to marry me. I stopped looking for a husband a long time ago. I'm just trying to explain that I can't...that you and I can't...that I won't...'

Suddenly Travis knew exactly what Cori was trying to say. She wasn't telling him that this wasn't the right time in their relationship to make love. She wasn't talking about a matter of a few days or weeks or even months. She was talking about...

Good God. Cori was talking about celibacy!

Dear Reader,

Spring is in full swing and so is Special Edition™, with a very special line-up!

We begin this month with our THAT'S MY BABY! title for April. It's *Of Texas Ladies, Cowboys...and Babies* by Jodi O'Donnell, where Glenna Dunn, a young and graceful grandmother-to-be is shocked to find herself pregnant! Graham, in *The Case of the Maybe Babies* by Victoria Pade is just as shocked to discover that someone has abandoned two babies in his bedroom—and apparently he's the dad! So, he calls in Lindsey Strummel of STRUMMEL INVESTIGATIONS...

Cori Cassidy finds it extremely difficult to resist temptation in *Not Before Marriage!* from Sandra Steffen, and three little girls get up to some serious matchmaking in *Thank Heaven for Little Girls*; the first of a great new mini-series, CUPID'S LITTLE HELPERS, by Tracy Sinclair. Look out for the next one, on the shelves in June.

Rounding off April's fantastic selection are *Keeping Kate* by Pat Warren, the last of her REUNION novels, where Kate at last finds her long-lost brother and sister, and *In a Family Way*, the first book from a talented new writer. Julia Mozingo weaves an emotional tale using both amnesia and the 'secret baby' theme—a stunning combination!

All the best,

The Editors

Not Before Marriage!

SANDRA STEFFEN

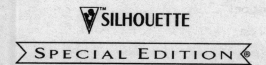

SILHOUETTE

SPECIAL EDITION

*Silhouette, Silhouette Special Edition and Colophon are
registered trademarks of Harlequin Books S.A., used under licence.*

*First published in Great Britain 1997
Silhouette Books, Eton House, 18-24 Paradise Road,
Richmond, Surrey TW9 1SR*

© Sandra E. Steffen 1996

ISBN 0 373 24061 9

23-9704

*Printed and bound in Great Britain
by Mackays of Chatham PLC, Chatham*

SANDRA STEFFEN

Creating memorable characters is one of Sandra's favourite
aspects of writing. She's always been a romantic and is
thrilled to be able to spend her days doing what she loves—
bringing her characters to life on her computer screen.

Sandra grew up in Michigan, the fourth of ten children, all
of whom have taken the old adage "Go forth and multiply"
quite literally. Add to this her husband, who is her real-life
hero, their four school-age sons who keep their lives in
constant motion, their gigantic cat, Percy, and her wonderful friends, in-laws and neighbours, and what do you get?
Chaos, of course, but also a wonderful sense of belonging
she wouldn't trade for the world.

Another novel by Sandra Steffen

Silhouette Desire®

Gift Wrapped Dad

THE MARRIAGE PACT

We the undersigned mother and daughter (and this was all Mum's idea!) do hereby declare not to consummate any relationship without first obtaining a licence of marriage. (In other words: There will be no wedding night without a wedding ring!)

Prospective partners will be screened for sincerity, faithfulness and the willingness to commit to happily-ever-after. If chosen party does not comply with the terms stated within The Marriage Pact, said party will be given the heave-ho.*

Signed:

X Corinna Cassidy, Mum

Corinna Cassidy

X Allison Cassidy, Daughter

Allison Cassidy

*Note that this stipulation is subject to change depending on the irresistibility of the man.

Chapter One

Travis Delaney moved a coffee cup aside and studied the blueprint spread out on his cluttered desk. He glanced up when the door opened, and muttered under his breath when the phone rang. Braden Calhoun, his friend and business partner in Northwood Builders, sauntered into the office and hiked one work boot onto a vinyl chair.

Minutes later Travis dropped the phone into its cradle and grumbled, "This is the last time we let Claudia take a vacation, agreed?"

Braden chuckled. "I'll let you be the one to tell her."

Travis's eyes shifted back to the blueprint. Chaos always erupted when their middle-aged secretary was away, and this week had been no exception. The air-conditioning was on the fritz, one of their best carpenters had fallen off a scaffolding and broken his right arm, they had yet to figure out Claudia's filing system, and the phone hadn't stopped ringing since eight o'clock Monday morning.

He opened his mouth to speak, only to clamp it shut again when the horrendous beeping sound of a dump truck backing up split the air from outside the open window. Braden dropped his foot to the floor and stretched lazily.

"Thank God it's Friday, huh?" he asked. "Pete and I are going to check out that new nightclub downtown tonight. It's supposed to be the hottest spot in Madison. Why don't you come along? It's probably just what you need to help you out of your mid-life crisis."

Travis clenched his teeth and folded the blueprint into a neat square. "How many times do I have to tell you? I'm not going through a mid-life crisis. I'm just in a little slump, that's all."

"Sure you are, and bears sleep in pajamas and this *slump* has nothing to do with the fact that your thirty-ninth birthday is only a few weeks away."

Travis didn't even bother scowling; his best friend was immune. Rising to his feet, he said, "Times like these, I don't know why I ever followed you home when we were kids, Calhoun. I sure as hell don't know why I stayed."

Braden chuckled out loud and said, "Sure you do."

A series of raucous catcalls and wolf whistles rent the air. Braden ambled over to the window and let out a long, quiet whistle of his own. "Now there's what you need to get you over your mid-life *slump*."

Travis rounded the desk and glanced out the window. A young woman was doing her best to skirt a group of workers who were putting in new curbs across the street. Most of the men were looking at her, and a few were making out-and-out nuisances of themselves.

"Guys like that give all construction workers a bad name," Travis grumbled.

"You aren't supposed to be looking at the guys."

Braden grinned and Travis swore under his breath. The truth of the matter was, he could hardly take his eyes off the young woman. From here, everything about her looked golden—her long, straight hair, her skirt and matching top, even the warm color of her skin.

"She looks awfully young," he said quietly.

It was Braden's turn to sputter under his breath. "For crying out loud, Delaney. As long as she's over twenty-one, she isn't too young."

"How old do you think she is?" Travis asked.

"I don't know. Twenty-two, twenty-three, maybe."

When she disappeared inside the dry cleaner's, Braden turned away from the window and said, "There will probably be a hundred women just like her at Roxy's tonight. If you won't come with me for yourself, do it for the guys in the crew. They've been tiptoeing around you for weeks and are starting to complain. What do you say?"

Travis pretended to think about it for a few seconds then shook his head. Braden left soon after, muttering about stubborn streaks and mid-life crises. Travis knew he should leave, too. But he stayed at the window, thinking.

He had to admit, thirty-nine sounded like a horrendous age to be. That's how old Braden's Uncle Artie had been when he'd started wearing black socks with his sandals and plaid Bermuda shorts. It was also the age his father had been when he'd finally left for good. Not that *that* had anything to do with anything.

His friend was convinced that Travis was going through a mid-life crisis. Although he wasn't looking forward to his thirty-ninth birthday, Travis hadn't told Braden the real reason he'd been barking everyone's head off lately. It had all started a month ago when he'd run into a guy who used to know his old man. Travis supposed that in a county of over three hundred thousand people, it was bound to happen sooner or later, but he hadn't been prepared for the old sense of anxiety and dread that had slipped inside him that day.

Bub Dooley was an overaged biker who'd come to the house a couple of times when Travis was a kid. Bub's hair was longer than it used to be, his arms beefier, his motor-cycle newer. Other than that, he was the same as Travis remembered. He thought he'd buried any hard feelings he'd had for either of his parents a long time ago, but something Bub said had hit home.

"You're the spittin' image of your old man. You look like him, walk like him, talk like him, you lucky dog. Last I heard, he was living in Ohio with a woman named Sue. He always was good with the ladies, and I'll bet you are, too."

Travis's stomach had turned, and it had nothing to do with the fact that Bub was missing a front tooth. The idea that Travis was *anything* like his old man had done that.

Across the street, the door of the dry cleaner's store opened and the golden-haired woman stepped onto the sidewalk. She looked both ways, as if trying to decide whether or not she wanted to go back through that mine field of men she'd passed on her way by.

He could see her back straighten with determination as she headed the way she had come. His own backbone straightened, too, his chest filling with a strange mixture of curiosity and admiration. She may be young, but she obviously had a lot of spunk.

Corinna Cassidy folded her dry cleaning over her arm and looked toward the men who were working a short distance away. She dreaded walking past them a second time, but she didn't have time to walk three blocks out of her way simply because a few men chose to ogle and leer. Allison would be getting hungry soon, and Cori hadn't even started supper. She took a deep breath and started down the street at a steady clip.

She made it past the first group without incident and was about to breathe a sigh of relief when the wolf whistles started all over again. She increased her pace, and had almost made it to her parked car when a shirtless man with the chest hair of an ape stepped into her path.

"Hey, baby, what's your hurry?"

She tried to skirt around him to the right, but the man took a quick step back and another to the side, effectively blocking her escape. She doubted that he posed any real danger on a busy street in downtown Madison, but nerves fluttered in her stomach just the same.

"I asked you a question," he taunted.

"I'm in a hurry," she answered, glancing nervously around.

Instead of taking the hint, he leaned closer and said, "In too big a hurry to tell me your name? That isn't very friendly. It's Friday, and I feel like partying, don't you?"

"Look, I um," she stammered, "don't want to cause any trouble. But I really do have to get home to my little..."

"Come on, honey," he cut in. "All I want to do is talk to you. I won't bite, unless you want me to."

The man's fingers snaked around her upper arm. Cori gasped, her trepidation turning to shivers of real fear. She tried to back away, but he held her firmly in place. She was about to open her mouth and scream at the top of her lungs when a voice came from behind her.

"Leave her alone."

It took a moment for the significance of those three little words to filter through her panic. She glanced behind her, catching a glimpse of another man with broad shoulders and brown eyes narrowed in warning.

"I said, leave her alone."

"Get lost, buddy. I saw her first."

Travis leveled his gaze at the greasy jerk and stepped ominously closer. He didn't know what he was going to do. He wasn't even sure how he'd ended up out here. One second he'd been staring out the window; the next he was halfway across the street.

Keeping his voice low, he said, "As far as I know, this is a public sidewalk."

The other man scowled in warning. Adrenaline surged through Travis's bloodstream, heating him from his chest to the tips of his fingers. It reminded him of all the fights he'd been in when he was a kid. Back then, he'd been so light on his feet the guys on the street had nicknamed him Lightning Delaney. It had been a long time since he'd used his fists to defend someone's name and honor, but he hadn't forgotten how.

With his shoulders squared and his elbows bent and ready, he met his opponent's stare and held his ground. The other man's eyes darted back and forth as if gauging Travis's bravery and stamina against his own.

Travis stood statue-still and ready. The other man raised his hands in a gesture of retreat, his beady little eyes sliding back to the young woman. "Baby, you don't know what kind of a chance you just passed up."

To Travis, he said, "Can't blame a guy for tryin'. Huh, buddy?"

Travis thought about telling the jerk that he was no buddy of his, but didn't want to waste his breath. He couldn't remember the last time he'd fought such a strong urge to flatten somebody's nose. Not trusting the man as far as he could throw him, he said, "Let the woman go and we'll forget this ever happened."

"Hey, Rex, get back to work," someone yelled from behind.

Other voices called similar orders. Travis paid little attention. He was aware that the woman had moved aside, but he didn't take his eyes from the man squaring off directly in front of him.

Experience and gut instinct warned Travis not to be fooled by the man's calm stance. A fist shot out. Travis moved fast, but not quite fast enough. Bony knuckles clipped his jaw. He staggered, but he stayed on his feet.

When the next punch came, he was ready. He jumped to the side like lightning, and brought his own fist up with a sharp hook.

The man's head jerked to the side. With a dazed expression, he keeled over backward.

Even as Cori forced her hands from her cheeks, everything seemed to be happening in slow motion. Two men half dragged and half carried the greasy-looking man away. The other man, the one who had stepped in on her behalf, was holding his fist.

She struggled to find her voice and finally asked, "Are you all right?"

He nodded, but she noticed that he was still rubbing his right hand.

"Are you hurt?" she asked.

"Nah. What about you?"

She meant to answer his question with a slow, steady smile, but her gaze caught on his mouth and the smile never made it to her lips. She'd never pretended to be a good judge of male character, but there was no denying the fact that she was innately drawn to the look deep in this man's dark eyes.

"Are you sure you're okay?" he repeated.

She blinked, trying to clear her mind of her wayward thoughts. She glanced at the red mark on his tanned jaw and finally said, "I'm fine, but I don't know how to thank you."

"Forget it," he answered.

"No, really, I don't know what I would have done if you hadn't stepped in," she confessed. "I'm afraid I've never been very good at telling a man no."

Travis looked down at the woman who had spoken, straight into the bluest eyes he'd ever seen. There was a faint spattering of golden freckles across her nose, and the hint of a self-mocking quirk on her lips. Taking a step closer, he said, "I'd say your message was loud and clear. It isn't your fault he didn't listen."

"That may be true," she said quietly, "but I still appreciate your intervention. I wish there was some way to repay you. I could buy you a drink."

For a man who almost never smiled, Travis had the strangest urge to do just that. A jackhammer burst on behind him, the sound covering the traffic on the street, not to mention his own thundering heartbeat. Feeling strangely buoyant, he said, "I hate to have to be the one to tell you this, but you barely look old enough to drink."

She pushed her hair behind her shoulders and said, "It's these freckles of mine. They've been the bane of my existence since I was twelve, but believe me, I'm older than I look."

He wondered what she meant by older. That she was closer to twenty-five than twenty-one? Suddenly, it didn't matter. Nothing did, except the glimmer in her eyes, and the flickering awareness deep in his body.

"I know what I can do to repay you," she said, suddenly rummaging through her small purse. The next thing he knew, she'd slipped a business card into his hand. With a butterfly touch, she curled his fingers over it, then gave him a whimsical smile that hit him right between the eyes.

"Thanks again for coming to my rescue. If you're ever in the neighborhood, I hope you'll stop in for breakfast. My treat."

With that, she turned, her long hair brushing his forearm, the material of her gauzy skirt trailing against the knees of his jeans. A kiss couldn't have left him more speechless.

"Wait!" he called. "I don't even know your name."

She turned at her car's door and smiled again. "Oh, you're right. My name's Cori Cassidy. What's yours?"

Travis wasn't sure how he managed to mutter his name. All he knew was that it hadn't been easy. Every male hormone in his body was on a rampage. His blood seemed to thicken and his heartbeat kicked into overdrive.

After she pulled away from the curb, he brought the card up for closer inspection. It was bordered with flowers in pink, rose, lavender and blue. In the center, intertwining gold letters spelled out Ivy's Garden. The words conjured up visions of paradise, of soft green fronds and fresh garden flowers, of long blond hair and long golden limbs wrapped around him. He wasn't sure why he brought the small card up to his nose, but as he inhaled the scent of lilacs and roses, the throbbing in his hand and jaw all but disappeared.

The sounds of jackhammers and street traffic barely registered in his mind because in his memory he could still hear the lilt in Cori Cassidy's sultry voice as she'd invited him to breakfast. He could still see the warm look in her eyes as she handed him that little card, and could still feel the gentle flutter in her fingertips when she placed it in his palm.

If you're ever in the neighborhood, I hope you'll stop in for breakfast. My treat.

Normally, he knew what a woman meant when she offered to fix him breakfast, because normally, the invitation was issued from a double bed. He didn't know what to make of such an invitation when it came without so much as a preliminary kiss.

Travis tucked the card into his pocket and turned to leave, suddenly incredibly hungry for breakfast—among other things.

The hinges on the antique mailbox creaked ever so slightly as Cori tucked her letter inside. Squinting against the bright sun, she closed her eyes. Her mind felt as wispy as the thin clouds in the Wisconsin sky, her thoughts on about a hundred different dreamy things. The aroma of the Peach Betty baking in the oven wafted to her nose.

Turning toward the smell, she opened the screen door and stepped into the inn's big old kitchen.

"You mailed another letter this year, didn't you?"

Cori jumped, one hand flying to her throat, the other to the screen door at her back. By the time her eyes began to adjust to the dimmer light in the kitchen, she saw the shadowy form of her friend standing on the other side of the big room, a stack of tablecloths in her hands. "Ivy, you nearly startled me out of my shoes."

"I'm sorry about that, but Cori honey, are you sure it's wise to send another letter?"

Emotions shimmered through Cori at the expression of worry in her dear friend's beautiful, wrinkled face. "Allison deserves to know her grandpa and grandma. Don't worry about me. I'll be fine."

Ivy made a clucking sound and shook her head. "Considering you're the daughter I never had, I can't help but worry. I hate what this does to you every year. Why, I can't tell you how many times I've thought about going to Green Bay myself and giving those people a piece of my mind."

Washing her hands at the deep porcelain sink, Cori said, "Until they're ready to forgive me, it wouldn't do any good. Now, would you like some help with those tablecloths?"

Ivy made a little sound at the back of her throat, blowing air out through her nose at the same time. "Only a fool would turn down an offer like that, and I'm no fool." With another huff, she pushed through the swinging door, taking her tablecloths and her dignity with her.

Cori dried her hands on a kitchen towel, listening to the swishing sound the door made as it swung into place, thinking about what Ivy had just said. Ivy Pennington was the dearest friend she'd ever had, but she didn't fully understand Cori's need to mail that letter every year. Sometimes, Cori didn't understand it herself. She only knew that it was something she had to do.

The older woman was already busy spreading a cloth on the farthest table when Cori entered the room. Late morning sunshine streamed through the lacy curtains, throwing intricate designs on a square of the old-fashioned carpet, spilling over onto the tables and their mismatched chairs nearby. Taking one of the pale yellow cloths from Ivy's stack, Cori shook it out, letting it billow down to the tabletop below.

"The O'Brians checked out of the Rose Room a little while ago," she said while she worked. "And the Donovans are packing their things in the Lilac Room right now. Everyone else has gone sight-seeing for the rest of the day, except Mrs. Abershankle, who's lying down with a bad headache. Anyway, I should have plenty of time to get those two rooms ready for our next guests."

Ivy nodded, and Cori smoothed another cloth on the next table as she said, "If I have time, I want to work in the garden later today."

Ivy made that sound again, the one that was a cross between a hum and a huff. This time she followed it up with a firm shake of her head. "Corinna, Corinna, Corinna. All you ever do is work. I saw you slip the books out of the office late yesterday. It was Saturday night, and how did you spend it? Working on our ledgers."

"I don't mind, Ivy. Besides, it looks as if we'll be able to afford at least some of the repairs this old house needs. If I'm not mistaken, this place is starting to show a profit."

"Humph. Weekends aren't for showing a profit. Weekends are for couples. According to Lisa and Jillian, you met a hunk when you were running errands Friday afternoon. You should have gotten his phone number and given him a call the first chance you got."

Cori couldn't help grinning at the way Ivy said *hunk*. When Travis Delaney's image flashed through her mind, she was glad her back was to her friend because Ivy would have noticed the way her grin changed to a dreamy smile. For some reason she wasn't ready to share these particular feelings with anyone. Her memories of Travis Delaney were too potent for her own peace of mind, her response to those memories too intense.

"Maybe you should go back to that street and see if you can find him," Ivy said. "Who knows, maybe you'll see him again...."

Cori only half listened as Ivy rattled on. She knew her friend would have been thrilled to learn that she'd invited a man to breakfast, but Cori was glad she hadn't mentioned it. After all, Travis hadn't come. She should know—she'd watched the door for his arrival two mornings in a row. She told herself she was lucky he hadn't shown up, lucky that she'd never see him again. For some reason, it felt like bad luck. That fact alone concerned her, but what worried her even more was the heat that had gathered deep inside her when she'd looked into his eyes that day. It scared her, because it brought out yearnings she thought she'd put behind her a long time ago, yearnings she had no intention of giving in to again.

"...and the next time you see him, buy him a soda. Why, you could even..."

"I'm not planning to go back to that street, Ivy. It was just a fluke that I met him in the first place. I'm sure I'll never see him again."

Changing the subject, Cori said, "Did I tell you that every room is booked for the next two weeks?"

It took her a moment to realize that Ivy had grown quiet. Smoothing a wrinkle from the last tablecloth, she said, "What's the matter, Ivy? Cat got your tongue?"

Ivy's answer was a long time coming. When she did finally speak, it was in a voice Cori hardly recognized. "I've never seen a cat this big before."

"What are you talking about?" Cori asked, wondering at her friend's strange answer. "Ivy?"

When Ivy didn't answer, Cori glanced over her shoulder, straight into Travis Delaney's dark brown eyes.

Chapter Two

Cori's mind wasn't playing tricks on her. This wasn't an aberration or a mirage. Travis Delaney really was looking at her from the other side of this very room. She knew she should say something, but standing there with her back against a high-backed chair, all she could do was stare.

He was incredibly good-looking—she'd noticed that on Friday—but she'd come across good-looking men before and none of them had caused her heart to lodge in her throat, leaving her speechless. Besides, the cut of his dark hair wasn't so unusual. Neither was the somewhat stubborn angle of his chin. And it wasn't uncommon to see a man with a good tan in June, just as his blue cotton shirt and pleated navy slacks weren't much different than a thousand other men's Sunday attire. So why did the breeze wafting through the open window suddenly grow ten degrees warmer?

"Hello, Cori."

The tone of his voice led her to believe that he was very aware of her struggle to recapture her composure. If he really wanted to help, he'd stop looking at her as if he was thinking very seriously about doing more than look.

After answering his greeting with a simple "Hi," she happened to glance at Ivy, whose thin eyebrows were raised curiously. The expression on her friend's face finally brought Cori to her senses. She took a careful breath and said, "Ivy, this is Travis Delaney. Travis, this is my dearest, and sometimes darnedest friend, Ivy Pennington."

Ivy stepped closer, smoothing her hands down the front of her ruffled apron. "Ah, yes. Travis. That's a fine name. It means 'at the crossroads,' you know. Would you say you've reached that point in your life? Never mind about that for now. Just let me look at you." Eyeing him up and down, she added, "So, you're the hunk Cori met the other day."

Suddenly, Travis felt the way he did when a tailor was measuring his inseam, a little afraid to move, and a little afraid not to. Casting a look at Cori, he asked, "You mentioned that we met?"

Cori shrugged, but the older lady declared, "As a matter of fact, Corinna here didn't breathe a word about what happened, not a single word. She happened to mention the trouble she had to two of her friends. It was Lisa and Jillian who told me about the man who was giving her a hard time and some hunk—it appears that would be you—who stepped in to help."

Travis tried not to grimace, but it wasn't easy. Finding out that Cori hadn't mentioned him to her "dearest and darnedest friend" wasn't easy to swallow. Especially since *he'd* picked up *her* business card so often it was getting worn around the edges.

He'd never doubted that he would come here to see her. The only question had been *when*. He'd tried to hold out long enough to keep from looking overanxious, but it hadn't been easy. When he couldn't get her out of his mind last night and again this morning, he knew he'd reached his limit. And here he was.

"Ivy, I'm pretty sure the Donovans will be ready to check out any minute."

He didn't miss the heavy hint behind Cori's words or the look she gave her friend. As a matter of fact, nothing about *Corinna* escaped him. Today she was wearing a sleeveless summer blouse tucked into the waistband of an airy-looking skirt that stopped just inches above her white canvas shoes. The golden freckles across the bridge of her nose looked every bit as faint and delicate as they had a few nights ago, but here against the backdrop of linen tablecloths, old-fashioned wallpaper and billowing lace curtains, there was a maturity deep in her eyes he hadn't noticed before.

Ivy moved, breaking the lock Travis had on Cori's gaze. The older woman made a strange, nasally kind of sound, then grinned and said, "I think I'll go on out to the front desk and get the Donovans checked out. It was nice meeting you, Travis, real nice."

With the creak of orthopedic shoes and the flutter of apron strings, she left the room. Travis raised one eyebrow and stepped around a square table, his hands automatically settling to the back of the chair in his path. "My name means 'at the crossroads'?"

The beginnings of a smile pulled at Cori's lips as she said, "Ivy claims it's a gift, but she knows the meaning of practically everyone's name."

Watching her walk steadily closer, Travis squeezed the back of the chair beneath his palms, feeling the rest of his body tighten with every step she took. "What does your name mean?" he asked quietly.

The way she rolled her eyes made Travis wonder if she was going to tell him. She stopped several feet away, crossed her arms and shifted her weight to one foot before finally saying, "You aren't going to believe this, but Corinna means 'maiden.' It's dumb, I know."

"You think 'maiden' is worse than 'at the crossroads'?"

She laughed, a rich sound that was marvelous and so darn uninhibited it took his breath away. Something intense flared through him, followed by an almost overwhelming need to move closer to her. Since he doubted that she was ready to be swept into his arms, he glanced around the room and said, "It looks like I'm too late for that breakfast you promised me."

Her eyebrows went up a moment before she turned in a half circle, gesturing toward another door. "All our guests have already eaten, but I'd be happy to fix you a plate."

He watched her hair and skirt swish into place, and once again breakfast was the last thing on his mind. Drawing an unsteady breath, he said, "I think I'll take a rain check. For now, would you show me the inn?"

Her features became more animated. Her eyes sparkled and her hands spread wide. "You've just hit upon one of my favorite topics. Come on, I'll give you a guided tour, but I have to warn you, I've been known to go on and on and on, so stop me if you get bored."

"I don't see how any man in his right mind would ever want to stop you from going on and on."

Slowly, Cori's arms lowered to her sides. The words he'd spoken might have been as innocent as could be, but the way his voice had dipped, low and husky, painted another picture entirely. She was already far too aware of the outdoorsy scent of this man's after-shave, of the way his fingers were toying with the back of the chair, and of the way her mind was toying with her senses.

After studying him for a long moment, she said, "The last thing I should do after hearing a comment like that is take you upstairs."

For a span of at least five seconds, he looked back at her. Then he shrugged one shoulder and said, "This wouldn't be the first time my mouth has gotten me in trouble. A friend of mine claims it's going to be the death of me someday. It wouldn't surprise me if he turned out to be right. It wouldn't surprise me if you asked me to leave, either. My ego's been taking a beating lately."

She wished he hadn't mentioned his mouth. Now that he had, she was having a difficult time looking anyplace else, especially when he began talking again. "I wouldn't blame you if you told me to go, Cori, but I have to tell you, I'd be undeniably disappointed."

With that, he picked up the misplaced chair and effortlessly slid it to a nearby table. He faced her, the space between them filled with emotions that swirled every bit as much as the breeze fluttering through the curtains.

"So, Cori, what do you think?"

What did she think? She *thought* she liked the way he moved, strong-limbed and easy, but she liked the slow smile he gave her even more because she had a feeling that Travis Delaney didn't smile very often. She couldn't help remembering the way he'd looked standing on that sidewalk Friday afternoon, one side of his face red. He certainly hadn't been smiling then.

A long time ago she'd learned what happened when a spark of attraction was allowed to burn out of control, but she didn't see what harm could come from showing this enigmatic man with the purple bruise on his jaw, and the invisible one on his ego, around her inn.

With that decision made, she glanced at the watch on her wrist and started for the door. "You're in luck. The next tour is about to begin."

Travis didn't realize he'd been holding his breath until it rushed out of him all at once. He knew he'd been pushing it with that innuendo about going on and on. That was why he wouldn't have been surprised if Cori had shown him the door, but damn, he was glad she hadn't.

Following her around tables topped with pale yellow cloths, he listened to every word she said. "Since you came in through the front door, you've already seen the guests' sitting room and the open stairway leading to the second floor. Come this way, and I'll show you the kitchen where Ivy prepares her specialties like Fidget Pie and Peach Betty and Gilded Apples."

They entered a big square room that had a deep sink, an old-fashioned oven and pots and pans hanging from hooks overhead. When she gestured to a closed door, which she explained led to the small apartment where Ivy lived, he asked, "Does Ivy own the inn?"

"Actually, we own it together. Her late husband, Baxter, bought it for a song fifty years ago, long after the doctors and attorneys who once lived on this street had moved to new houses in more elite neighborhoods. Ivy and Baxter were newlyweds and had planned to fill all its bedrooms with children. When the babies never came and heating costs rose, Baxter partitioned the back part of the house into an apartment for them and closed off the rest of the rooms.

"After Baxter died, Ivy began to take in boarders to make ends meet. I stayed in one of the rooms. By then the entire house was in need of repair, but I still fell in love with it. Ivy and I both envisioned it as a bed-and-breakfast so we scrimped and saved to buy paint for the exterior. We hired someone to replace the roof, but we did most of the other work ourselves. A couple of my friends helped whenever they could. We scrubbed and sanded the floors, and painted and papered the ceilings and walls. We found wonderful old furniture at garage sales and auctions, and well, like they say, the rest is history. Ivy's Garden was born. Ivy said it was my dream as much as hers, so she put my name next to hers on the deed."

Someone else might not have heard the almost imperceptible note of loyalty and appreciation in Cori's voice when she spoke of Ivy Pennington. Although he didn't know the story behind those emotions, he did know that a person didn't acquire that particular combination without being knocked around by life. Friday he'd sensed that there was more to Cori Cassidy than golden freckles and a perfectly proportioned feminine body. Now he was sure of it, and even more intrigued.

"Come on," she said, starting up a narrow back stairway. "The inn has eight bedrooms for guests. Two on the first floor, four on the second, and two more on the third. Only the Rose and Lilac rooms are unoccupied right now, but I'll show you those if you'd like."

Since the steps were too narrow to walk side by side, he followed her up, listening to a story of how she and someone named Jillian had dropped an antique headboard down an entire flight of stairs the week before the inn opened for business. Before he and Cori reached the top, Travis was sure he was smiling at the picture she portrayed of herself and her friend.

They emerged onto a narrow landing that stretched down the center of the second level. An ivy green sofa, the color at the heart of every room he'd seen so far, was tucked into an alcove along one side of the hall where the wall slanted beneath another stairway. Running her hand along a long crack in the plaster, she said, "One thing about old houses is that the repairs are never-ending. Ivy's Garden has slowly climbed out of the red, and it's a good thing, because there are some things we absolutely have to fix this summer."

"What sorts of things?" he asked, falling into step beside her.

"Well, that crack in the plaster, for one, and the floor in one of the bathrooms, for another. A couple of the shutters on the second- and third-story windows are loose, a few doorknobs stick, and the back porch is sagging. If there's any money left, I want to have a gazebo built in the gardens," she said, turning a crystal knob on the second door they came to.

She pushed the raised-panel door to the wall, and Travis had his first glimpse of a room where lilacs in full bloom adorned wallpapered walls, and dried flowers and straw hats hung from pegs near the ceiling. He walked on in, the soles of his shoes thudding softly on the whitewashed wooden floor.

The house was a relic, but as he smoothed his hand over a piece of old-fashioned molding above the door, he couldn't help being impressed with how well it had been cared for. "This trim has to be at least a hundred years old," he said quietly.

"A hundred and twenty-five. Are you familiar with old houses?" she asked. Leaving the door wide open, she strode inside, closing a dresser drawer and straightening a hand-crocheted doily.

He was all set to answer her question when his gaze fell to the toe of her shoe as she smoothed it over the edge of an ivy green rug. Whatever he'd been about to say caught in his throat, along with his breath. His gaze climbed higher, over the narrow ridge of her knee visible beneath the thin fabric of her skirt, upward over the smooth line of her thigh. He had a sudden burning desire to cover her knee with his hand then follow her leg all the way up to the curve of her hip, and down again to the inside where her skin would be soft and supple.

He swallowed tightly and forced his feet to remain planted where they were. It took incredible concentration to ignore the desire surging deep inside him, and even more to gather his thoughts.

She'd asked him something, but what? After an interminable moment, his mind cleared enough for him to recall her question. *Are you familiar with old houses?* He was familiar with them, all right, but what he really wanted was to become more familiar with her. It was probably a good thing a board creaked beneath his right foot as he strode closer. The sound helped bring him to his senses.

Stopping next to her, he said, "My friend Braden and I started our own construction business ten years ago."

"Then you build houses?" she asked.

He nodded. "Now we do. In fact, these last several years we've worked exclusively on new houses, but when we were first getting started, we remodeled our share of these old beauties. Our company is called Northwood Builders. I came up with the name. You wouldn't believe some of the things Braden wanted to call it. I keep telling him I'm the brains *and* the brawn behind our operation. It's my favorite way to needle him."

"How does he react to your needling?" she asked.

"By getting in a shot of his own every chance he gets. Lately he's been telling everyone that I'm going through a mid-life crisis. One of these days I'm going to get even."

"Are you?" she asked. "Going through a mid-life crisis, I mean."

Travis watched as she smoothed her hand across the white wrought-iron bed frame where a sleep-rumpled comforter in muted shades of purple hung half on and half off the mattress. Her fingers were long and tapered, and slowly followed an S-pattern over the smooth surface. Unable to look away, he became increasingly aware that they were the only two people in the room, the only two people on the entire floor.

Clearing his throat, he said, "I may have been experiencing a little slump these past few weeks, but I've been feeling younger by the minute ever since I set foot inside this room."

She stopped suddenly, looking up at him. He was pretty sure the sudden stiffness in her posture had as much to do with finding herself shoulder-to-shoulder with him at the foot of an unmade bed as with his huskily spoken words. Regardless of the reason, he knew what he saw in the depths of her eyes. She wanted him. It wasn't a revelation that came to his mind, but to his body, because deep in the center of him, he wanted her, too. The difference was, Travis wanted to turn her into his arms and fall with her to the bed, and *she* seemed to be doing everything in her power to resist the attraction between them.

His sharp intake of breath was at odds with the gentle swirl of the breeze as it trifled with the curtains at the open window. He tried to focus on the lace-tipped shade, but it wasn't easy. Cori was so close and the bed was so inviting. His body was at war with his integrity. After interminable seconds, it became apparent that his integrity was winning. He didn't know whether to be proud or disappointed.

Sliding one hand into his pocket, he pretended to study the furnishings in the room and tried to come up with a topic of conversation that wouldn't lead to hazy thoughts and thick desires. "You mentioned the Lilac Room and the Rose Room. What do you call the other rooms in your inn?"

He knew his voice was low, but he couldn't help it. That was where his thoughts had pooled. It was going to take more than a little distance between him and Cori to get his mind back above his neck where it belonged.

Cori nearly sighed out loud when Travis moved to the other side of the bed. Maybe it hadn't been a wise decision to show him the inn. Maybe there was no maybe about it.

You're weak of the flesh, Corinna. Weak. You've made your bed, now lie in it. Even after all this time, the memory of her mother's words hurt as deeply as if she'd uttered them only yesterday.

Taking advantage of his sudden preoccupation with the antique dresser across the room, she strode to the door where she finally said, "We call the other rooms on this floor the Apple Blossom Room, the Oz Room, and the Buttercup Room. The two downstairs are the Marigold Room and the Daisy Room."

He turned around slowly and asked, "The Oz Room?"

"It's decorated with poppies. You know, like the poppies Dorothy fell asleep in in *The Wizard Of Oz*. We couldn't very well call it the Poppy Room. That made it sound like only grandpas could stay in it. So we called it the Oz Room, and everyone loves it, even the kids."

"Which one is your favorite?" he asked.

For a long moment, Cori didn't say anything. He'd looked at her this way when she first saw him standing in the dining room downstairs, as if he was thinking about doing a lot more than just look. The light in his eyes told her that he knew darned well what he did to her. And there wasn't a hint of guilt anywhere, not in the curve of his lips, not in the lofty tilt of his chin, certainly not in the confident set of his shoulders or the way his hands rested lightly on his hips. She wanted him. And he knew it. Bother the man!

Suddenly, her dormant wits renewed themselves. *You're not weak,* she told herself, at least not anymore. Determination washed over her, lifting her chin, not to mention her confidence. Sending him an insolent look to rival his, she said, "My favorite room would have to be the Morning Glory Room on the third floor."

"Is that floor as empty as this one?" he asked, slowly drawing closer.

Now that her self-confidence was back, his slow, steady approach failed to fluster her. She pushed her hair behind her shoulders and stepped into the hall. With a mild shake of her head, she said, "Mrs. Abershankle, one of the guests, is in bed with a headache in the Morning Glory Room. I can show you the Rose Room, as long as you promise to..."

"Behave?"

That one little word slowed her steps.

"Be good?"

Those two stopped her in her tracks. Despite her resolve not to allow it, heat coursed through her body, shimmering into strategic places along the way. She turned around slowly and faced him.

With one hand on his hip and the other in his pocket, he took another step and slowly said, "Believe me, Cori, I'd promise to do everything in my power to be good."

The man was already good. Too good.

Crossing her arms at her ribs, she tilted her head and said, "I was going to show you if you promised to be quiet."

"Does that mean I don't have to behave?"

Cori fought the urge to grin, and lost. Gazing at the anything-but-innocent expression on his face, she couldn't help it. She couldn't remember the last time she'd spent time with a man who could make her laugh and blush in the same breath.

Without giving him any warning, she did a neat little U-turn in the middle of the hall and said, "On second thought, I think I'll show you the gardens instead. Come on, a breath of fresh air will do us both good."

Travis stopped abruptly and turned around, thinking that Cori *was* a breath of fresh air. He would have told her so, if she hadn't been halfway to the other end of the hall by the time he came out of his befuddled state. Although he was disappointed that she wasn't going to show him the secluded third floor, he couldn't help but admire her pluck.

Everything about this woman drew him. And it had as much to do with what was on the inside of her mind as the way her hips moved underneath her summer skirt. He'd never been so completely captivated or utterly entranced by a woman he'd just met, had never been so certain that he wanted to get to know her better—a lot better.

By the time he caught up with her by the back door, his heart was beating hard and his breathing was deep. And it wasn't from hurrying down the stairs. His galloping pulse rate didn't diminish as they walked out the door, down two steps, and along a winding path made out of beautiful old flagstones. Neither did his certainty that she was as aware of the attraction between them as he was.

He tried to listen as she gestured toward what she called "the perfect place to build a gazebo," then pointed to roses and hollyhocks and daisies and about a hundred other kinds of flowers he couldn't name. He vividly recalled the fantasy he'd had when Cori had placed her business card in his hand Friday night. At the time, Ivy's Garden had conjured up images of soft green fronds and fresh garden flowers, of long blond hair and long golden legs wrapped around him. In this case, three out of four simply wasn't enough. He wanted the last part of his fantasy so bad he ached.

The sun shone overhead and birds sang from the rooftops and trees. It was a beautiful day to be outdoors. Travis had a burning wish to forget about the sunshine, to take Cori's hand and retrace their steps over the curving garden path, through the back door and up two flights of stairs to a shadowy, secluded room. Once the door was closed, he was certain they wouldn't talk about flowers. They wouldn't talk at all.

He clamped his mouth shut and did his best to ignore his erotic fantasy. Even so, trying to carry on an intelligent conversation was becoming more difficult by the second.

"We're almost to the end of the property. See that lilac hedge?" she asked. "It marks the northern border of Ivy's Garden. That hundred-year-old oak tree over there..."

"Have dinner with me tonight."

"...is smack-dab in the middle of the lot line on the western border. Of course, it was on one side or the other when it was planted, but now it's grown so big," she continued as if he hadn't spoken.

Travis studied her thoughtfully. God, the woman was smooth, and so steadfast and determined he would have been in awe, if he hadn't been so aware of her sultry voice and the effect it was having on his body. She'd heard him the first time he'd asked her to have dinner with him, and the second and third. Although she hadn't said a word about his requests, her eyes gave her away.

"I know what you're doing," he said quietly.

Travis's voice was deep-timbred and so husky Cori could practically hear its sensuous echo in the wind high in the trees. They'd reached the end of the flagstone walkway, and she had reached the last of her diversions.

He stepped directly in front of her, leaving her with no place to look except at the width of his shoulders and the column of his neck where his blue shirt lay open against his tanned skin. The man was extremely persistent. She knew she should have simply told him no and meant it. Why was it so difficult for her to do that?

"You've been ignoring my invitations to dinner," he said with quiet emphasis.

She didn't see much point in feigning innocence, and she wasn't about to lie. Pushing a strand of hair out of her eyes, she looked up at him and simply said, "Yes."

His eye brows rose fractionally. By the time they lowered again, a reckless light flickered in his eyes.

In a voice barely above a whisper, he said, "Ignore this."

His hands cupped her shoulders, slowly drawing her near. Watching his face come steadily closer, she was struck with wonder. She'd known this was going to happen since the moment she'd seen him standing across the dining room less than an hour ago. She'd tried to tell herself she could stop it. Now she knew she wouldn't. She'd tried to tell herself that she wasn't so weak that she couldn't show Travis her inn without going all warm and breathless. But she did feel unusually warm and her breathing *was* shallow. Good heavens, hadn't she learned anything about restraint?

Evidently not.

"The way I'm feeling, Cori... It's all because of you. Only you."

She went willingly into his arms. He didn't have to raise her chin; she did that on her own. He didn't have to draw her into his embrace; she swayed closer the instant his mouth touched hers. Rays of golden sunlight shimmered through her closed eyelids. Or maybe it was another kind of light, one that was radiating from within.

Her lips parted under his, his kiss hot and demanding and exciting. She gave in to it with the thirst of a woman a long time denied. Their mouths broke apart only long enough to drag in soul-drenching breaths of air, then clung together again more fiercely and needily than before.

Her hands found their way to his chest, her fingers spreading wide before gliding to his back. She wasn't surprised at her own response. She wasn't even surprised when his hands left her shoulders, smoothing down the sides of her waist, kneading her flesh, cupping the curve of her backside and drawing her ever closer to the hard length of him.

A groan escaped her at the intimate invitation. Everything about him felt wonderful, the strength of his hands molding her closer, the contour of his chest, the flatness of his stomach, even the scent of his after-shave. She reacted to every one of those things, undeniably wanton, unbelievably responsive.

When she groaned a second time, he captured the sound in his own mouth. The kiss deepened, spinning away out of control. His breathing mingled with hers, almost as much a part of the garden as the songs of birds high in the trees and the breeze fluttering through leaves, whispering in a language all its own.

Somewhere, a car honked its horn. On the other side of the lilac hedge, a door slammed, a girl giggled and a boy's deep voice answered with laughter. All those sounds seemed hazy and far away compared to the echo of Travis's deep breathing and her own thundering heart.

"Mom?"

A thread of reality filtered through Cori at the sound of that young voice. She dragged her mouth away from his, her entire body tensing.

"Mom? Are you out there?"

Good heavens, that was Allison's voice.

Cori yanked her mouth away from Travis's and tore herself from his chest. When his hands fell from her waist, she straightened her hair and clothes with shaky fingers. Taking a shuddering breath, she strode the remaining distance to the edge of the neat lilac hedge.

She knew that Travis was watching her, but she couldn't look at him. Her blood was still thundering through her body, making her feel pale and strangely weak in the knees. Pasting on a smile, she somehow managed to find her voice.

"I'm here, Allison. I'm right here."

Chapter Three

Travis surfaced more slowly than Cori did. Still in the throes of a strong passion, he was having a difficult time gathering his wits. He stayed in a narrow strip of shade near the lilac bushes, out of sight. From this position, all he could go by was sound, and from the sound of things, Cori was talking to a girl who called her Mom.

The wanton woman he'd held in his arms seconds ago was someone's mother?

His thoughts jumbled all over again. Before he could make sense of the situation, a girl's dreamy voice carried to his ears. "Ross and I are going to Lake Mendota for the afternoon. We thought we'd walk the trails and then go swimming."

"Okay," Cori answered. "Have fun, you two. And try not to get sunburned."

"We won't. I have the sunscreen right here. 'Bye, Mom."

"'Bye, honey. Drive carefully, Ross."

"Yes, Miz Cassidy."

A few moments later, Travis stepped out of the shadows. A girl with hair a shade lighter than Cori's was strolling hand in hand down the driveway with a boy wearing a black muscle shirt, his baseball cap plunked onto his head backward.

"That's your daughter?" he asked softly.

Watching them walk away, she nodded. "Her name is Allison. She's sixteen."

"Tell me you weren't seven years old when she was born."

"You're off by ten years," she answered, a strange expression on her face.

Doing some quick mental math, he said, "You don't look thirty-three."

"I told you I'm older than I look."

So she did. "Who's the boy?"

"Ross Gentry. He's a nice enough kid, but the way he looks at her worries me," she answered.

"Why's that?" he asked, striding ever closer.

"Because he's seventeen."

"Ah," Travis said with a dawning note of understanding.

"And because, just now, Allison had the dreamy look of a girl who's just been thoroughly kissed."

Travis took the remaining few steps separating them, his voice dipping low all over again. "So do you."

His simple statement brought her head up with a start. Now that he had her attention, he traced her cheekbone with one finger and smoothed a lock of hair off her forehead. His gaze roamed her entire face, finally homing in on her mouth. Tipping his head toward the small house nearby, he asked, "Is that cottage part of Ivy's Garden?"

She nodded slowly. "At one time it was used as a guest house. Now Allison and I live here."

Travis digested the information, trying to focus on the fact that he was undeniably attracted to a woman who had a sixteen-year-old daughter. Somehow, the significance faded next to his need to touch her all over again. Glancing from Cori's dark blue eyes to the cottage and back again, he whispered, "Invite me inside."

She didn't move a muscle, but he saw the negative answer in her eyes. Trying again, he said, "Then have dinner with me. Right now or tonight. It doesn't matter when."

"I can't."

He studied her thoughtfully for a moment. She'd said "I can't." Not "I don't want to." It wasn't much encouragement, but it looked as if it was all he was going to get.

"Why?" he asked. "Are you married?"

"Hardly."

Desire was still thick in his body. So was need. Not caring that she knew what she did to him, he shifted his body closer to hers and said, "Then I don't see any problem."

When she didn't answer, he said, "Let's go someplace out of the way, someplace quiet and private where we can talk. Maybe to the park."

It was happening again. Cori felt her body going soft, her thoughts turning dreamy. All because Travis was touching her and talking to her in that low, shimmery voice of his.

"You can tell me anything, Cori, anything you want. After all, you must have one helluva life story, and I'd love to hear every last word."

That last statement filtered into her brain like ice water, clearing her thoughts and her mind. He'd made her nervous in a sensual sort of way since the moment he'd set foot in the inn. Now, she understood why. It was because she felt so much when she was with him. And feelings like these were dangerous.

His mention of her life story brought to mind the letter she'd mailed to Green Bay, the one she prayed would finally be answered this year. It reminded her of all the things she'd done wrong in her life, all her weaknesses.

Once again, the memory of the last thing her mother had said to her flickered through Cori's mind. *You're weak of the flesh, Corinna. Weak. You've made your bed. Now lie in it.*

"Come on, Cori. What do you say?"

Dazed, Cori looked up at him. His voice was still husky, and had all the invitation of an incredibly virile man. This time, she didn't give in to it. Taking a step backward, she said, "I'm awfully busy, Travis."

His eyes narrowed stubbornly as he said, "It's a lazy Sunday afternoon. Surely you can take a few hours off."

Out here in the bright sunshine, Cori could see the faint purple bruise he'd received on Friday. Fighting the impulse to touch that bruise with the gentlest of fingertips, she said, "Perhaps I could. But I'm not going to. No hard feelings, all right?"

She saw him swallow tightly, and closed her eyes. Opening them again, she said, "I don't know what else to say, Travis. I've never been very good at telling a man no."

Travis wanted to argue, but he was torn by conflicting emotions. He would have continued to try to change her mind, if he hadn't heard the almost imperceptible note of pleading in her voice when she said she wasn't very good at telling a man no. She'd said something similar Friday when that jerk hadn't wanted to take no for an answer. Could she really believe there was anything about that episode that had been her fault?

Travis wasn't one of those men who thought a woman meant yes when she said no. He'd come across a few men who'd bragged about using force to change a woman's mind. The thought alone sickened Travis. *He* understood what no meant. He also understood how willing she'd been when they'd kissed mere minutes ago, how she'd melted against him. What had changed her mind?

Regarding her thoughtfully, he said, "For a woman who claims she's no good at telling a man no, you're doing an awfully good job of it with me."

Her eyes opened wide, the grim set of her lips slowly changing into a smile. "I am, aren't I?"

"You don't have to look so happy about it."

After a long pause, she said, "You don't know how long I've worked to perfect this, Travis. I said no, and not just to anyone. I said no to *you*."

Travis knew there was absolutely no reason for him to suddenly feel like strutting, no reason for him to feel taller, smarter, stronger. No reason, except for the fact that Corinna Cassidy had insinuated that he wasn't just *any man*.

"I hope you enjoyed the tour of the inn, and I want you to know that I really appreciated the way you came to my rescue Friday afternoon."

Travis came out of his trance far enough to realize that he didn't like what he was hearing. She was trying to let him down gently, but he was being dismissed just the same.

"Well," she said, "thanks again, for coming to my aid on Friday, I mean. Um, I have a lot of work to do so I'd better be getting back inside. Have a nice summer, Travis. Goodbye."

Without another word, she strode away.

A bumblebee buzzed around his head. Since he didn't want the fat little bugger to mistake his gaping mouth for a hole in a tree, he clamped his lips together and watched Cori round a bend in the garden path.

Have a nice summer?

That was it? She was just going to walk away and forget about the passion between them?

No, Delaney. She wasn't going to. She already did.

The banging of the screen door pretty much accented the end of their brief acquaintance. He didn't need to be hit over the head. Cori had no intention of seeing him again. None.

Fine. He had *some* pride, after all. He didn't date women who had teenage daughters, anyway. Turning on his heel, he headed for the street where his Jeep was parked, an unwelcome tension tightening the muscles between his shoulder blades.

He started the engine and glanced at the big gray house with its steep roof, painted porches, and the green grass that led to the gardens containing all those colorful shrubs and flowers. Of their own accord, his eyes strayed to the back of the property, to the small white cottage where Cori lived.

Forcing his gaze back to the street, he told himself to forget about her—forget about the way her eyes lit up when she was trying to make a point, forget about the way they darkened when he was about to kiss her. Forget about the way the sun glinted off her honey blond hair, and the way his blood heated just thinking about her.

He shifted in his seat uncomfortably, then pulled away from the curb. With the wind rushing in his open window, he realized that there were a lot of things about Cori that weren't going to be easy to forget. Unfortunately, she hadn't left him much choice.

The eight ball rolled neatly across the table, thudding as it dropped into the corner pocket.

"Yes!" Braden shouted. "Calhoun remains supreme. That's the third game in a row I've won, Delaney. Delaney?"

Travis turned. "Huh?"

Braden shook his head and took a long swallow from the bottle in his hand. Lowering it to the table behind him, he said, "It really takes all the fun out of beating you when you don't even notice."

"Oh, did you win?"

"Yeah, I won. Again."

"I guess I'm a little distracted tonight," Travis confessed.

Racking up the balls for another game, Braden said, "A *little* distracted? I'd say you're more than a little distracted, Delaney. Your mind's been in the outer limits all week."

Braden knew him too well.

Coins clinked to the bottom of the jukebox halfway across the room. Seconds later, a twangy country song filled the bar. Listening to the lyrics, Travis didn't bother answering.

Both Braden and Pete Macnamara, one of Northwood Builders' best carpenters, had strolled into the office just as he'd ground the phone into its cradle after talking to Cori late that afternoon. Pete had taken one look at his boss's face and backed out again without saying a word, but Braden hadn't been the least bit put off. He'd arched one sandy brown eyebrow and said, "That was either Uncle Artie, or a woman."

Travis had answered with a succinct curse. Funny, staring through the smoky haze in Bruno's, their favorite hole-in-the-wall bar, he couldn't remember which word he'd used.

He'd been feeling as edgy as a cat pulled backward all week long. When that had happened in the old days, he found himself a good fight. In the years since the Calhouns had taken him in, he'd picked up a hammer and spent as many hours as it took, working and sweating until the feeling passed. For some reason, hard work hadn't helped this time. He and the crew had roughed in an entire house in four days, but he still felt as if someone had a hold of him by the tail.

Braden shoved a cue stick into Travis's right hand and a bottle of beer in his left, saying, "Drink up, Delaney. I promised the crew I'd either get you drunk or kill you, and I'd hate to have to kill you."

Travis gripped the cue in his hand, placed the untouched bottle on a stand behind him, and leaned over the pool table to line up his next shot. "Are the guys really starting to complain?"

Shaking his head because not one single ball found its way into a pocket during Travis's turn, Braden said, "They *started* complaining two weeks ago. Now they're working their way up to a full-scale mutiny. Come on, Travis. You know they all respect you. They're just worried about you, that's all. How long's it been since you've taken a vacation? Two, three years?"

Instead of answering, Travis asked, "You ever miss remodeling old houses, Braden? You know, like we did when we were just getting started?"

"You mean back when we were kids? For crying out loud, Travis. I don't know how much more of this mid-life crisis of yours I can stand."

Travis took his shot, lucking out when the cue ball bounced off the fourteen, which just happened to fall sloppily into the side pocket. He missed the next one by a mile, and while Braden sank three in a row, Travis's mind wandered.

Although he'd told himself he wouldn't, he *had* called Cori and invited her to dinner. Again. He'd tried to be nonchalant about the entire thing, but she'd turned him down anyway. Again.

He knew that wanting a woman who had a teenaged daughter should have made him feel older. But it didn't. The way Cori kissed him had felt good, frustratingly good. No matter how much he'd tried not to think about it, he couldn't get her or her kiss out of his mind. Maybe he *had* taken to slamming doors and kicking through piles of lumber at work. Maybe the guys in the crew *had* been steering clear of him. They probably all thought he was going through a mid-life crisis. Hell, he didn't know what he was going through.

But enough was enough. Whether Cori kissed like a dream or not, he wasn't going to call her again. With that decision made, he took a good look at Braden, who was standing on the other side of the pool table, his hands on his hips, a disgruntled expression on his face.

Both men were a little over six feet tall; both were strong. There, the similarities ended. Travis's hair was dark, Braden's was sandy brown. Travis was lean and muscular, while Braden was thicker, more like an oak tree—and right now that oak tree looked pretty darned frustrated.

Braden laid his stick down and heaved a great sigh. "You just scratched on the eight ball and beat yourself. Your concentration has 'blonde' written all over it. Are you about ready to talk about it?"

Standing there, Travis almost smiled for the first time that week. Almost. Although he liked to spout that he didn't know why he ever followed Braden home when he was seventeen, Travis knew why he did it. Braden Calhoun was his best friend, and the closest thing to a brother he'd ever had.

Holding the long-necked bottle loosely in his hands, he sauntered around to the other side of the table. Resting on its edge, he crossed his ankles and finally said, "You're right about what's on my mind. The blonde, as you refer to her, invited me over for breakfast, remember?"

"Yeah, did you go?"

"As a matter of fact, I did."

"I don't see why that should have you slamming around like a carpenter with a sore thumb."

"I'm getting to that. I stopped in for breakfast, but toast and eggs weren't really on my mind, if you know what I mean. She showed me around her inn, and then she kissed me senseless."

The jukebox chose that instant to change songs, so that Travis's declaration was heard from one corner of the bar to the other. The handful of Thursday-night regulars who were scattered throughout the room all turned and gave him different gestures of encouragement, from thumbs-up signals to idiotic grins. Travis shook his head and scowled.

The next song started, and Braden said, "I still don't see the problem."

Travis ran the blunt tip of his finger down the neck of the bottle in his right hand. Watching a bead of condensation zigzag its way down the label, he said, "The kiss was interrupted. By her sixteen-year-old daughter."

Braden whistled between his teeth. "Is that the problem? You don't want to date a woman old enough to have a kid that age?"

"I know that wanting a woman who has a sixteen-year-old daughter should make me feel old, but I feel about eighteen every time I think of her. No, that isn't the problem. The problem is that she won't go out with me, not to dinner, not to the park, not to the lake. She didn't say she didn't want to, only that she won't."

"Do you know why?" Braden asked.

"Not exactly, but I have a pretty good idea, and I'd sure like to find out if I'm right."

"Then maybe you're going to have to find some other way to be with her."

Braden's simple statement brought Travis's head up. Ideas popped into his mind like pool balls scattering in a good break. Maybe Braden was on to something here. Maybe there was another way to see Cori besides taking her to dinner.

Braden was studying him expectantly. "Well? I know you've got something in mind. Are you going to tell me what it is?"

Finding his feet, Travis said, "If you really meant it about that vacation I have coming, I might need to take some time off next week."

Braden slapped him on the back and, with a swash-buckling leer, said, "Welcome back, Delaney. Take all week if you need it. The guys are gonna be thrilled. Just kidding, but listen, if it doesn't work out with the blonde, Veronica, the woman I met at Roxy's last weekend, has a friend with long red hair, legs up to here and a chest out to there. She'd be happy to fix you up. I guarantee that *that* woman will get you out of your mid-life crisis. When she's through with you, you won't even know you're about to turn thirty-nine."

Travis shook his head. "I'm not interested, Braden. And for the hundredth time, I'm not going through a mid-life crisis. As far as my birthday goes, nobody had better be planning any kind of party, do you hear me?"

Braden shrugged sheepishly.

"Calhoun?"

Holding his hands up as if he could possibly be innocent, Braden said, "Hey, none of this was my idea. Just keep the last Sunday of the month open. And you didn't hear it from me."

Travis turned toward the door, grumbling. "I knew I should have followed Chad Peterson home when we were seventeen."

"Chad Peterson was a wimp!" Braden shouted.

Travis kept on walking.

"Good luck, Delaney," Braden yelled to his back. "Keep me posted. If things don't work out, remember, there are redheads in the world, too."

Travis called him a choice name or two, then pushed through the outer door. Walking to his Jeep, his thoughts weren't on any redhead. He had plans to make, and one amazingly stubborn, incredibly sexy blonde to sweep off her feet.

If Braden could have seen his face, he would have glimpsed a twitch of amusement, and the beginning of a smile.

Thunder rumbled outside the kitchen window. Moving the lacy curtain aside, Allison said, "Oh, no. It looks like it's going to rain any minute."

"Our flowers need rain," Cori said from her position at the deep kitchen sink.

Allison went back to her task of placing cut garden flowers into the eight vases on the tray in front of her. "I know, but Ross and I were planning to go back to the lake this afternoon."

Ivy clucked her tongue. "Don't worry, Allison, honey. It won't rain all day."

Cori cast her friend a sharp glance. As she lifted her gaze from the piecrust she was rolling out, the expression on Ivy's face said, *Well, it won't.*

The hinges on the old mailbox just outside the door creaked with the arrival of the mail. Ivy and Allison exchanged a silent look before peering at Cori. Ignoring the conspiratorial exchange, Cori said, "I'll be right back."

With hands still dripping, she turned and hurried out the door. She was back again seconds later, dropping the mail onto an empty space on the counter. "Fliers, junk mail and bills. Lots of bills."

"That's all?" Allison and Ivy asked in unison.

Gazing at her two favorite people, she shook her head slightly and said, "Will you two stop worrying? I'm going to be fine. Besides, my letter to Green Bay just went out on Monday, so it's too soon to expect a reply, right?"

Ivy made her sound again, and Allison visibly relaxed and cast her mother a wink. Cori's heart melted. Ivy was truly a wonderful person, and it never ceased to amaze her that the other truly wonderful person in the room, the one with long blond hair and intelligent gray eyes, was her daughter. She'd been struck with the wonder of it every day for the past sixteen years.

"So, Mom, it's okay if Ross and I go to the lake this afternoon, isn't it?"

Turning back to the sink, Cori took a deep breath. Allison was not only beautiful and intelligent, she was also persistent and stubborn. Ivy claimed those last two qualities alone made her her mother's child. Being careful not to chip the plate in her hand, Cori tried to feel her way around the subject.

"Why don't you call Laurie and Heather and go to the mall this afternoon?"

A tinge of exasperation came into Allison's voice as she said, "Laurie's family has been on vacation for the past week and a half, and Heather was just here yesterday. I want to be with Ross, Mom. You just don't understand how I feel."

Cori closed her eyes. There was a time when she would have known that one of her daughter's best friends was on vacation. Back then, Allison told her mother everything. She knew her little girl was growing up, but that didn't make letting go any easier. And whether Allison realized it or not, Cori *did* understand exactly how her daughter felt, how her young body yearned for her boyfriend's touch, how grown-up Allison *thought* she was. She was sixteen, the exact age Cori had been when her child was conceived.

Steam rose up from the sink, but it wasn't the hot water that caused a sheen of perspiration to form on the back of her neck and along other places on her body, places she was trying not to think about. Normally, those places weren't so difficult to ignore, but ever since Travis Delaney had kissed her...

She reached for another dish, hoping the movement would steady the erratic rhythm of her heart. She tried to listen to Allison's plea that she allow her to go out again this afternoon, but Cori's thoughts kept straying to one tall, dark-haired man whose eyes spoke a full five seconds before he did, whose subtle wit and wry humor had a way of sneaking up on her as much as her desire.

Everything about Travis seemed to be indelibly etched into her memory. Rinsing another plate, she reminded herself how proud she should be of the way she'd handled the situation with him last Sunday. She told him no, and meant it. Although he'd called again yesterday, Travis, bless his heart, had taken her refusal to see him like a man.

She closed her eyes against the onslaught of yearning her thoughts evoked. He'd taken it like a man, and if she'd have let him, he'd have taken her the same way.

Trying to ignore the images dancing in her head, she reminded herself that she had done the right thing by not becoming involved with Travis. She happened to have a wonderful, full life. She had an inn to run, a sixteen-year-old daughter who needed her, and a few terrific friends. If she was lucky, this year, she'd receive an answer to the letter she'd mailed to Green Bay. And she'd have a family again. If she had to sacrifice in other areas of her life to make that one wish come true, so be it.

"Can I go? Please?" Allison begged, stretching the last word as far as she possibly could.

Cori turned to face her daughter. "You saw Ross on Sunday and Tuesday and again on Wednesday..."

"But it's Friday," Allison cajoled. "It's the weekend. You always let me go out on the weekend. My work's all done here at the inn, and my room's clean at home. We're just going to go swimming. Please?"

Where this issue was concerned, Cori felt as if she were tiptoeing through a mine field. Allison was as stubborn as *she* was. Saying "Absolutely not, uh-uh, no way" would be like waving a checkered flag at the beginning of a race. After all, Cori had reacted the same way when she was her daughter's age. Unlike Cori, Allison had never given her mother any real trouble. But that didn't mean Cori didn't worry.

"Come on, Mom. You trust me, doncha?"

Cori took one look at that impish face and knew she was lost. Evidently, Allison knew it, too, because a smile fluttered to her lips.

"You, young lady, are too sure of yourself," she declared with a grin.

Allison picked up the tray of fresh flowers and put all the joy of youth into her voice as she said, "Thanks, Mom. You're the greatest."

"Remember that," Cori called as Allison floated up the back stairway.

"Remember what?"

The rhythmic thuds and thunks of Ivy's rolling pin ceased. In a room that had gone completely quiet, Cori slowly turned toward the dining room door.

There stood Travis, his jeans worn white at the stress points, his navy T-shirt tucked in above a scuffed leather belt. He had work boots on his feet, and a go-ahead-and-make-something-of-the-fact-that-I'm-here glint in his eyes.

Ivy could have been following a tennis match, the way her head moved in Cori's direction, then in Travis's, and back again. After an interminable moment of silence, she laid her rolling pin down and made noises about being needed somewhere else. With a grin that was far too knowing, she bustled from the room.

Cori and Travis were alone.

"What are you doing here?" she asked, wishing her voice hadn't come out sounding quite so breathless.

Walking steadily closer, he said, "You promised me breakfast."

"Breakfast?" she asked inanely.

"You know," he answered. "Breakfast. The first meal of the day. The one you promised me on Friday."

He stopped a few feet away, his gaze roaming over her face. She didn't notice the papers in his hand until he pushed them into her fingers. With a wink a gentleman would never get away with, he turned on his heel and strode through the swinging dining room door.

Cori was left standing there with her mouth open, listening as the door slowly stopped swishing back and forth. Thunder rumbled outside. An answering emotion rumbled deep inside her chest. She clamped her mouth shut and brought the papers closer to her face.

Riffling through first one page and then another and another, her mouth dropped open all over again.

Chapter Four

Travis took a seat at an unused table near the window in the otherwise empty dining room. The windows were shut against the approaching storm, but the anticipation deep inside him was quaking every bit as much as the thunder rumbling around in the ever-darkening sky.

If he lived to be a hundred, he wouldn't forget the expression on Cori's face when she'd looked up and found him standing on the other side of that door a few minutes ago. There had been surprise, yes, but there had also been excitement, the same kind of excitement that had been building inside him ever since they'd kissed five days ago.

He figured she had good reasons for telling him she wouldn't go out with him, but whether she admitted it or not, the attraction between them was as real as the storm brewing outside. He didn't know why she was fighting it so hard, but the way she'd stiffened when he'd mentioned her life story could only mean that it had something to do with that. Somewhere along the way, somebody had hurt her. The last thing he wanted to do was add insult to injury, but damn, attraction like this didn't come along every day. All he wanted was to get to know her better, and see where it would lead.

Corinna Cassidy was stubborn. Good Lord, was she stubborn. She'd told him no and meant it. Fine. She didn't have to *have dinner with him*. There were other ways to get to know a woman, even an obstinate one like her.

He adjusted his breathing to the adrenaline pumping through him. Strumming his fingers on the table, he kept his eyes trained on the door, and waited. He tried not to appear overanxious when the door burst open, but it wasn't easy. Cori was a sight for sore eyes.

The storm gearing up in the western sky was nothing compared to the commotion she caused as she strode into the room. She made short work of wending her way around tables, planting her feet so abruptly it took a moment for her skirt to swish into place around her knees. It took a moment longer for the yellow sheets of paper pinched tightly in her hand to stop fluttering.

"What do you think you're doing?" she asked.

He'd come to her rescue the first time they met, but now Travis wondered if that had been necessary, after all. The person standing before him could take care of herself. He liked that in a woman—at least, he liked it in Cori. Since he doubted she was ready to hear what else he liked about her, he shrugged in a noncommittal way and waited for her to make the next move.

She plunked the papers in front of him, rapping the table with her knuckles in the process. "These estimates for repairs to the inn are too low."

Holding her gaze, he said, "That's good, isn't it?"

"You'll lose your shirt."

Travis felt himself go as still as the air. During that interminable span of time, thunder didn't roll, floors didn't creak, doors didn't swish, and neither of them made a sound. The lights weren't on, and with all the clouds blocking the sunlight outside, he couldn't quite make out the golden freckles on Cori's nose. He sensed, more than saw, the indecision in her eyes. She was fighting a battle against restraint. He'd made her an offer, and she was having a difficult time refusing.

Cori's mind floundered, and she could think of nothing to say. It would be so easy to get lost in the way Travis was looking at her, so easy to give in to the invitation in his eyes. Her heart was doing crazy things in her chest, erratic things, slowing down and speeding up at whim. All because the image of Travis Delaney, shirtless and sexy, had flashed through her mind.

She felt a blush tinge her cheeks. In comparison, he appeared inordinately calm and self-assured. She finally managed to break the hold he had on her senses, and glanced around. Although it was only ten o'clock in the morning, shadows stretched from the corners of the room. Raindrops trailed down the windowpanes, her thoughts trailing right along with them.

Not more than ten minutes ago she'd assured herself that she'd done the right thing when she'd refused to have dinner with this man. She had her hands full running the bed-and-breakfast, not to mention raising a daughter who always managed to stay one step ahead of her mother.

Looking down at the papers on the table, she knew that if she had any sense at all, she'd tell him exactly what he could do with his offer. Staring at the figures scratched in his bold handwriting, she knew she couldn't do that. The inn needed these repairs, and Travis's prices were too good. The problem was, so was he.

Casting him a wary glance, she asked, "*If* I hire you, when could you start?"

"Would Monday morning be soon enough?"

Despite her resolve to remain unflustered, her eyebrows rose fractionally. "So soon?"

"I would have started today, but I *am* half owner of the company and I do have a few loose ends to tie up."

Cori found herself extremely conscious of the grin lurking around the edges of his mouth. Thinking about everything *she* would have to do in the inn to prepare for a few days off, she asked, "You could really be ready to start by Monday?"

"I've already talked to Braden about this. He agrees that I should take a few days off. In fact, he insisted."

She didn't quite know what to make of his self-mocking little snort, but then, she didn't quite know what to make of those prices, either. "Why would you offer to work here on your days off?" she asked.

He shrugged casually and said, "Because I want to, and because seeing this inn last weekend reminded me how much I used to enjoy working on old houses. I jotted down a few names there on the last page. If you want references, go ahead and give those people a call."

Cori didn't have to call anyone. She'd already asked her friend, Lisa, about Northwood Builders. Before starting her own catering business, Lisa had done payroll and basic accounting for another builder. She said she'd heard a lot of things about Northwood, and not one of them had been bad. With eyes twinkling and a voice that had gone low and secretive, she'd added, "Sometime when you have a few hours, I'll tell you what I've heard about the owners."

Cori hadn't had to ask what Lisa had meant. After all, she'd spent enough time alone with Travis to interpret the dreaminess in her friend's expression. It was the same way *she'd* felt when she'd shown him the inn, when they'd strolled through the gardens, and when they'd kissed.

She bit down on her lip, irritated with her own wayward thoughts. It was no wonder she'd made so many mistakes in her life. She couldn't even handle one sexy carpenter's overtures. And Travis *was* sexy. He may have been too rugged-looking to be considered classically handsome. Maybe he was a little rough around the edges, but he was definitely virile everywhere else.

"So, am I hired?" he asked.

She watched as he stretched his legs out more comfortably underneath the table. He gazed back at her with that old I'm-here-now-what-are-you-going-to-do-with-me look of a man begging for trouble. It occurred to her that he knew exactly what he was doing. Suddenly, so did she.

Her chin went down and her tenacity went up. She wasn't a confused teenager anymore, and she certainly wasn't a young girl trying to make sense out of her parents' stringent rules and her own body's newly felt yearnings. Now, she had a business to run and a much, much stronger resolve. She was a mature woman. It was about time she acted like one.

After a long pause, she said matter-of-factly, "All right. You're hired. Since guests come here to sleep, I'll want you to keep the noise down until after 10:00 a.m. By then, everyone is usually finished with breakfast and off to go sight-seeing or to enjoy the day on the lakes in and around Madison. Now, what would you like for breakfast?"

His gaze settled to her mouth.

For a moment, she felt her lips begin to soften. Then she let out a little huff, redistributed her weight to one foot, planted her hands on her hips, and waited.

Seemingly beyond intimidation, he shrugged. "Bring whatever's easiest. I'm not fussy, at least not when it comes to food."

He didn't say *women were a different story,* but the way his eyelashes dropped down and one corner of his mouth lifted insolently, he might as well have. Rather than making her angry, his attitude infused her with energy. She cast him her own brand of innocent smiles and said, "I'll bet you have quite a way with women."

"You really think so?" he asked.

Cori snorted her answer. She didn't think so, she knew so, and the way he settled his shoulders more comfortably along the back of his chair, so did he.

Thunder rumbled again, this time much, much closer. Within seconds, the storm's first forks of lightning streaked across the sky. Travis glanced casually out the window, his fingers absently curling the edges of the estimates in front of him. Without looking at her, he said, "You're beginning to sound like Braden. He wants to fix me up with a long-legged redhead. I told him I wasn't interested."

"What's the matter? Don't you like red hair?" she asked.

He didn't smile the way she expected. He didn't even shrug in an offhand manner. Instead, he looked directly at her and said, "I think there's something you should know. This," he motioned to the price lists on the table, "has nothing to do with the color of your hair."

Cori didn't know what to say. The man had a way of unnerving her with the truth. Even so, she was proud of the way her backbone straightened and her eyes flashed in challenge. She spun away, stopping at the kitchen door where she glanced over her shoulder and said, "I'll bring your breakfast right out. And Travis? There's something you should know, too."

"What's that?" he asked.

"I think you should consider taking your friend up on his offer with that redhead, because this arrangement between us is going to be strictly business."

Without another word she turned around again and marched into the kitchen. Travis sat staring at the place she had been. He felt his eyes narrow, and his heart rate quicken, and it had nothing to do with the thunder and lightning outside.

Peering into the shadows in the room, he said to himself, "We'll see about that, Cori. We'll definitely see about that."

Cori held the door for the Averys, a family from Ohio who just happened to be the last guests to set off for a day of sight-seeing. "Have fun," she called. "I'll see all of you tonight. Don't forget—Billy, Justin and Ryan—Ivy is going to bake two kinds of cookies this morning and will be wanting your opinion before you go to sleep tonight."

All three boys' eyes grew large as they exchanged a look, grinning from ear to ear. Mr. and Mrs. Avery shook their heads affectionately then set off down the steps with their active brood in tow.

Still smiling, Cori closed the door and hurried into the dining room where she quickly began stacking used dishes onto a plastic tray. She'd almost finished clearing the first several tables when the door burst open and Lisa Markman, one of her closest friends, strode into the room. Glancing all around, the slender brunette whispered, "All right, where is he?"

Holding a stack of plates in one hand, Cori lowered her own voice to match her friend's. "Where is who?"

"Don't play innocent with me, Corinna Cassidy. You know exactly to *whom* I'm referring. Travis Delaney. Jillian called last night and told me you've hired him to do the repairs in the inn. And I want to know where he is."

All things considered, Cori thought she did a fair job of feigning disinterest. She nodded somewhat absently then went back to her task. "Lisa, aren't you supposed to meet with a prospective client this morning?" she asked.

"Don't try to change the subject. Just answer the question." After interminable seconds spent waiting, she prodded, "Well?"

"Well, what?" Cori asked.

"Is he as virile and to-die-for sexy as they say?"

Cori placed the stack of plates on the cluttered tray, then strode to the other side of the table where she thrust the tray into Lisa's hands. Motioning toward the next room, she said, "He's fixing the latch on the back door. Why don't you take these dirty dishes into the kitchen and find out for yourself?"

Raising delicately arched eyebrows over round brown eyes that sometimes appeared too large for her face, Lisa asked, "You really don't mind?"

Cori gestured toward the door. "Now why would you think I'd mind? By all means, be my guest."

With a grin that could only be described as impish, Lisa clutched the tray of dishes close to her body and turned toward the door, saying, "I don't mind if I do."

Moments later Cori heard the soft murmur of voices filter into the dining room. Lisa laughed at something Travis said. As far as Cori could tell, Travis didn't laugh in return. She was just putting the last few stacks of dishes on another tray when the door opened again and Lisa reentered the room.

It was Cori's turn to say, "Well?"

After a few moments of silence, Lisa heaved a long sigh. "There's nothing like a man in work boots, is there? He has bedroom eyes all right, and those muscles in his arms and shoulders..."

Lisa's words sent blood rushing into Cori's head. She'd spent a good share of yesterday trying *not* to think about the muscles in Travis Delaney's arms and shoulders. She was already far too conscious of his appeal, of the way her heart did a slow slide into her stomach every time he came within ten feet of her.

"The rumors don't really do him justice, though, do they?" Lisa asked, her soft voice cutting into Cori's reverie. "They were partially right. He *is* a little standoffish and he *does* have a bad-boy smile. What a combination.

Unfortunately, there's no sizzle, no spark and alas, no attraction.''

From the other side of the room, Cori did a double take. Lisa had just described Travis to a T, at least right up to the part about there being no spark.

Shaking her head ruefully, Lisa smoothed her hands down her red jacket. "Oh, well," she said. "There may be no attraction, but I still envy you the scenery around here these next several days."

At Cori's gasp, Lisa winked and headed for the door, muttering that if she didn't hurry, she was going to be late for a meeting with prospective clients and her catering business would go down the tubes. Within seconds, Cori heard the front door slam, and listened for the honk of the horn that was bound to follow. Little more than half a minute later, she smiled to herself at the sound of the two short and one long beep.

With a mild shake of her head, she picked up the last pieces of silverware and placed them on the cluttered tray. Although Lisa was a little younger and ten times more brash, they'd both grown up fast when they were too young to know better. They'd struck up a friendship when Lisa had rented a room here at Ivy's more than a dozen years ago, and they'd been close ever since.

Lost in long ago memories, Cori picked up the tray and shouldered her way into the kitchen. Barely inside the door, she stopped. She wasn't sure how long she stood there staring at the *scenery* Lisa had mentioned, but, mesmerized, she couldn't look away. Travis was on his knees, at eye level with the latch on the back door, fiddling with the lock's tricky mechanism. His jeans stretched tight over his thighs, his T-shirt molding to his midsection like a second skin.

"Did I pass inspection?" he asked.

Horrified to be caught staring, Cori jerked her gaze away and hurried toward the sink, the sudden movement causing the tray in her hands to clank to the counter. "What do you mean?" she asked, righting the teetering dishes.

"I was just wondering if I passed inspection. With your friend, I mean. I think she said her name was Lisa something or other."

Cori could feel Travis's gaze on her. Instead of looking at him, she bent at the waist and reached for the dish soap, glad she had something constructive to do. "Markman," she said, squirting a generous portion of soap into the streaming water. "Her name is Lisa Markman, and yes, I guess you could say you passed inspection with her."

"What about with you, Cori?"

His question drew her around to face him, just as he seemed to know it would. He wasn't really smiling, but she knew that depending upon what she said, a smile wasn't far away. In that instant, she realized that there was something different about this man, something invigorating and dangerous and exciting. It was a scary combination, one that could easily be her downfall.

She'd done her best to steer clear of him yesterday. Somehow, he still managed to be in whatever room she was in. He'd repaired the crack in the plaster when she was vacuuming the upstairs hall. He'd replaced the rotted floorboards in the bathroom off the Marigold Room late yesterday afternoon. While she'd prepared the room for the next guests a little while ago, he'd applied the first coat of paint to the new floor. And now he was in the kitchen when she needed to do the dishes. Each time she found herself alone with him, her heart did a crazy flip-flop. Strangely, something else had happened to her, too. Her wits revitalized themselves, and so did her resolve.

She reached behind her to turn off the water and finally said, "I'm reserving judgment until *after* you've finished all the work in the inn."

The soles of his leather work boots creaked as he slowly rose to his feet. Wearing that bad-boy smile Lisa had mentioned, he said, "If my work passes inspection, will you have dinner with me?"

She watched him come closer. Crossing her arms at her ribs, she shook her head and said, "You're persistent, I'll give you that much."

"Then I'm in good company. Now what do you say?"

Travis Delaney did *not* beat around the bush, and he didn't seem to expect her to, either. Feeling the steam rise from the sink behind her, she crossed her ankles and leaned more comfortably against the edge of the counter.

"Having dinner with you wasn't included in your quote," she pointed out.

"I knew I forgot something when I was figuring those prices. But tell me the truth, Cori. Were my prices *really* the only reason you hired me?"

Rather than make her feel nervous, his slow, steady advance heightened her awareness of him as a man, and of herself as a woman. Raising her chin to look directly into his eyes, she said, "No. There was another reason."

Travis stopped an arm's length away. It was hotter than blazes outside. Here inside, there was something in the oven, as usual, and steam rose up from the sink at Cori's back, clinging to her hair and cheeks like dew. All those things combined to raise the temperature in the kitchen, but even if snow had been falling and the temperature had been hovering near zero, he still would have felt overheated. All because of Cori.

Someone else might never have suspected that behind her angelic blue eyes lurked a stubborn streak a mile wide. He happened to know it for a fact. This woman's cussed obstinacy had been wreaking havoc with his plans since the first time she refused to have dinner with him. He'd been doing everything in his power to get closer to her for the past two days. Now, finally, he was making progress.

"Are you going to tell me about that other reason, Cori?" he asked quietly.

She wet her lips. Travis's mouth went dry.

"You're not going to like it," she said hesitantly.

"Try me."

"It's selfish," she added, shaking her head.

"I like it already," he said, his voice becoming as low and husky as his thoughts.

Taking advantage of her silence, he boot-scooted a little closer and asked, "Are you going to keep me in suspense all day?"

He loved the way she raised her chin, but he loved the spark of intelligence and spirit deep in her eyes even more. Yes, indeed. Now he was definitely getting somewhere.

"Okay," she replied. "Here goes. I hired you because your prices were right, because you're a respectable carpenter, and because..."

"Yes?" he prodded, ever so huskily.

"...because I wanted to practice my newly acquired skill."

Blood pounded out of Travis's brain, making his senses feel short-circuited. At least ten possible *newly acquired skills* popped into his mind, every one of them X-rated and so erotic he could hardly think straight.

"Are you sure you want to hear this?" she asked.

He didn't know how he ever managed to nod. Holy Mary, queen of saints, he was absolutely positive he really wanted her to continue, although *hearing* about her newly acquired skill was fast becoming *second* on his want-to-do list.

"Okay," she said. "You asked for it. My newly acquired skill is my ability to say no."

Travis heard a loud noise. It was either thunder, or a jackhammer going off inside his skull.

"Your what?"

"My newly acquired skill," she repeated, "is my ability to say no, more specifically, my ability to stand firm behind my decision to say no."

Suddenly, he wished he hadn't asked, because, studying her expression, he realized that she was serious. He couldn't remember the last time he'd been so disappointed. *Saying no* was the last skill he wanted her to perfect, especially when she was saying no to him. By the time the bells and bombs stopped going off inside his brain, he realized she was trying to explain.

"You see, every mistake I've ever made has been a result of my inability to say no and mean it. My parents said I was undisciplined and unmotivated, but what I really was was weak. Have you ever been weak, Travis?" she asked.

He swallowed, hard, and shrugged.

"I didn't think so. Well, I have, and it's the worst feeling in the world."

"Corinna, honey, could you give me a hand up here?"

Cori didn't move, and neither did he. In some far corner of his mind, he recognized the voice drifting down the stairs as Ivy Pennington's.

With stunning clarity, he realized that Cori wasn't simply playing hard-to-get. She truly believed she was weak. He wanted to tell her that wasn't so, but he had a sneaking suspicion that mere words would never be enough.

"Corinna? Can you hear me?"

Ivy's second summons finally broke their concentration. They both turned toward the stairs, but Cori was the first to find her voice. "I'll be right there, Ivy."

Without another word, she turned and strode up the back stairs. He couldn't help noticing how perfectly straight she held her spine. He couldn't help noticing that she didn't look back, either.

Cori stepped off the back stoop and made a beeline for the ornate mailbox several feet away. Releasing the latch, she peered into the empty space inside. That's strange, she thought to herself. Walt, the middle-aged mailman with the noticeable paunch, wasn't usually late.

The shrill screech of an electric drill drew her attention to a place high over her head. She shaded her eyes with her hand and tipped her head back, peering up at Travis, who was standing near the top of an aluminum ladder.

One thing she'd learned during these past three days was that Travis Delaney wasn't a man to sit around when there was work to be done. He'd plowed through the jobs on his list with skill, efficiency and a great deal of noise. As a result, he'd finished nearly everything on the inside and would soon be ready to start building the gazebo in the backyard.

She'd gone over the books again last night. Most of the rooms were rented in advance for much of the summer and on into the fall. Winter was always slow, but if they were careful and watched their spending, the inn would still be operating in the black come spring. If all went well, they'd have enough money to buy a big dishwasher and update the kitchen next year.

The drill screeched again, the noise sounding even louder in the still of late morning. Travis was drilling holes through one of the old wooden shutters that had come loose during a thunderstorm last spring. As usual, he was making a lot of commotion.

Eyeing the chips of paint and splinters of wood fluttering from the second story, she called, "Who says it never snows in June?"

He gripped the electric drill with one hand and the ladder with the other. Peering down at her, he said, "Probably the same person who said it never snows in hell."

With the bright sun in her eyes, she couldn't see the expression on his face, but from here it looked as if at least one corner of his mouth was pulled up in wry humor. His white T-shirt looked slightly damp and was clinging to his upper body. No wonder. The sun was shining directly on him, and with temperatures that were fast approaching the mid-eighties, the humidity was only making matters worse.

"Why don't you take a break and cool off?" she asked.

He stepped down onto a lower rung. "Is that an invitation for an early lunch?"

She answered with a mild shake of her head and an indulgent smile. Squinting up at him, she said, "There's some of Ivy's Fidget Pie left from supper last night. You're welcome to have some."

Being careful not to lose his balance, Travis contemplated Cori's offer. He hadn't talked to her, at least not in any deep and meaningful way, since she'd told him about her *newly acquired skill* yesterday. He still grimaced every time he thought about it, and he still had no idea what to do about any of it.

He'd spent his first three days off in nearly two and a half years working on her inn just to be close to her, and he wasn't much closer to getting to know her than he'd been the first night they met. He'd run into Braden at Bruno's last night. As usual, his friend was full of suggestions, among other things, and in his own straightforward way had told him that the redhead was still available. The problem was, Travis didn't want another woman. He wanted Cori.

"What do you say?" she asked, bringing him back to the question of lunch.

Since he couldn't very well say what he was thinking, he asked, "You really eat something called Fidget Pie?"

She laughed at that, the sound rousing his desire all over again. When her laughter trailed away, she explained. "It's an old English recipe for a deep-dish meat, potato and apple pie. It may not sound good, but it tastes great. Do you want me to warm some up for you?"

"Would you be joining me?"

She shook her head slowly, exactly as he was afraid she would. Clenching his teeth, he said, "In that case, I think I'll finish this before I take a break."

She seemed to breathe a huge sigh of relief that he'd dropped it at that. Glancing back up at him, she said, "If you're sure. Let me know if there's anything you need, okay?"

He answered under his breath, but he knew the shrill screech of the electric drill drowned out his words. He figured it was just as well, because he'd cursed her newly acquired skill from here to there and back again.

Travis watched as she went toward the cottage where she and her daughter lived. She plucked a garden flower on her way, breathing in its scent. He remembered when she'd told him that her parents used to say she was undisciplined and unmotivated. As far as he was concerned, uninhibited and undisciplined were two entirely different things. He wanted to get closer to her, and prove to her that her parents had been wrong. Accomplishing that wasn't exactly going to be a picnic when she refused every overture he made.

High on the ladder, he went very still, an idea taking form in his head. Watching her duck inside the cottage's side door, he thought that maybe this was going to be a picnic, after all.

Cori pulled the screen door shut behind her, and turned, only to find Allison striding into the room from the opposite direction. Wearing cutoffs and a baggy knit shirt that drooped off one shoulder, she looked innocent, and far too sexy for her mother's peace of mind.

Stifling a yawn, she said, "Oh, hi, Mom."

"Hi, yourself," Cori returned warmly, softly placing one of the season's first daisies on the table. "How was class today?"

Allison shook her head. "The same as usual."

"That bad?"

Allison swished her long blond curls behind her shoulders and shuddered. "Taking geometry during the school year was bad enough, but trying to learn it in the summer is awful."

Now that Cori's vision was adjusting to the dim interior of the tiny kitchen, she noticed the fire in her daughter's eyes. Allison was a good student, but she'd gotten mono last winter and had missed over a month of school. She'd managed to catch up in all her other classes, but geometry had somehow gotten away from her. Now, she was taking it over in summer school.

"Hang in there, kiddo. Nothing lasts forever. Not even summer school. Mmm," she murmured when their paths crossed. "You smell good."

"It's that new jasmine shampoo you bought. Ross absolutely loves it," Allison replied, peering into the refrigerator.

"That sweet scent doesn't come out of any bottle. *That* is all you."

The grin Allison gave her over the top of the refrigerator door reminded Cori of how her daughter had looked when she was eleven years old. Her gray eyes crinkled at the corners, her lips stretching to meet the cutest dimples Cori had ever seen. Grinning back, she wished she could take her daughter into her arms the way she had back then, when all of Allison's hugs had been reserved for her.

Instead, Cori asked, "What are you hungry for, breakfast or lunch?"

"Breakfast, I think. But I can fix something for myself."

Allison's declaration came as no surprise to Cori. Her daughter had practically been born independent, and had been precocious since before her third birthday. Nudging her aside, Cori said, "I know you can, but if I help, it'll give us a chance to talk."

Allison cast her mother a quick look before asking, "What do you want to talk about?"

For a moment, Cori studied her daughter. The expression in those gray eyes was wary, making Cori even more convinced that there was something bothering her daughter. She'd had a feeling that Allison had been on the verge of telling her something for weeks. In the past, she'd always shared everything with her mother. This time was different, and Cori wasn't entirely sure what to do about it.

Reaching for the eggs, she said, "We can talk about anything you want, kiddo, anything at all."

"I know, Mom," Allison said. The statement was followed by silence.

As they had at least a hundred times before, mother and daughter worked side by side in the small kitchen. In no time, Allison had her place set and Cori was cracking the eggs. Instead of broaching a difficult subject, Allison began chatting about some "majorly cool" guy Laurie met on horseback on one of the trails in the Grand Canyon.

"He's a cowboy," she said breezily. "A real live, modern-day cowboy. Can you believe that? Heather and I are going over to Laurie's house to look at her pictures and the home videos her parents took."

Although Cori knew that this wasn't the topic that had been putting that pensive expression in Allison's eyes, there wasn't much she could do about it until the girl was ready to open up to her. In the meantime, all Cori could do was be there and hope Allison came to her when she was ready.

Reaching into a drawer for the spatula, Cori said, "A real cowboy? I'll bet Laurie had fun. Would you get that yellow bowl out of the bottom cabinet for me?"

Allison bent over to do as her mother asked, reaching to the back of the shelf for the bowl. In the process, her hair swished to the front of her shoulder, baring the side of her neck. Without thinking, Cori brushed her fingertips across the small red splotch on the pale skin a few inches below her daughter's ear.

Allison jerked to her feet as if she'd been stung, bringing the plastic bowl with her. Color flooded her cheeks. Her eyes darted to the floor, to the counter, and back to the floor again.

Cori forced herself to finish her task, trying not to let her worry show. Allison had gone out with Ross last night. She'd come in right at curfew. Cori knew because she'd been waiting up. Once again her daughter had worn the look of a girl who'd been thoroughly kissed. That little red love-bite proved that the kissing hadn't been confined to her lips.

As if Allison had heard her mother's thoughts, she said, "Ross didn't mean to, Mom. Honest. He just got a little carried away, that's all."

Making sure her back was to her daughter, Cori closed her eyes and took a deep breath. Of all people, *she* knew how it felt to get carried away, and wouldn't dream of sitting in judgment. That didn't mean she wouldn't do everything in her power to protect her child. Oh, Allison, she thought to herself. That was so much easier when you were small.

She finally turned around. With the saltshaker in one hand and the cheese in the other, she said, "You know that I think Ross is a nice boy, but fair or not, kiddo, if he isn't strong enough to know when to stop, you're going to have to be the strong one."

"I know, Mom. I know. You've told me at least a hundred times."

Cori heard the rising defensiveness in Allison's voice. Since she didn't think it would be wise to say anything else, she put the finishing touches on the omelet then placed it on the table next to the daisy she'd dropped there a short time ago.

She told Allison about Lisa's latest visit, and a phone call she'd had from Jillian. Except for a cursory nod or two, Allison ate her breakfast in silence, the warm camaraderie that used to be second nature to them little more than a distant memory. It nearly broke Cori's heart, but she didn't know what she could say to bring it back.

Once again, she wished she could take her daughter in her arms and keep her safe. With a stab of sorrow, she knew she could no longer do that. She could guide her, and help her, but ultimately, Allison was going to have to make her own choices.

Sitting across from the woman-child who was her daughter, Cori prayed that, when the time came, Allison would do a better job of it than she had.

Chapter Five

Cori stretched as far as she could and reached for the sneaky weeds that were hiding behind the antique lamp-post in the center of one of her flower beds. Half an hour ago, she'd waved goodbye to Allison, who was on her way to spend the afternoon with her friends. Although Allison had returned her wave, there hadn't been much enthusiasm behind it. Her daughter was still sulking, and Cori was still worried.

The sun was almost straight up in the sky. If there had been any breeze earlier, it had died away, leaving the leaves on the trees and bushes utterly motionless. Most people tried to stay indoors during the hottest time of the day. Ivy, who, at seventy-two, was a flutter of activity the rest of the time, always rested in front of her soaps between twelve and two. Even the birds seemed to be sleeping right now, leaving Cori alone with only the bees and butterflies for company.

Normally, the quiet and solitude suited her. Today, it left her with too much time to think, too much time to badger herself with things she *wished* she had said to her daughter. Why didn't she tell Allison how much she trusted her, and admired her, and loved her?

She knows, a voice whispered in Cori's mind. Although that thought calmed her, she vowed to tell Allison all those things the next chance she had. With that decision made, she tried to turn her attention to the task at hand.

After last week's soaking, everything in the garden had grown. As usual, the weeds seemed to be faring better than anything else. Carefully pulling the spires out by their roots, her thoughts once again turned to Allison and the telltale mark she'd found on her neck. Until today, she'd tried to tell herself that Allison and Ross were just kids who liked each other and happened to have a lot of fun together, but Cori couldn't deny the evidence any longer. Now she had to face the fact that Ross and Allison had passed the point of sharing chaste kisses.

She could hardly blame Allison for kissing a boy she'd been dating for four months when *she* had kissed Travis the second time they met. That kiss had been far from chaste. Even now, nearly a week later, she felt a passionate fluttering at the back of her neck at the memory alone.

Being careful not to yank out the flowers with the weeds, Cori tried to put that kiss out of her mind. It wasn't easy. After all, Travis Delaney wasn't an easy man to forget, and neither were his kisses.

The ladder he'd been using earlier had been moved, but he was nowhere in sight. He must have finished refastening the shutters and gone to lunch as he'd said he would.

Thoughts of Travis started it, that warm softening in her chest, swelling upward until it touched her throat, lower until it engulfed her entire body. A bead of perspiration trailed down her neck, over her collarbone, skimming the outer swell of her breast. Suddenly, her clothes felt too tight, her cropped T-shirt too warm.

She dropped another weed onto the pile and drew herself up to her knees. Peeling one glove off, she swiped her hand across the side of her neck and, with eyes closed, arched her back and raised her face to the sky. Strangely, the sun's golden rays didn't peep through her closed eye lids or warm her upturned face. That was odd. The last time she looked, there hadn't been a cloud in the sky.

"Break time."

Those words came from a place directly in front of her. She opened her eyes, but the act of looking was just a formality. She already knew who had spoken. After all, she'd recognize Travis's low, smooth baritone anyplace, anytime.

No wonder she couldn't feel the sun on her face. His broad shoulders and tall body were blocking it from view. He had a way of disappearing without a sound, only to materialize the same way. What was a woman supposed to do with a man like that?

She peered up at him from beneath the wide rim of her straw hat. He'd changed into a pair of clean jeans, and a black T-shirt had replaced the white one he'd worn earlier. He had the look and smell of a man who'd recently stepped out of the shower, and was gripping a wicker basket in one strong hand.

He lowered the picnic basket to the ground, dropping to his haunches at the same time. Despite her resolve not to allow it, her heart did a crazy little flip in her chest.

"What are you doing?" she asked.

Glancing down at the wicker basket, he said, "You know what they say. If you can't bring Muhammad to the mountain, take the mountain to Muhammad."

"You mean you made lunch?" she asked.

"Not me, exactly," he said.

With that, he grabbed the basket's handle and rose to his feet, all in one motion. Watching him walk away, she asked, "Then who?"

"Ginny."

Cori tried to remember if she'd ever heard him mention anyone named Ginny. Suddenly, the image of red hair, legs up to here and a chest out to there flitted through her mind. Since she didn't want to examine her reaction to that particular image, she simply stared at Travis's broad back.

This wasn't the first time she'd watched him walk away from her, nor was it the first time she'd noticed how good he looked from behind. His shoulders were broad, his waist was trim, and his faded jeans were just threadbare enough to mold to every long, lean inch of him. As usual his gait was sure and easy, and far, far too masculine. Bother the man!

Travis would have loved to look over his shoulder, to glance into Cori's face so he could gauge her response to his arrival. Luckily, he'd learned his lesson when she'd turned down his invitations to dinner, the park, the lake, even a simple lunch. Oh, no, he wasn't about to blow this now by appearing overanxious.

Instead of asking her to join him, he'd tossed the idea in front of her, then strode away. Now, all he could do was hope that her curiosity got the best of her.

Keeping his back to her, he pulled a faded summer quilt from the basket and shook it out, letting it flutter to the grass in the shade of a nearby maple tree. Trying to portray a sense of calm he didn't necessarily feel, he lowered himself to his knees on the blanket and began removing items from inside the picnic basket.

"Who's Ginny?"

He heard the curiosity in Cori's voice, and felt his chest expand with a unique mixture of excitement and relief. Even as he fought the urge to grin, he swore the beating rhythm of his heart changed. He took his time spooning a generous helping of homemade potato salad onto his plate, then finally raised his gaze to hers.

She was standing in the sun near the edge of the blanket, just outside the line of shade. Light filtered through the tiny holes in her straw hat, dappling her face like golden tweed. Looking up at her, he knew he'd never had so many responses to a woman in his life. She captivated him and intrigued him, irritated him and baffled him. More than anything, she turned him on. It was happening right now.

If he ever wanted the chance to get to know her better, he decided he'd better get his hormones under control. He took a deep breath, then pulled a bowl of fresh strawberries from the bottom of the picnic basket. Holding one ripe, red berry between his fingers, he looked up at her and said, "Nice hat."

The casual observation seemed to surprise her and put her at ease at the same time. She shrugged one shoulder and explained, "I love to be out in the sun, but if I don't wear a hat, I freckle."

Travis swallowed, hard, and popped the strawberry into his mouth. He'd seen the freckles across her nose, and couldn't help wondering if she had a few anyplace else. He didn't see any on her arms or on the skin visible above the scooped neck of her shirt, but was careful not to let his gaze stray below her shoulders for too long. Not that it was easy. He'd noticed her legs the moment he'd set foot in her garden, not to mention the patch of pale skin she'd bared at her waist when she'd reached for those weeds a few minutes ago.

Deciding it might be best if he didn't think along those lines, he dropped from his knees to a sitting position and answered her first question. "Ginny—that's short for Virginia—is Braden's mother. I stopped in on my lunch hour and asked her if she'd fix me a picnic lunch. She's a phenomenal cook, but I have a feeling her payback is going to be murder.''

Cori had no idea how she ended up sitting on one corner of Travis's blanket, a plate of food on her lap, a grin of pure whimsy on her face as she listened to his description of his friend and business partner's mother, Ginny Calhoun. According to Travis, the woman was a plump five foot two and a powerhouse of pure feminine audacity.

''Sam, her husband, is a brute of a man,'' Travis declared. ''He's a good foot taller than she is, yet I've seen her chase him out of her kitchen with a broom. He may wear the pants in that household, but she definitely rules the roost.''

Cori was laughing too hard to take a bite of the stacked turkey sandwich in her hand. Lowering it to the plate, she asked, ''What type of payment do you think she'll demand in exchange for your picnic lunch?''

Travis released a breath that would have befitted the most tortured martyr. ''For one thing, I'm going to have to pretend to be happy about the surprise party she's throwing for my birthday this weekend.''

Holding out her glass, thereby accepting his silent offer of ice-cold lemonade, Cori found herself responding to his exasperated tone. ''This upcoming birthday of yours wouldn't have anything to do with that mid-life crisis you mentioned, would it?'' she asked.

Travis looked mildly disgruntled as he said, ''Don't you start in, too. I'm *not* going through a mid-life crisis.''

She laughed all over again, saying, ''Of course you're not.''

''Finally, someone who believes me. Just wait until I tell Braden's family.''

Watching Travis flick a tiny ant off the quilt, Cori wondered about the man behind those warm brown eyes and serious expressions. She'd heard him mention Braden and his family before. Although every reference had contained wry humor and more than a hint of exasperation, he obviously had strong ties to the Calhouns.

Her gaze strayed to the bead of condensation clinging to the bottom of her glass. Within seconds, the droplet of water plopped to the quilt, darkening a spot as it soaked in. Smoothing her fingertip around the tiny circle it made, she quietly asked, "What about *your* family, Travis?"

"What about them?"

She was a bit surprised by the raw edge in his voice, but she certainly recognized its counterparts. Old baggage, old disappointments, old pain. She looked over at him and found him studying the deviled egg in his hand.

She was curious about his behavior, but even more curious about Travis Delaney, the man. Trying for a tone of voice that was somewhere in between blatant noisiness and general concern, she quietly asked, "Do you have any family, Travis, other than Braden's, I mean?"

He stared straight ahead, as if he was trying to decide how much to tell her. Finally finding his voice, he said, "As far as I know, my parents, if you want to call them that, are still living. Somewhere. Not together. I haven't seen them in a long, long time."

Cori wasn't aware that she'd moved closer. She only knew that his slow words and mellow voice drew her, evoking a response from deep inside her at the same time. This was something very few people went through. It was also something she understood all too well.

"What happened?" she whispered.

For a moment, Travis felt as if he were peering through a thick fog. He turned his head, wondering when Cori had removed her hat. Slowly, she came closer, watching him, waiting for him to continue. This wasn't how he'd planned to spend his lunch hour, and his past sure as hell wasn't something he wanted to dredge up. But he wanted to get to know her better, to get closer to her. Looking at the emotions deep in her blue eyes, he figured this was as good a place as any to begin.

"I don't have many memories of my childhood, at least not good ones," he said, keeping his voice level. "I guess my clearest memory is of the night my old man finally left for good. He and my mother were fighting, as usual. It was his thirty-ninth birthday, and my mother had found out about another of his girlfriends. He said he wasn't going to spend the rest of his life with a woman who did nothing but nag him from the inside of a bottle. They yelled some more, and he left."

"What did your mother do?"

"She took one look at the dreary apartment, reached for her open bottle of Scotch, and disappeared into her bedroom."

"Were you there?" she asked quietly.

He nodded, and she closed her eyes.

"How old were you, Travis?"

He shrugged, shifting uncomfortably on the blanket. "I was ten, but it's really no big deal. I learned to take care of myself, and I did a pretty good job of it, too."

Cori knew he was leaving a lot out, but he'd told her enough for her to picture the incident in her mind. He'd been in some dreary apartment when some man who couldn't have been much of a father left for good, and he'd watched as a woman who wasn't much better had reached for her bottle instead of her son. Although his mother hadn't left in the physical sense, Travis had been deserted by both his parents that night. And he'd only been ten years old.

Wishing there was some way for her to tell him she understood, she glanced at him, but he'd turned his attention to the rose trellis nearby, giving her free rein to study him unhurriedly. Even in profile, his face was full of strength, his forehead, his angular jaw and chin. Instead of the coffee-colored highlights one might expect in hair so dark, his glimmered with threads of auburn, chestnut and bronze.

Although he'd said that witnessing his father's desertion and his mother's retreat into her bedroom all those years ago hadn't been a big deal, Cori happened to know better. That incident, along with others she could only imagine, had shaped the young boy he'd been into the man he was now. Because of it or in spite of it, she wasn't sure which, he'd become quite a man.

He turned his head, his gaze unerringly settling to hers. In that instant, everything else receded to another plane. For that moment, she and Travis were the only two people in the garden, the only two people on the street, quite possibly the only two people in the world. Even as she told herself she'd done the right thing when she'd decided she couldn't become involved with him, her gaze strayed to his mouth.

Lisa had said he had a bad-boy smile. He wasn't smiling now. Instead, his lips were set in a straight line. She knew what those lips felt like, all warm and masculine and responsive, and she knew how they tasted. Her heart thudded, and her breathing became shallow, because she wondered what he'd say if he knew she wanted to kiss him again.

Travis liked the way Cori was watching him, studying him, memorizing him. Somewhere nearby, a bee buzzed in its never-ending quest for nectar. Farther away, he heard the occasional sound of street traffic. Otherwise, the garden was utterly still, utterly quiet.

Cori was sitting at a ninety-degree angle to him, her knees drawn up, her face turned toward his. Her innermost feelings played across her features: understanding, empathy, attraction. Especially attraction. Concentrating on that, longing stretched over him, until he was unable to fight his growing need to touch her. He placed most of his weight on one hand and leaned toward her. Reaching for her fingers with his free hand, he gently pulled her closer.

She swayed toward him easily, willingly. Her chin came up as his went down, their timing so perfect it could have been choreographed in some other lifetime. Her mouth opened on a soft sigh, meeting his halfway. Her lips were petal-soft, and like the other time they'd kissed, desire radiated in every direction the moment she touched them to his.

With his eyes closed dreamily, he relied on his other senses, and his other senses were filled with wonder. The garden was alive with the mingled aromas of flowers, a scent that seemed to be the essence of the woman herself. The air was warm, the blanket beneath him smooth and soft. His hand found its way to her upper arm, where he kneaded the small muscles before moving on to her shoulder, to her back, to her waist, where his palm finally came into contact with bare flesh.

He'd never be sure how it happened, but somehow, she was leaning toward him and he was leaning back, until he was stretched out on his side on the soft, quilt-covered patch of grass. Cori's warm body fit his perfectly, hip to hip, waist to waist, chest to chest.

The flowers and soft green fronds in Ivy's Garden hid them from view of the inn, the thick maple leaves overhead their only ceiling other than the sky. In their own secluded corner, the kiss went on and on.

Need grew strong within him, thick and primal and lusty. His hand smoothed over the soft skin at her waist, then higher, around to her back then up one side, his fingers skimming the outer swell of her breast through the soft lace of her bra. She leaned into his hand, a deep-throated moan escaping her, the lusty sound nearly his undoing.

Her hands started an exploration of their own, roaming from his shoulders to his chest, kneading and skimming and bringing him so much pleasure he was sure he'd explode with the onrushing of emotions her touch evoked. Somewhere high overhead a jet broke the sound barrier. Moments later a mellow, slightly out-of-tune whistle found its way into their haze of passion.

Cori heard the familiar sound, and went perfectly still. She lifted her mouth from Travis's as if in slow motion, and finally opened her eyes.

Lying there, her face only inches from his, she listened as that out-of-tune whistle came steadily closer, then stopped altogether. In the ensuing silence, she tried to get her breathing under control, not to mention her thoughts. Long before she'd accomplished either, she heard the distant creak of the mailbox's hinges.

She rolled to her side and went up onto her knees. Peeking around the rose trellis and through the hollyhocks and daylilies, she saw their friendly mailman pull the inn's mail from his brown leather bag. Seconds later, he turned and headed back up the sidewalk on stocky legs visible beneath the hem of baggy shorts. The whistling started up again, fading away as steadily as it had come.

"The mail just arrived," she said.

"So that's what that noise was." When she didn't make a single move, he asked, "Do you want to go check it?"

Cori glanced down into Travis' brown eyes, feeling sideswiped by her emotions. Until Travis, she hadn't thought of brown as a warm color, but until Travis, she never would have believed that *anything* could make her forget about the letter she so desperately hoped would arrive any day.

"Go ahead," he said. "I'll just stay here a minute and catch my breath."

His voice had dipped so low she imagined she could feel it brushing over her bare knees. Her emotions followed its trail like rose petals scattering in a warm summer breeze.

Of its own volition, her gaze left his, skimming his body from head to toe.

She averted her eyes quickly, cursing the blush she felt rising to her cheeks. Suddenly needing something to do with her hands, she plucked her straw hat from the quilt and quickly rose to her feet. "I think I will go check the mail. I'll, um, only be a minute."

Travis saw the soft pink color spread to her cheeks. God, the woman was incredible. She'd been unbelievably brazen, undeniably responsive, practically kissing him senseless mere seconds ago, and here she was blushing at the effect she'd had on his body.

Her lush curves had fit him so perfectly, and her kisses had been so delicious, he wanted to pull her to him all over again, to roll her underneath him and pick up where they'd left off. Instead, he rose to a sitting position and watched her wend her way over the curving garden path to the other side of an ornate picket fence and on to the old-fashioned mailbox near the inn's back door.

She was wearing shorts and a peach-colored shirt that stopped an inch or two above her waist. It was the first time he'd seen her in anything other than a skirt. He'd wondered if there were freckles anyplace except on her nose. He hadn't noticed any, but then, at the time, he'd been going more by touch than sight. And everything about her had felt wonderful.

Until today, she'd been awfully adept at fluttering away, out of his reach, every time he came near. He wondered what she'd do after she'd had a chance to think about what had just happened between them.

The mailbox creaked as she opened it, her trepidation at what she might find clearly evident in the slight shake in her fingers. The expression on her face when she didn't find whatever it was she was looking for was a little more difficult to decipher, but the word she uttered cleared everything up. As far as he knew, *dammit* had a universal meaning.

Rising to his feet, he watched as she turned and made her way back toward him. When she'd reached the half-way mark, he called, "What were you expecting? Notification that you've won a clearing-house sweepstakes?"

"Hardly."

"Good," he answered, walking closer. "Because there are a lot of people who think those things are scams."

"Oh, really?"

She was smiling, albeit grudgingly, and Travis was trying to decide how far he should push his luck. When she stopped in the middle of the flagstone walkway, he said, "Really."

"Look, Travis . . ."

Thinking fast, he said, "And if Ginny had heard you swear just now, she'd have you saying two Hail Marys."

He saw a trace of humor in her smile, and found himself smiling back. "Are you ready to finish lunch?" he asked.

Eyeing him skeptically, she said, "I think I've had enough."

If Travis had been a fool, he would have argued that she couldn't possibly have had enough, not when they were just getting started. But he wasn't a fool. Opting for another tack, he said, "Ginny isn't going to like that."

With a mild shake of her head, she asked, "Are you making this up?"

He dropped down to the quilt and casually reached for his plate before making the sound men everywhere make when thinking about an exasperating woman. "No, Ginny Calhoun is a lot of things, but she isn't a figment of my imagination."

This time her laughter was real, and so was her curiosity. She didn't walk over and drop down to the quilt next to him as he'd hoped she would, but she did sit on one corner and reach for her plate.

"How long have you known the Calhouns?" she asked.

"Since I was a kid. I was on my own a lot while I was growing up, and got in more than my share of trouble. I met Braden in the principal's office. Believe it or not, we struck up a friendship, and I ended up at his place most weekends. When I was seventeen, I followed him home for good. By then I'd acquired a rather *extensive* use of the English language."

"Every other word was a swearword?" she asked.

He nodded. "Ginny said a prayer every time I cussed. There were a lot of whispered incantations in the air those first few months, believe me."

Taking a long drink of lemonade, Cori couldn't believe she was sitting here casually talking to Travis after the way they'd just kissed. He, on the other hand, didn't appear to think that anything unusual was taking place. It was almost as if he believed it was the most natural thing in the world. The strange thing was, spending time with him *felt* natural. How could that be? What was there about this man that drew her and baffled her at the same time?

He was too brash to be a complete gentleman, too quiet to be truly arrogant, and just sure enough of himself to think nothing of any of it. She was discovering that he had good reasons for his bad-boy smile, his occasional brooding silences. She could almost picture him as he'd been at seventeen, tall and lanky, slightly belligerent, lost, but too proud to admit it. Although he'd undoubtedly filled out in his adulthood, he was still tall, belligerent and proud, and Cori had a feeling that she was on the verge of discovering the heart of a very special man.

Their gazes met, one moment stretching to two. Nerves clamored in her stomach, and worry furrowed her brow, because she wasn't sure she could ever say no to him if she got to know him all the way to his heart.

"What are you thinking?" he asked quietly.

She swallowed and glanced down at her plate. "That you could complicate my life, not to mention confuse me."

A strange tension settled over Travis. Truth be told, he *liked* complications, and he *wanted* to confuse her, if it meant she'd see him, and kiss him, and...

Desire was still thick inside him. He wanted her. The world's biggest understatement. But that wasn't all there was to what he felt for her. If it had been, he could have walked away last week after that first kiss right here in this very garden. After all, he wasn't stupid. He was a man, with a man's sensitive ego, and he didn't happen to relish the idea of giving anybody the opportunity to stomp on it. But he hadn't walked away from her before, and he didn't now. He couldn't, because whether she admitted it or not, she wanted him, too—the world's second biggest understatement.

Those kisses they'd shared had been spontaneous, her whispered sighs so throaty and deep his eyelids dropped down at the memory alone. He'd made a lot of progress today. Unfortunately, he didn't know what to do to keep from losing ground.

Without any warning, she placed her hat on her head, and quickly rose to her feet, saying, "It's time for me to get back to work."

He rolled up to his knees and said, "Cori, wait!"

She stopped several feet away.

Once again sunlight shone through her hat, dappling her face with golden color. He couldn't make out the expression in her eyes, but if he was reading her body language correctly, she was expecting him to ask her out again, and was gearing up to say no all over again.

Since he wasn't especially fond of the word *no*, he decided to steer the conversation in a different direction. "What did you think of Ginny's cooking?"

Surprise registered on her face, and a smile found its way to her lips. "I think Ginny Calhoun must be an incredible woman, and her potato salad was almost as good as Ivy's. Everything was perfect. Thank her for me, okay?"

Thank *her?* Travis said to himself, mentally going over everything *he'd* done to bring Cori this picnic lunch, not to mention what he was going to have to put up with from Sam and Ginny as repayment. "Is that all you have to say?"

"Well," she said, "I am curious about one other thing."

"What's that?"

"You mentioned an upcoming birthday. How old are you going to be, when Ginny throws that surprise party, I mean?"

Of all the things she could have been interested in, she'd brought up the sorest subject of all. Biting down a string of expletives that would have cost him more Hail Marys than he wanted to think about, he finally said, "According to Braden, Ginny's planning the *surprise* party for this Sunday, but my birthday isn't until the following day."

"And?" she prodded.

"And then I'll be thirty-nine."

She cast him a knowing look that made him the tiniest bit uncomfortable. He might have questioned her about it, but he had something else on his mind.

"Cori?" he called. "As long as we're asking personal questions, I have one for you. If you aren't hoping to win a sweepstakes, what do you look for in that mailbox every day?"

He could tell from the deep breath she took and the way her shoulders shook that she was having a difficult time forming an answer. Finally, she simply said, "I'm waiting for a letter."

"I figured that much out for myself. Who are you waiting to hear from?" he asked quietly.

It was her turn to look uncomfortable with the question, her turn to spread her lips in a thin line before answering. "I'm hoping to hear from my parents."

"Why, do they live far away?"

"No, they live right here in Wisconsin, but I haven't seen them in almost seventeen years."

Without another word, she turned around again and strode into the inn. Feeling dazed, Travis climbed to his feet and watched her go.

She hadn't refused to go out with him this time, but then, this time, he hadn't asked. Somehow, that didn't matter. She'd had lunch with him, and she'd kissed him. She'd talked with him, and she'd looked into his eyes as if she thought he was someone special. He didn't know the whole story behind the letter she was waiting for, but he doubted he'd ever forget the tremor in her voice or the quiver in her chin just before she'd turned away. No wonder she'd been so curious about his life story. She had a turbulent one of her own.

That woman had a way of turning him upside down and inside out. He never quite knew what to expect from her, never quite knew what she was going to do or say. Good Lord, she could smile like the first morning and kiss like a dream, but there was another side to her, a side that had been hurt so deeply that she seemed to have lost her faith in herself and in her own strength.

She may have had him going around in circles, but all in all, the picnic had been a huge success. Unfortunately, he didn't know what he was going to do for an encore.

He set to work scooping up their used plates and stacking them inside the picnic basket. Long before he was through, a grin was pulling at his lips. Corinna Cassidy was going to go out with him, or he was going to die trying.

And he was feeling much, much too young to die.

* * *

Allison waited for a break in the traffic before crossing to the shaded side of the street. Setting off at a normal pace, she caught sight of a black car as it turned the corner up ahead. By the time the '87 Camaro pulled to a stop at the curb next to her, a smile had spread across her face.

"Hey," Ross called.

"Hey, yourself," she answered, striding closer. "I thought you were going waterskiing with the guys."

"I took my turn a couple of times, but I couldn't stop thinking about you."

"Oh, Ross."

He threw the gearshift into park and opened his door, meeting her on the grassy slope between the curb and the sidewalk. "Do you have any idea what you do to me when you say my name like that?"

"I have a pretty good idea." She cocked her head at him the way she always did, but the area surrounding her heart softened and swelled in a most peculiar way.

"How were Laurie's home videos?" he asked.

"They were great," Allison answered. "The Grand Canyon was spectacular, but Laurie swears the guy she met there was the best scenery she saw."

"Better than me?"

Shrugging playfully, she said, "I'll have to let you know."

He groaned, and reached for her hand. Looking up into his light blue eyes, she was almost sure the rhythm of her heart changed. She wondered if he could tell just by looking into her eyes.

He was wearing a muscle shirt that showed off his arms and shoulders to perfection. His dark hair was on the long side, his attitude a little bit cocky. He was a grade ahead of her in school, and since she'd started dating him four months ago, she'd become the envy of every girl in both the sophomore and junior classes. She didn't think any of those things were what made him truly special. He was her first real boyfriend, so she didn't know much about guys, but she knew she'd never felt this way before, and she knew it had everything to do with Ross.

"Have you thought about what we talked about last night?" he asked.

She nodded.

"Have you thought about how much I love you?"

There was something so incredible about the way she felt when he said that. She wasn't dainty like Laurie, or chesty like Heather, and Ross didn't wear a Stetson like that guy Laurie met in the Grand Canyon, but Ross Gentry could make her feel feminine and cherished by simply saying her name.

His body was hard where hers was soft, rough where hers was smooth. Oh, she'd always known there were differences between boys and girls. The school nurse had covered that in the sixth grade, and her mother had always been open to discussions about sex. But nothing had prepared her for Ross.

"I can't think about anything else," she said shyly.

A car full of guys honked its horn as they drove by. Allison and Ross both waved. When he turned his attention back to her, his voice was less husky, but the warm glint was still in his eyes. "Let's go for a drive."

"I can't," she answered. "Mom's expecting me for dinner."

"I'll give you a ride home."

Shaking her head, she said, "I'd better not. She's not too happy about the mark on my neck. I don't want her to think I'm seeing you behind her back."

"You know you're driving me crazy."

Feeling at once infinitely strong and weak in the knees, she ran a finger along his jaw and shyly said, "I don't mean to, Ross."

Taking several backward steps, she waved, one finger at a time, then blithely turned around and strode toward home.

Travis gripped the steel bar with both hands, carefully leaning into it with most of his weight. As soon as he finished leveling this porch floor, he planned to go to the lumber company and pick up the boards and flagstones he'd need to build the gazebo and extend the sidewalk.

It felt good to be working on his own this week. It felt even better to be working close to Cori. His confidence had spiraled during their picnic yesterday. After the way she'd kissed him, he couldn't help it. He knew the alteration in their relationship had as much to do with their conversation as with those kisses. Regardless of how it had happened, a wavering connection had formed, and a fledgling alliance had sprung up between them.

He had a growing admiration for the way she dealt with her busy life. Although she didn't seem to recognize her own strength, she handled her guests with innate calm and genuine friendliness, keeping up with the never-ending tasks with apparent ease. Her friends, Jillian and Lisa, were in and out of the inn as if it was their second home. The three younger women joked and laughed with Ivy, but it was the relationship Cori had with her daughter that truly made him stand up and take notice.

Even though there were no more than seventeen-odd years between their ages, Cori was a wonderful mother who was both mature and surprisingly open with her child. He'd spoken to Allison Cassidy several times during these past four days. Each time, he was amazed at how much the girl reminded him of her mother. God, he bet Cori had been a beauty at that age, but there was no way she could have been more beautiful than she was right now.

He didn't fully understand what was happening to him, but he couldn't seem to get her out of his mind. There was more to this than hormones, although he couldn't deny that every time Cori came near there were plenty of those pulsing through his body. What was a man to do?

The old porch creaked and groaned as he slowly brought the sagging corner up flush with the rest. He studied the level in the center of the floor, applied a little more pressure to the metal bar beneath his hands, then turned to search for the two-by-fours he'd placed on the ground before starting the project. Unfortunately, the pieces of lumber were out of his reach.

Catching a movement out of the corner of his eye, he turned and saw the younger Cassidy wandering aimlessly back and forth near the lilac hedge. "Hey, Allison!" he called. "Could you give me a hand?"

The girl's blond head came up with a start, as if she'd been lost in her own world and suddenly resurfaced. "Oh, it's only you, Travis," she said.

"Sorry to disappoint you," he answered sardonically.

"I didn't mean it like that," she said, flicking her long, waving hair behind her shoulders and striding toward him. "I was just thinking, that's all."

Cori claimed Allison was ten times the spitfire *she* ever thought of being. He wasn't sure about that, but the girl *was* normally full of female energy. Today, she was unusually quiet and subdued. Motioning to the two-by-fours a few feet from her feet, he said, "Hand me one of those, would you? While you're at it, you might as well tell me what's bothering you."

"What makes you think something's bothering me?"

He raised one eyebrow the way men everywhere did when faced with a similar question from a member of the opposite sex. "Did you and Ross have a fight?" he asked.

"No. Not exactly. Well, sort of. Not in person, but when he called me last night. How did you know?"

"I've learned enough about women over the years to know when one has a man on her mind."

Allison crouched down close to the ground. Reaching for one of the pieces of wood, she said, "That's what I like about you, Travis. You don't think of me as a child."

She was wrong there. As far as Travis was concerned, Allison was little more than a baby. Since no sixteen-year-old wanted to hear that, he took the two-by-four from her hands and slid it underneath the raised porch wall.

"So," he said conversationally, "what did Ross do?"

"He hasn't really done anything," she said shyly.

He'd heard that one before.

"Travis?" Allison asked after a long pause. "How old were you the first time, you know, the first time you..."

The question came from so far out of the blue he almost dropped the second board. Even though her voice had trailed away, he knew exactly what she'd meant. Gulping in a breath of air, he said, "Well, um, gee..."

"That's okay," she said soothingly. "You don't have to tell me. But have you ever been in love? Really and truly in love?"

Not caring whether the porch sagged back to its former position, Travis let go of the lever and the second two-by-four and held up both his hands to ward off more questions. "I take it back. I don't know the first thing about women, and to be honest, I know even less about love. I think you should talk to your mother about this, not me."

"I've been thinking about that, but I'm scared, you know?"

"I thought you had more spunk than that. Just yesterday your mother told me that you grew an inch taller than her on purpose. I don't know the whole story about your mom, but I know you're sixteen and she's only thirty-three. Somehow, I think she'd understand whatever it is you're going through, don't you?"

"You really think so?"

Travis nodded. "I think she and Ivy are in the kitchen, so it looks to me as if this is your golden opportunity."

Allison leaped to her feet and spun around. In a voice that was part-child, part-woman, she said, "Thanks, Travis, you're the greatest."

"Does that mean you're going to talk to her?"

"I can't very well walk away from such a golden opportunity, can I?" she said, her old sass shining in her voice and in her eyes.

Travis shook his head and smiled.

Allison strode up the porch steps and added, "I'm going to talk to Mom, and when I'm through, I'm going to call Ross."

The porch boards creaked and groaned. Within seconds, the two-by-four tottered over and the floor sagged back to its former position. Seemingly unaware that *she*'d caused it, Allison waved to him then let the screen door bang shut behind her.

Shaking his head, he had a feeling that Cori didn't stand a chance against that girl's charm, and neither did Ross. Travis didn't begrudge the kid her sass. He only wished he'd stumble upon a golden opportunity of his own.

Voices carried to his ears from the kitchen—Cori's and Ivy's and Allison's. Travis backed away, so as not to eavesdrop, but he couldn't help overhearing the bits and pieces of the conversation drifting into the garden on the warm, still air.

His hands settled to his hips, and his thoughts formed, one at a time. He'd wished for a golden opportunity. If he wasn't mistaken, one was unfolding on the other side of that door this very minute.

Chapter Six

"Ivy, would you mind if Mom and I talked . . . alone?"

Cori wasn't sure what to make of the note of shyness in Allison's voice. After all, her daughter was a lot of things, but she was almost never shy. Cori glanced at Ivy, the expression in her dear friend's eyes only adding to her own sense of unease.

"Allison, honey, I don't mind a bit," Ivy said, taking her time wiping her hands on her yellow apron. "Your name means truthful. I know that isn't always an easy expectation to live up to, yet you've managed to do a remarkable job of it. You just let me know if there's anything you need. And that goes for you, too," she added, turning to Cori. Then, making her own special sound that was half huff and half hum, she left the room.

Cori continued to rinse the fresh blueberries in the deep sink. Keeping her voice light, she asked, "Whatcha want to talk about, kiddo?"

"It's about Ross."

"What about him?"

"Well, we talked last night, about a lot of things," Allison began, her voice gaining in volume and speed. "I've never felt this way before. It's incredible. What's even more incredible is that he feels the same way about me. He's special, Mom. I think he's the one. Last night he told me he wants to marry me."

Cori swung around to face her daughter.

"N-not now," Allison stammered. "After high school, maybe even after college. In a long time."

Cori forced herself to relax. Okay, so Allison wanted to get married, years and years from now...

"But he loves me now, Mom, and I love him."

Cori went very still.

"Do you remember all those times when you told me I could always come to you with anything, anything at all?"

Cori nodded, but it wasn't easy.

"Well, I want..."

Allison's voice trailed away, so that the only sound in the room was Cori's thudding heart.

"I mean, I think I should..."

Once again, Allison didn't finish, and Cori didn't know what to say. She'd been fearing this moment for years, and expecting it for weeks. How could she be so unprepared for it now that it had arrived?

"...um, Ross doesn't... I mean, I don't... I mean, we don't want to wait until we're married. It'll be such a long time until then, and..."

Suddenly, Cori remembered the first time she'd looked into her newborn daughter's trusting eyes. At the time, she'd been little older than Allison was now. Ivy had gone home, and Cori had been sore and weepy, alone and afraid. She'd brushed one finger over her baby's soft cheek. Allison had made a tiny sound, almost like a sigh, and turned her face into her mother's touch. Cori's heart had turned over, and in that instant, everything had changed.

Her baby had barely weighed six pounds, but Cori would never forget how it felt to hold her in her arms. During the wee hours of that dark winter morning, she'd promised her child that she'd always be there for her, would always love her, support her, accept her. More than anything, she'd promised to protect her. That wasn't the kind of protection Allison was asking for now.

"Do you want to see a doctor?" Cori whispered, her heart so heavy she was sure it would drop down into her stomach any second.

When Allison didn't answer, Cori whispered, "Is that what you're trying to say, Allison? Is it?"

Allison nodded once.

Cori closed her eyes and took a shaky breath. In a voice thick with emotion, she said, "I know it must have taken a lot of courage to tell me this, and I want you to know how much I respect you and admire you and especially how much I love you. You're so much stronger than I was at your age, and I swear there's nothing you could ever do to change the way I feel about you. But baby, you're only sixteen. I'll do whatever I have to do to keep you safe, but are you sure, absolutely sure that you're ready to take this step?"

"Ross and I have talked about it before. I've given it a lot of thought, Mom."

Cori took a step closer. She started to reach up to smooth a strand of pale blond hair from Allison's cheek. The stiffness in her daughter's slender shoulders and the set of her chin halted Cori's hand. Allison was setting her own boundaries, and while Cori knew it was normal, her heart ached, and she couldn't keep her voice from breaking into a whisper as she said, "I'm sure you have, but you can be grown-up for the rest of your life. You don't have much longer to be a child."

"That's just it," Allison retorted, her voice rising. "I'm not a child. I'm already more mature than most kids my age."

"But we have an agreement, kiddo—Allison. A pact."

"That pact's not fair!" the girl cried, her voice rising to a full-scale wail. "It was okay before I met Ross. But he and I are in love. It's easy for you. *You're not even dating anyone.* I want out of it. Out, do you hear me?"

Allison's outburst drained the blood from Cori's face. She'd messed up a lot of things in her life, but she'd been there for her little girl every day for the past sixteen years. She'd rocked her to sleep when she was afraid, cleaned her scratches and cajoled her out of an occasional bad mood. She'd loved her with everything she had, and so far, she'd kept her safe. Their pact was the only way she knew to protect her now. And Allison wanted to dissolve it. What in the world was Cori going to do?

A sound near the door drew her attention. Turning, she saw Travis slowly step into the room. He nodded at both of them then closed the screen door behind him.

"I hope I'm not interrupting," he began.

"What is it, Travis?" Cori asked, her voice sounding oddly quiet after Allison's outburst moments ago.

"I couldn't help overhearing, and I was curious about something," he said, sauntering farther into the room. "Cori, why don't you tell Allison here that I've asked you to have dinner with me?"

Except for two sharp intakes of breath, the room was so quiet Travis could have heard a pin drop. He struggled to maintain an even, conciliatory expression, which wasn't easy with the excitement strumming through him.

He glanced from one Cassidy to the other. Both their eyes were round, their mouths slightly open. He wasn't sure which of their faces was more pale, but Allison was the first to find her voice.

"Is this true, Mom?" she asked. "Has Travis asked you out?"

Apparently, Cori was still having a difficult time thinking coherently, because all she did was nod.

"M...o...m!"

Travis wasn't certain what finally drew Cori from her befuddled state, the way her daughter stretched the word "mom" from one M to the other, or the smile he was having a hard time keeping off his face.

"This is so weird," Allison declared to her mother. "You never date."

He noticed Cori's shakily drawn breath, but was proud of the way she pulled herself together as she slowly turned to face her daughter and say, "Does this mean our pact still stands?"

Allison gave a long, long-suffering sigh, even for a teenager. Shrugging, she said, "Yes, I guess it does." Stiffly backing toward the door, she added, "I promised Ross I'd call him this afternoon. So...well...I guess I'll go do that now."

She cast both her mother and Travis an oddly shy look, then hurried from the room. Within seconds, the door closed, leaving Travis and Cori alone.

Travis didn't know what sort of pact was between mother and daughter. It wasn't exactly the kind of thing he'd ever experienced with either of his parents, but if it made Cori proud of her kid, he figured it had to be something good. It probably had to do with trust, honesty, and heart-to-heart talks about boys and God only knew what else.

In that instant, he wouldn't have minded a little heart-to-heart with Cori, only he wasn't thinking about doing a lot of talking. Taking a step closer, he quietly said, "I don't know how you keep up with her, but I can see why you're proud."

Cori never would have believed such a softly spoken compliment could cause so many feelings to swell in her chest. Pride and amazement and pleasure all came together to send a giddy sense of relief coursing through her. Not caring that she gushed, she grinned at him and declared, "You probably don't know it, but you just saved the day. Thank you, Travis. Thank you so much."

He didn't give her an innocent shrug as she'd expected. Instead, he faced her from halfway across the room. In a voice that was low and composed, he said, "There's no need to thank me, Cori. I'll pick you up at seven."

Without another word, he followed the same path Allison had taken across the old linoleum floor. With her heart thudding and her lips parted on a sharp intake of breath, Cori could do nothing but watch him go.

She didn't remember walking to the door, but peering out, she couldn't help noticing Travis's lean-hipped swagger as he stepped over a level and some boards then ambled around the corner of the house. Narrowing her eyes, she realized that he hadn't strolled in here and innocently saved the day by telling Allison about his invitation to dinner. In fact, there was nothing innocent about anything he'd said or done.

Travis Delaney knew exactly what he was doing.

Bother!

Cori slipped the post of one earring through her earlobe and reached for the other one, her thoughts once again turning to Travis and their upcoming date. After he'd ambled out of the inn's kitchen late that morning, she'd done a lot of thinking about his motives and her reaction to him. In fact, she'd thought of little else.

His timing had been perfect where Allison was concerned, his mention of dinner such a relief she'd grasped it like the golden opportunity it was. When she'd first watched him walk away, she'd felt as if he'd tricked her into having dinner with him. After a time, she knew that wasn't so. She had a choice. She could have turned down his invitation. Again. Or she could have let Allison believe she'd gone out with Travis. But she could never lie to her daughter. She couldn't lie to herself, either. And the truth was, she was attracted to one tall, rugged carpenter whose smiles were rare and whose expressions were dark and the tiniest bit insolent.

How many times had her parents told her she was weak of the flesh? She'd been as righteous as Sunday school these past sixteen years, but that was before she met Travis Delaney. How in the world was she going to keep her pact with Allison when she went all warm and pliant every time he touched her?

By the time she finished applying her lipstick, she'd reached a decision. She would let him know, in no uncertain terms, that this was going to be the first and last date they ever had.

Feeling strengthened by her convictions, she strode to the kitchen and smiled at Ross. He returned her greeting, but it was obvious that his heart wasn't in it. Although she was immensely pleased with Allison's decision, she remembered how it felt to be a kid. Ross was a nice boy. She only wished, for both their sakes, that he and Allison would have met ten years from now, when they were both older and wiser, and ready to deal with their emotions and desires.

They were much too young to get serious, to take on the responsibilities of adulthood, although, right now, she doubted that either of them would appreciate hearing her say it. Still, she trusted Allison. If her daughter said she would honor their pact, she would. Cori's relief was so pure she was sure she was practically floating. Now, all she had to do was handle her date with Travis.

The moment she heard his knock, she raced into the front room. She called a quick goodbye to both kids and still managed to beat Allison to the door. "Be good," she whispered.

"You, too."

Cori gave Allison a sidelong glance, her own face breaking into a smile despite her hurry. That daughter of hers had always been quick-witted and wily. She gave Allison a kiss on the cheek. Within seconds she turned the handle and stepped out onto the front step.

She hid her smile to herself at the look on Travis's face. His eyes widened, and the hand that was still poised in midair following his knock slowly lowered to his side. She'd surprised him by greeting him on the front step instead of inviting him inside.

Good. She had every intention of staying one step ahead of him. That didn't mean she'd be nasty or rude, because no matter what his ulterior motives were, he *had* come to her rescue with Allison. She was grateful, but she planned to be extremely careful not to appear overly so.

"Hi, Travis," she said breezily. "You're early, just as I *expected*."

Travis took a backward step down to the ground. Something about Cori's behavior rendered him speechless. Her smile was genuine enough, but a little too knowing for his peace of mind. And the way she'd accented the word "expected" made him think she was *expecting* more from him than his early arrival. He wouldn't be at all surprised if she was *expecting* a seduction scene, too.

The fact that she was right didn't make him feel any better. He'd been looking forward to having dinner with Cori, but he'd been even more anxious to get her alone *after* dinner. In fact, he'd harbored a good share of fantasies in which he encircled her wrists with his long fingers and slowly drew her to bed.

From the look on her face and the tone of her voice, that was exactly what she *expected* him to do. She'd been ready and waiting for his knock, and she hadn't invited him in.

She certainly hadn't wasted any time on small talk. They were only twenty seconds into their date and all his carefully made plans were already going awry.

Until that moment, he'd thought that getting her to agree to go out with him had been his biggest challenge. Now he knew that wasn't so. Getting her to go out with him *again* was going to be his biggest challenge. She would never do that if he went through with his plans for the evening, plans that included a quiet, intimate dinner for two at a dimly lit restaurant, followed by a walk in the moonlight and a night of passion back at her place or his.

Damn.

"It's a beautiful evening, now that the temperature and humidity have dropped," she said conversationally, falling into step beside him.

He made an agreeing sort of sound without moving his lips. Seemingly satisfied with his answer, she continued to talk about inconsequential things. Barely listening to her conversation, he frantically searched for an alternative plan, discarding every notion as quickly as it formed.

By the time they reached his Jeep at the end of her narrow driveway, he had run out of ideas and patience, and was about ready to climb out of his skin. He couldn't take her to a fancy restaurant and he couldn't seduce her. What in the hell was he supposed to do?

Out of the blue, an idea popped into his head. *Do the last thing she would expect.* Within seconds, a plan was full-blown, and he started to relax. Cori thought she could read his mind? Well, he'd see what she read into what he had in store for her tonight.

"Since I didn't know where we were going, I wasn't sure how to dress. I hope this is all right," she said, standing aside while he opened her door.

For the first time that evening, Travis turned all his attention to her, taking full advantage of the opportunity to look her up and down. As on the first day he saw her, everything about her appeared golden. She wore another long, airy skirt, this one in shades of brown and gold. Her blouse was sleeveless and scoop-necked. It matched the gold in her skirt, and lay against her curves like a whisper. Her feet were ensconced in flat, strappy sandals that somehow made her seem delicate and infinitely feminine.

"I don't see how you could go wrong with that outfit," he answered, cursing the huskiness he couldn't quite keep out of his voice.

There was a trace of laughter behind her smile as she thanked him for the compliment, and a trace of feminine wiles behind her shining blue eyes. In that instant, he knew her delicateness was just an illusion. If he'd learned one thing these past two weeks, it was that Corinna Cassidy was as stubborn as she was tall. As aggravating as it could be at times, he liked that in a woman. At least, he liked it in her.

"Where are we going, anyway?" she asked coyly.

It took incredible willpower to keep from kissing that knowing grin off her face then and there. Since she probably *expected* him to do that, too, he simply said, "I think you're in for quite a surprise. But why don't you tell me what you think after we get there?"

Her chin came up and around. He pretended not to notice. He didn't, however, even pretend to try to keep the jauntiness out of his stride as he hurried around to the other side of the Jeep.

Hot damn and Hail Mary! They were both in for quite a night!

Cori smoothed her skirt around her and clicked her seat belt into place, keeping her eyes trained on Travis every second. She was sure he'd been surprised when she'd greeted him on the front step instead of asking him in. Watching him now, she didn't know what to make of the change in him. In the blink of an eye, his apprehension had disappeared into thin air and his jauntiness had come back in full force. It wasn't anything he'd actually said. It was more the way he walked, the way he climbed onto his seat and started his vehicle's engine, the way he sat as he effortlessly pointed the Jeep south, all loose-limbed and comfortable, at ease and invigorated at the same time.

This was the first time she'd seen him in a tie. If anything, it made him appear even more handsome, but it did nothing to tone down his ruggedness, or to chase away the sensuous light in his eyes. The man was up to something; of that she felt certain.

Half an hour later, she wondered if maybe she'd been a little hasty, a tad judgmental, and completely wrong about his intentions. She'd fully expected him to take her to a dimly lit restaurant where there would be husky murmurs and dusky scents and long, searing looks.

Peering past the rows of semis parked helter-skelter in the huge lot, she asked, "We're having dinner at a place called Mel's Truck Stop?"

He pulled into a parking space near the door and said, "I happened upon this place a couple of years back when we built a house a few miles from here. Mel makes the best curly fries I've ever tasted, and his blueberry pie, well . . ."

Cori couldn't help smiling at the congeniality in Travis's voice. Relaxing by degrees, she was fairly certain that curly fries and blueberry pie were hardly the stuff seductions were made of. Evidently, she'd been wrong about his intentions and his barely-there smiles.

He, on the other hand, had been right, at least about a couple of things. Mel did make the best curly fries she'd ever tasted, but every once in a while, when Travis's gaze settled on her mouth, she was almost sure his thoughts shimmered into erogenous zones along with hers. It wasn't anything he said, and it certainly wasn't the atmosphere inside the truck stop where he'd chosen to take her to dinner. It was something else, something she couldn't quite put her finger on.

The restaurant was old but clean. The same could be said for Mel. Cori wasn't the only woman sitting at one of the many booths and tables, but she was the only one who wasn't wearing a T-shirt advertising motor oil or tires. She was also pretty sure she was the only woman Travis had looked at since setting foot inside the building. His unwavering attention made her feel interesting and feminine, and brought out emotions she was afraid to analyze.

"What do you think of my choice in restaurants?" he asked, his deep voice at odds with the smell of greasy food and the raucous laughter coming from the back of the room.

Cori traced a pattern around the label on the bottle of ketchup sitting in the center of the table. Travis was watching her. Her own gaze slowly strayed to the two-hundred-and-eighty-pound man with the dirty-dishwater beard and ponytail who was leaning over the pay phone. Sitting there in silence, she tried to remember how long it had been since she'd been within hearing distance of a trucker murmuring sweet nothings to his sweetheart.

She swept her hand through the air in front of her and said, "This place isn't fancy, but there's a unique feeling here, a kind of welcome for all these men and women whose work takes them far from home. That alone puts a unique brand of class and charm on the place, don't you think?"

He looked at her for a long time before saying, "You're probably the only person who's ever found this place charming, Cori, but if there's any class in Mel's tonight it's all because of you."

Warmth surged through her at the sincerity behind Travis's softly spoken words. His compliment touched her in ways she hadn't anticipated. Her heart thumped, seeming to rise to her throat. As if he knew, or as if he was feeling it, too, he smoothed a hand down his tie and leaned back in his chair. His gaze was as soft as a caress, the look in his eyes as fleeting as a wish.

It was incredible and heady and dangerous, and it threw her off-balance. Hoping he didn't notice how strained her voice sounded, she reached for her coffee and said, "Actually, my mother always said I'd end up in a place like this. Or worse."

Travis didn't know what had put the sudden stiffness in Cori's shoulders, but he would have recognized the self-deprecation in her voice any day of the week. Motioning for the frizzy-haired waitress to bring more coffee and a generous helping of blueberry pie, he said, "I think Ivy's Garden is better suited to your personality."

"That's what Ivy says."

He was a little surprised when she didn't elaborate, and immensely relieved when she reached for her fork and took a small bite of the pie in front of her. A dozen feet away, the trucker made kissing sounds into the mouthpiece then hung up the phone. Taking a deep, lonely breath, the poor guy turned and ambled away. The chain hooked to his wallet clinked with every step he took, but at least his departure awarded them a little more privacy.

The desire that had been uncurling deep inside Travis since the moment Cori had agreed to have dinner with him hadn't gone away. In fact, he swore it was stronger now than it had ever been. When he'd decided to do an about-turn and bring her here, he'd had every intention of keeping things light. There hadn't been anything light in the tone of her voice moments ago. It looked as though his plans for the evening were about to take another turn. At this rate, there was no telling where it would end, but Travis was pretty sure it wouldn't end in passion the way he'd hoped it would.

Not this time, a voice whispered inside his head. But soon.

Not sure how much longer he could ward off the need to touch her, he scooped up a forkful of his own pie and tried to think of a safer topic of conversation. "How long have you known Ivy?" he asked.

Pushing a berry around on her plate, Cori said, "I met her on the beach at Lake Mendota when I was sixteen. We've been friends ever since."

"Where were your parents?" Travis asked quietly.

"Back in Green Bay, but they'd washed their hands of me. Those were my father's exact words."

Clenching his jaw, Travis asked, "Because Allison was on the way?"

Cori nodded and said, "I was a constant source of embarrassment to them. As far as I know, my father is still a professor at the University of Wisconsin in Green Bay. My mother dabbled in local theater. They're very steadfast and proper, meticulous and intelligent. My father could analyze numeric equations in his head and my mother could memorize every line in an entire play by reading it twice. Imagine their dismay and disappointment when I couldn't subtract without using my fingers, and when I fell off the stage during the third-grade play."

Suddenly, Travis's pie tasted like seaweed. These new feelings twisting in his stomach were even worse than unspent desire. He listened as Cori talked about her childhood, but he couldn't help noticing how she put herself down in every incident. So she wasn't a short and petite actress like her mother or scholarly like her father. So she'd had bruises on her knees and couldn't stay on her toes in ballet class. So what? Her strengths lay in other areas. Why hadn't her parents seen that? Why didn't she?

Pushing his plate away, he said, "If either of Braden's sisters had fallen off the stage during their school plays, Sam and Ginny would have given them a standing ovation."

For a moment, Cori stared wordlessly across the table at Travis. His mention of Braden's sisters intrigued her. For some reason, she'd assumed that Braden was an only child, too.

"Braden has sisters?" she asked.

"Two," Travis answered. "Anne and Rachel. You wouldn't believe the fuss they caused! They were seven and nine when I went to live with the Calhouns, and I swear those girls went through every emotion in the book every day of the week."

Cori smiled at the mixture of dismay and affection in his voice. "Girls do tend to be very demonstrative," she agreed. "To this day I can tell what kind of day Allison has had by the way she walks into the house."

"Did she fall off any stages when she was younger?" he asked.

Shaking her head, she said, "No, but I'll never forget what she did when she was in the seventh grade. Her teacher was a huge Shakespeare fan, and gave Allison the role of Juliet in *Romeo and Juliet.* My darling daughter thought the whole thing was boring, so the night before the play, she talked Jimmy Johnson into switching roles with her. He played Juliet, and she was Romeo. It was so hilarious it practically brought the house down, but I don't think Mrs. Anderson, her teacher, has ever fully recovered."

Travis found himself laughing along with Cori as she told one story after another of her daughter's antics. The kid definitely had a lot of spunk. He didn't blame Cori for being proud, and he definitely liked the laughter in her voice more than the disparagement he'd heard earlier when she'd been talking about her own childhood.

She continued to reminisce while he paid for their meal. By the time he pulled into her driveway and turned off the Jeep's engine half an hour later, she was finishing yet another story.

"...Allison inherited my mother's flair for memorizing lines. Too bad she didn't inherit my father's mathematical genius. If she had, she wouldn't have gotten so far behind in geometry after having mono last winter."

Travis heard the traces of sadness and guilt tucked inside Cori's words, and bit back a curse. He thought he'd had a crummy childhood. He had. But at least his parents hadn't had any expectations of him. Consequently, he'd never felt as if he'd let them down. Cori's childhood, although not as rough, was beginning to sound even worse than his, because *her* parents had made her feel inadequate, uncoordinated, stupid. He doubted his old man or lady had known better, but he'd bet his and Braden's company that Cori's had.

The windows were down in the Jeep, an occasional voice or two carrying to their ears from the garden and a neighbor's yard. Cori's head was turned slightly so that part of her face was in shadow. Her eyelashes were charcoal-colored, the freckles across her nose barely visible. A portion of her hair was fastened high on her head with a golden comb, leaving that side of her face bare, the dainty ridge of her ear exposed. She'd been wearing lipstick when the evening had started. Now her lips were a natural, pale pink.

Fighting the impulse to smooth his thumb over the pouty curve of her lower lip, he said, "Anybody can see how much you and Allison look alike. What else did she inherit from you besides her blond hair and winning smile?"

Cori pulled a face. "Let's just say my daughter came by her stubbornness naturally."

"You? Stubborn?"

She laughed along with him for a moment. When their laughter trailed away, she said, "I realized early on that I'm more stubborn than most people. How many girls do you know who were stubborn enough to ignore everything they'd been taught and get pregnant when they were only sixteen?''

She pulled up on the handle and pushed her door open as if she didn't expect an answer. Without another word, she slid to her feet and closed the door behind her.

Travis caught up with her near the front of the Jeep. Keeping his voice quiet so that the few guests who were strolling through the gardens wouldn't hear, he said, ''I got the scoop on sex the usual way, Cori—from my locker-room buddies in Junior High. Since then, I've done a little research, and in case you've forgotten, it takes *two* people to make a baby. So no matter how stubborn you were, you couldn't have done that on your own.''

In the gathering twilight, Cori didn't know what to say. Shadows stretched from one corner of the garden to the other, their shapes every bit as dark and dusky as Travis's voice had been. Warmth settled to her throat, around her heart, and down past her stomach. This time, it wasn't entirely unexpected.

She'd told Travis more than she'd planned to or should have. Yet he wasn't holding it against her. Somehow, that wasn't unexpected, either. There was something scary about that, something the tiniest bit dangerous. There was also something inviting, like a warm stove on a cold day, or a familiar voice when you were all alone.

For a moment, she wished her parents could see her the way Travis did. That thought made her heart ache around the edges. It also reminded her of the letter she'd mailed to Green Bay, the letter she so desperately hoped they would answer this year.

What if they don't respond? a voice whispered inside her head.

Cori didn't want to deal with that possibility tonight. She didn't even want to think about it. Fumbling with the clasp on her purse, she said, ''I think I've bored you with my past for long enough, Travis. Thanks for dinner. Mel's

Truck Stop was truly a place to remember, diesel fumes, greasy French fries, and all.''

She turned and started up the sidewalk, hoping he wouldn't follow, praying he wouldn't expect a good-night kiss. She was too vulnerable right now, too needy, and too aware of how good they could be together.

"Cori?"

His voice stopped her movements, his warm hand on her arm slowly drawing her around. As she looked up into Travis's lean face, yearning washed over her, yearning that was every bit as strong as loneliness and need.

"Please," she whispered.

She didn't know how he could have known what she meant by that one small word. *Please kiss me? Or please don't?*

Suddenly, it didn't matter, because his face was lowering to hers, her eyelashes were fluttering closed, and her body was swaying ever closer to his. His mouth brushed hers, his lips grazing hers for but a moment in a kiss that was so soft and fleeting she wondered if she could have imagined it all, his warm breath, his soft mouth, the musky scent of his after-shave.

By the time she managed to open her eyes, he had lifted his face and had taken a backward step. He smoothed a finger down the bridge of her nose, slowly brushing it across her cheekbone before letting his hand glide to her shoulder, down her arm, finally ending up at his side.

He glanced at her cottage behind her, then brought his gaze back to hers and said, "I don't think the things you told me about your childhood sound so unusual. But then, for years I held the record for being the youngest boy in school to get caught smoking in the bathroom, so I guess I'm hardly a good one to judge."

Cori cast him an amused look and asked, "What grade were you in?"

"Fourth. From that day forward, there was a chair in the principal's office with my name on it. After that, everybody's parents were worried sick every time my name was mentioned. A few of the boys tried to mimic me, and, of course, all the girls wanted me."

She shook her head, wondering how much of what he told her was true, and how much of it leaned the tiniest bit toward Irish bull.

"So," he said, casting her that bad-boy smile that probably got him in trouble with every teacher he'd ever had. "Do you think you might want to have dinner with me again one of these days?"

Another time she might have thought he had something up his sleeve, an ulterior motive. Tonight, she didn't believe that was true. He'd asked her an honest question, and he deserved an honest answer.

Winsomely winding her arms like pretzels at her waist, she cast him a small smile and said, "I might."

Travis looked at her for a good five seconds longer than a *nice* man would have, his gaze starting at her eyes, and ending on her mouth. Just when she thought he wasn't going to say anything, his mouth opened, and his words finally came. "Then I might ask you sometime. Good night, Cori. I'll see you in the morning."

He didn't quite smile, and Cori realized that smiling wasn't his style. He simply turned on his heel and, with that slow masculine swagger she was coming to recognize, strode back the way he'd come. He nodded to a few of the guests who had noticed his presence, then crawled into his forest green Jeep, and drove away.

Hidden from view by the lilac hedge, Cori felt her chest fill with wonder. She'd had every intention of staying one step ahead of Travis tonight. Somehow, they'd ended the night on even ground. It was strange, but in all her memories, this was the first time she'd ever been on even ground with a man, especially a ruggedly handsome, virile one like Travis Delaney.

She didn't know what was happening to her, and she certainly didn't know where it would lead. As she made her way toward the inn to relieve Ivy of a hundred and one evening tasks and make sure all the guests had what they needed for the night, she was sure of only one thing.

Having dinner with Travis had not been what she'd expected.

Chapter Seven

"Listen to this, Lisa," Jillian Daniels said, looking up from the magazine in front of her. "According to your horoscope, a large man is looming in your future. Do you suppose they could be referring to that deli owner you met when you catered that Polish wedding last weekend?"

"Puh-lease," Lisa grumbled.

"What's the matter?" Jillian teased. "Do you have something against large men?"

Lisa slanted her a look that would have chilled a lesser woman. "Of course not, but that guy is married and has seven kids."

"Oh, I didn't know," Jillian said quietly.

"Besides," Lisa said, her voice getting huffier, "if there is a man, any man, in my future, it won't have anything to do with the malarkey in that magazine."

"You never know," Jillian retorted.

Ivy's rolling pin continued to thump as she smoothed out an oval of dough, and Jillian and Lisa continued to argue about astrology and astronomy and fates decided in the stars. Cori drained the last mugful of coffee from the coffee maker and shook her head at her two best friends.

These late Friday morning coffee klatches had started years ago when Lisa had first rented a room at Ivy's, and Jillian had lived next door with her grandfather. A lot had changed since then. For one thing, the girls used to drink cola instead of coffee. They'd all grown up a lot in the ensuing years. Today, Lisa was taking a break from a busy day in her own catering service. Jillian, who had recently graduated from college after years of hard work, was waiting to hear on about a hundred resumés she'd sent out. And Cori and Ivy were both doing odd jobs in their bed-and-breakfast inn, which was turning into a profitable business.

Now that Cori thought about it, there were still a lot of things that hadn't changed. Jillian and Lisa still bickered like old fishwives, and while Lisa claimed she was always on the lookout for a single man, neither she nor Jillian had found one to their liking.

All three of them had had heartache in their pasts. Jillian had grown up right here in Madison, but both Cori and Lisa had left home at an early age. Cori had been pushed out, and Lisa had run away. They'd all wound up at Ivy's, and all three had become great friends. Jillian, with her curly hair and blue eyes, was a sweetheart with a typical redhead's temper, and no one set it off better than Lisa, whose big brown eyes only looked innocent.

Cori took a sip of her coffee, feeling lulled by the rhythmic swish and thump of Ivy's rolling pin and the normal bantering between Jillian and Lisa. She'd been in a euphoric mood since last night, and she wasn't completely sure why. She only knew that it had something to do with blueberry pie, the aftereffects of a Delaney smile, and something else. But what? All her pondering was making it difficult for her to follow her friends' conversations this morning. Not that she'd ever admit that to them.

"I think we should go to a nightclub tonight," Lisa insisted, drawing Cori's attention back to the present.

"Ugh!" Jillian groused.

"Where else are we going to meet single men?" Lisa insisted.

"I never said I wanted to meet single men," Jillian sputtered.

"Come on, Jillian. You've got to get back on the bicycle sooner or later," Lisa said, her voice unusually soft. "Doesn't seeing Travis here day after day stir your romantic imagination just a little?"

The mere mention of Travis had Ivy, Jillian and Lisa all peering out the window where one tall, rugged carpenter was working. Cori shook her head, but in the end, her gaze, too, strayed to the other side of that long row of kitchen windows.

The sun picked up the rust and bronze highlights in Travis's hair. It was probably also responsible for the way his shirt clung to his back and shoulders like a second skin. Cori happened to know that those golden rays of sunshine had nothing to do with the warmth that had gathered deep in her chest after he'd walked away last night. The man, himself, was responsible for that.

She'd gone to bed thinking about him and had woken up with a smile on her face and hazy memories that had made her blush when she tried to recall them. He'd strolled into the inn at nine this morning just as he had every other day this week. But today, the smile on his face and the expression in his eyes had matched hers.

Day by day, she was coming to know him, and day by day, a bond was forming between them. There was still the pull of attraction—she supposed there would always be that where Travis was concerned—but there was something else, too. She'd felt it the first time she saw him weeks ago, a kind of understanding and camaraderie that was at once new and exciting and as old as time itself. It was one of the things that had scared her, and drew her to him at the same time.

"Now there's an impressive man," Lisa murmured, her low, soft voice breaking into Cori's reverie.

"He is that," Ivy agreed.

Completely oblivious to his admirers, Travis bent at the waist, the material of his washed-out jeans stretching taut over his thighs and backside. Lisa made a quiet sound in the back of her throat. Ivy and Jillian hummed in agreement.

Cori closed her eyes.

"Too bad there weren't any sparks between us," Lisa said forlornly.

"Ah, yes," Ivy said. "Not every good man is attracted to every good woman, which is a good thing, don't you think? I mean, just imagine the mayhem! It would be like alley cats on the prowl."

"Yeah," Jillian said quietly, still watching Travis. "You don't want an alley cat, do you, Lisa?"

"Travis doesn't strike me as the alley-cat type," Lisa said.

"I think you're right about that," Ivy said. "Although he's quiet, brooding almost, he reminds me of my Baxter."

With that, Ivy launched into a story about what a magnificent man her late husband had been. Although he'd died before either Cori or Lisa came to live at Ivy's, they'd all heard every one of Ivy's stories countless times.

"Baxter Pennington had a lot of truly wonderful qualities, but nobody ever accused him of being patient. Oh, no, not my Baxter. When he decided he wanted something, he went after it with everything he had. Guess you could say I was one of those things. Why, he told me he wanted to marry me on our second date. Couldn't even wait a few short weeks for a proper wedding. That man swooped into my life and swept me off my feet.''

Once again, Lisa, Jillian and Cori nodded their heads during the appropriate pauses, and otherwise generally let Ivy have her say. Ivy was on a roll, and she barely slowed down to take a breath.

''I thought my daddy was going to aim both barrels of his shotgun at the seat of Baxter's pants when he found out we'd eloped. Would have, too, if I hadn't said, 'If you shoot him, Daddy, I'll never forgive you, because I love him, the way you loved Mama.' ''

When Ivy ended her story with a sigh, Lisa said, ''Travis may remind you of Baxter, but looking at all that muscle and brawn reminds me that I've been a long time without a man.''

This time Cori didn't have any trouble keeping up with the conversation. It hit her right between the eyes, the words turning into images that turned into heat that started at the back of her neck and slowly shimmied lower.

''In fact, he reminds me that I've been a long time without so much as a date,'' Lisa said dejectedly. ''Won't you go to Roxy's with me tonight, Jillian?''

''I don't think so,'' Jillian answered quietly. ''Why don't you and Cori go. After all, it's been almost as long since Cori's had a date as it's been for me. Isn't that right, Cori?''

''Hmm,'' Cori hummed noncommittally, watching the play of muscles across Travis's back and thighs as he wrestled one of the large, flat stones from the bed of an old pickup truck.

''It hasn't been long since Corinna has been on a date,'' Ivy declared.

Just like that, three pairs of eyes were on Cori like glue.

''You've been on a date?'' Jillian asked.

''When?'' Lisa asked.

''With who?'' Jillian said a second later.

"Why haven't you told us?" they said at the same time.

Cori had to fight the urge to roll her eyes at Jillian and Lisa, and narrow them at Ivy. Giving up any hope she'd had of keeping last night a secret, she finally said, "There isn't that much to tell."

"Let us be the judge of that," Lisa admonished.

"Now out with it," Jillian insisted.

"Every last detail," Lisa said firmly.

There wasn't much Cori could do except stand there looking at her friends' expectant faces. "What do you want to know?"

"Start with when," Lisa said.

"Okay. Last night."

"No, wait," Jillian declared. "Start with who."

"It's too late. She already told us when."

"Oh. Shoot. All right then," Jillian conceded. "Now tell us who."

Cori had a feeling that at this rate, talking about her date with Travis would take all day. Deciding on the surest, most direct route, she said, "Look. I went out with Travis last night, but it wasn't any big deal."

Her friends exchanged a disbelieving look, and Ivy made her own special sound before all three of them turned to watch Travis work a hundred feet away. Cori groaned out loud.

"What is it Ivy always says about a person who denies too loud and too vehemently?" Lisa asked.

"It isn't what you're thinking!" Cori exclaimed. "Allison came to me to talk about, well, um, protection. I tried to reason with her, and she said she wanted to dissolve our little pact. Travis was working outside and overheard, so he came to my rescue."

"That is so romantic," Jillian said, her voice floating away on a sigh.

"So," Lisa interjected, her eyebrows arched coyly. "How was he?"

Ivy sputtered. "Lisa Markman, if your name didn't already mean oath of God, I'd swear that mouth of yours had been cursed at birth. Goodness gracious, some things between a man and a woman are sacred, not to mention personal."

Not looking the least bit contrite, Lisa winked at Ivy, exchanged a knowing look with Jillian, and grinned inanely at Cori. "At least tell us what kind of a kisser he is."

Despite her resolve to remain unflustered, Cori's hands flew to her cheeks. For heaven's sakes, Travis had barely kissed her last night, yet she was still blushing. And Cori knew why. It wasn't because of the kiss he'd actually given her. The flush that was creeping into her face was a result of the kisses she'd dreamed about all night long.

With her hands still on her cheeks, she said, "In my next life, I'm going to go about choosing my friends a lot differently."

Horoscopes forgotten, Jillian said, "You love us and you know it. But it's no wonder you've been so quiet this morning."

"Hmm," Lisa agreed. "And it certainly explains the light in your eyes and the *Mona Lisa* smile on your lips. He kisses like a dream, doesn't he?"

Cori wished Lisa hadn't used the words "kiss" and "dream" in the same sentence. The truth was, Travis did kiss like a dream, when Cori was awake, and when she was sleeping.

"Well?" Lisa prodded.

"Are you going to keep us in suspense all day?" Jillian asked.

Actually, Cori would have preferred to keep them in suspense all summer. She just wasn't sure how she was going to accomplish that. After all, Jillian Daniels and Lisa Markman were very persistent.

"To tell you the truth," Cori said, "his good-night kiss was quite . . ."

The phone rang, jarring them all. They all jumped, but Cori was secretly thankful for the interruption. She raced the few steps to the end of the counter and snatched the receiver up.

The first time she tried to speak, no sound came. Clearing her throat, she tried again. "Ivy's Garden," she finally croaked into the mouthpiece.

After listening to the hurried explanation on the other end, her thoughts cleared and her professionalism returned. "Yes, yes of course," she said. "Would you hold for a minute?"

"Quite what?" Lisa whispered the moment Cori laid the phone down. "His kiss was quite what?"

Aware of the three pairs of eyes following her every movement, Cori whispered, "Chaste. It was quite chaste. Now are you satisfied?"

Cori had to pass by Lisa on her way to the screen door. Although she couldn't be sure, she thought she heard her dark-haired friend say, "The question is, are you?"

Ignoring the answer that sprang to her lips, and the one deep inside her, too, Cori opened the door and stepped outside.

"Travis. There's a phone call for you."

Travis swung around to face Cori and dropped the gloves he'd been wearing onto the tailgate of the old truck he'd borrowed from Pete Macnamara, one of the guys from work. Squinting against the sun, he didn't quite smile, and neither did she, but he was pretty sure a smile wasn't far away for either of them.

This wasn't the first time he'd caught her looking at him like this. It had happened after he'd brushed his lips across hers last night, and again this morning when he first set foot inside the inn's big old kitchen. Their date had gone nothing like he'd initially planned, but it certainly had brought him and Cori to a better understanding. It hadn't, however, done anything to relieve the need that was steadily growing inside him. He could think of only one thing that would relieve that particular need, one thing with one woman.

"Did they say who it was?" he asked, striding closer.

"It's Braden," she answered. "And it sounds important."

He swiped at the bead of sweat trickling down his forehead then held the door so Cori could precede him into the inn. It took a moment for his eyes to adjust to the dim interior, but it didn't take him long to become aware of the three women staring at him from different positions throughout the room. Standing there in the doorway, he gritted his teeth and fought the uncommon urge to check his zipper.

All three of Cori's best friends had different shades of hair and different-colored eyes. And all three were smiling as if today was a feast, and he was the fatted calf. Suddenly, he knew how Cori had felt that time when she'd been unfortunate enough to wander too close to that construction sight.

Pulling his thoughts together, he strode to the counter, where he grabbed the phone. "Yeah, Braden, what's up?"

He turned his back on the women. For some reason, it didn't make him feel any less ogled. Since there wasn't much he could do about it, he concentrated on what Braden was saying.

"Uh-huh," he said, his monosyllabic answer followed by a thoughtful "Hmm".

Within a minute and a half, he said goodbye and replaced the phone. Turning around, he once again found several pairs of female eyes on him. Looking stricken to have been caught staring, Ivy picked up her rolling pin and proceeded to do whatever it was she was doing to that piece of dough. The other two women, Lisa and Jillian, didn't make the slightest effort to pretend that they weren't watching him openly.

He almost grinned when Cori jabbed them both with her elbow, and barely managed to keep his countenance when the brunette and the redhead both began rubbing their upper arms. Until today, he'd only glimpsed this side of Cori's personality. He wasn't surprised he liked it.

"Is everything all right?" she asked.

Her question brought him up short for a moment. His heart thudded and his ears rang, because, for the life of him, he couldn't remember what he'd been doing.

The phone.

Oh, yes, he'd had a phone call. From Braden.

Blinking to clear his mind, he said, "A problem has come up at one of the building sites. I'm going to finish unloading the flagstones then head on out to Lake Waubesa to check it out."

Cori nodded, watching as he strode toward the door once again. With one hand on the screen, he looked over his shoulder and added, "I'll be back later today, but I don't really know when."

He spoke to everyone in the room, but his eyes had been on her, only her. Something shifted the tiniest bit deep inside her, like a rosebud softly uncurling its first petals.

"Wow," Jillian whispered after the door clanked shut behind him.

"I take it back," Lisa sputtered. "You don't have to tell us what sort of a kisser he is. I think we already know."

Before Cori could say anything, two young voices, one soft and mellow, the other deep and masculine, carried into the kitchen through the screens. "Travis, look out!" Allison and Ross called together.

A blur of red skimmed the top of the rose trellis, heading right for Travis. His head jerked back and his hand shot out in front of him, stopping the speeding Frisbee mere inches from his throat. The resounding thud of a spinning piece of hard plastic glancing off flesh-covered bone never came.

"The man's got moves," Jillian whispered.

A wan shaft of sunlight caught on his face as he cast a smile at Allison and Ross, who were several yards away. In the kitchen, the breath caught in the throats of the women who were watching.

"And a killer smile," Lisa added.

"M-a-n," Jillian said, dragging the word out from here to there and back again.

"Ditto."

"Good grief, you two," Cori grumbled. "Maybe you should go to Roxy's tonight and look for a man."

"That's what I was trying to tell you before all this . . ."

Travis sailed the Frisbee back toward Ross, and Lisa's voice trailed away. He really was a sight, Cori thought to herself, from the way the muscles bulged in his arms, to the way his shirt clung to the washboard ridges on his stomach, all the way down to the worn soles of his leather work boots.

Before anyone said anything else, Allison, the little showstopper, caught their attention. She pretended to run to the right then doubled back to try to head the Frisbee off before Ross could catch it. She reached it a split second before he did, her screech of pleasure and feminine wiles ringing out across the entire garden. Laughing, Ross tackled her from the side. His baseball cap flew off as they went down in a playful tangle of bare arms and legs.

"They remind me of lambs in the spring," Ivy said with a smile.

As if Travis knew his part in the game of Frisbee was over, he turned his back on the kids and headed for the tailgate of his truck. The wrestling match continued with shrieks from Allison, and a low rumble of laughter from Ross. Allison still had hold of the Frisbee, but suddenly, the atmosphere changed, their laughter fading, their play-fulness slowly giving way to something much less child-ish.

"Um," Lisa said. "I don't think they're quite as inno-cent as lambs, Ivy."

The Frisbee fell out of Allison's hand as she reached up and spread her fingers through the hair at Ross's nape. They were evidently oblivious to anything except each other as their kiss became more intense.

"She really came to you to talk about protection?" Jil-lian asked.

Cori nodded, wishing there was something she could do to interrupt the long-winded kiss that was still going on and on. And on.

"She's in love," Ivy said.

"She's boy-crazy," Lisa declared.

"Why wouldn't she be?" Jillian asked. "She's never had the attention of an adult male." Glancing at Cori's stricken face, she continued. "Not that you haven't done a won-derful job of raising her, Cori. You have. Allison's one of the happiest, most well-adjusted teenagers I've ever met. But I just read an article the other day that said girls who grow up without a father figure are twice as likely to seek male attention at a young age."

"You can't believe everything you read," Lisa admon-ished.

"What if all Allison really wants is some male atten-tion, some adult male attention, some fatherly adult male attention?" Jillian inquired, her redheaded temper flar-ing just a little.

"Jillian could be right," Ivy said, holding her rolling pin in midair.

Suddenly, Cori felt every bit as inadequate as she had the first time she'd tried to bathe her newborn daughter be-fore leaving the hospital all those years ago. The nurse had assured her that in no time at all she'd be completely adept and at ease handling her slippery, wet scrap of a baby. She'd been terrified that she'd drop her, or even drown her. This was worse. Now, there was no nurse to show her what to do, nobody to tell her everything was going to be all be all right in the end. This wasn't just a bath they were talking about. This was her daughter's future happiness and well-being.

"Do you really think she's been craving fatherly attention all these years?" she asked on a whisper.

"No."

"Yes."

"Maybe."

Cori had the presence of mind to cast each of her friends a sardonic look before saying, "It's so nice that you're all in agreement."

"Just like always," Lisa said with an impish grin.

"Then you think it's possible that I've let her down?" Cori asked.

"Of course not," Lisa insisted.

"At least not intentionally," Jillian said softly. "And besides, it isn't too late."

That gave Cori pause.

Lisa shot Jillian a quelling glare, and Jillian did look uncomfortable with the fact that she'd undoubtedly hurt Cori's feelings. "Lisa's probably right," Jillian said. "You probably can't believe everything you read in these magazines."

Undeterred, Cori still asked, "What if it's true? Where am I going to find a man who's willing to lavish adult fatherly attention on my sixteen-year-old daughter?"

"You're the one who went on a date last night," Lisa said, arching one eyebrow.

"You mean Travis?"

"He said he's coming back," Jillian said. "And we all saw how nice he was to Allison just now."

Cori turned to Ivy, who put the finishing touches on a raspberry pie before opening her mouth to speak. "I already told you he reminds me of my Baxter," she declared, as if that said it all.

"Then I guess that settles that," Jillian said, rubbing her hands together as if she were brushing away the day's work.

Glancing at her three closest friends, Cori could think of nothing to say. She let her head fall forward into her hands and made a low groaning sound deep in her throat, wondering how in the world she was ever going to be able to ask a man who was going through a mid-life *slump* to spend a little quality time with her sixteen-year-old daughter. Just how did one go about requesting this kind of favor from a man like that, a man who just happened to kiss like a song, and whose most innocent look and fleeting touches caused her to have the strangest dreams?

The topic changed and conversation resumed all around. Cori didn't participate. She just sipped her lukewarm coffee and tried to think.

Travis dimmed the truck's lights and pulled into the narrow driveway that ran parallel with the side yard of Ivy's Garden. The engine groaned for a few seconds after he turned the key, the door creaking as he pushed it open and slid to his feet. Pete Macnamara's truck was a piece of junk, just the way Pete liked it.

It was a little after eleven, which was a lot later than Travis had planned to come back for his things. Except for the insects that were starting to hum and chirp from the bottom of flower beds and the branches of trees, the garden was utterly quiet.

The problem Braden called about had proven to be a lot more involved than either of them had realized. The landowner and one of the subcontractors were at each other's throats. One was threatening a lawsuit, the other was threatening murder. He and Braden hadn't gotten to the bottom of it yet, and would have to put their heads together again in the morning. Tonight, Travis's mind was on other things. Tonight his mind was on Cori.

Being as quiet as possible, he picked up his hammer and tool belt, carefully laying it on the bed of the truck. He added a two-by-four, a level, his shovel, and several other items he'd need to finish laying the flagstones and building Cori's gazebo. Spotting a power saw that was nearly hidden amongst some tall fronds, he looked around the garden for anything else he might have forgotten.

Soft yellow lights glowed from several windows in the inn. He imagined that on the other side of those windows, guests were getting ready to turn in for the night. Here in the garden, small white lights delineated the curve of the rose trellis and the slats on the picket fence. Other lights, these a little larger, were strategically placed so that he could follow the winding paths with ease.

Starlight was just beginning to penetrate the darkness overhead, but it was the light in Cori's cottage all the way to the back of the lot that truly captured his attention. He caught a movement through the gauzy curtains, and saw a woman's shape on the other side.

Rubbing the dust from his hands, he closed the tailgate on the truck, and slowly ambled down the driveway as if being drawn by a powerful force field. He knew what that force was. Desire. Not for just anyone, but for one tallish blond with a stubborn streak a mile high, a heart that practically overflowed with caring for those around her, and a body that tempted him with every movement, every sweeping gesture, every little smile.

She must have heard the crunch of his shoes on the crushed stones beneath his feet, because suddenly she appeared on the other side of the screen door. "Oh," she said. "You're not Allison."

He placed his foot on the first step, the same step she'd met him on when he'd knocked on her door last night. "I've been called several things in my time," he said, keeping his voice quiet and at one with the still night. "But I can't say I've ever been mistaken for a sixteen-year-old girl."

His words had the desired effect on her. She shifted her weight to one foot and smiled at him from her side of the screen. "I didn't say I mistook you for Allison. I'm just expecting her any time, that's all."

"The kid's not home yet, huh?" he asked.

She shook her head.

"Is she out with Ross?"

She nodded.

"What?" she asked, evidently picking up on his little sneer.

"It's nothing."

The screen door creaked the tiniest bit as she pushed it open. "No. Tell me," she said, worry evident in her voice. "If there's something about Ross you don't like, *I'd* like to know about it."

Stepping to one side to make room for her on the small stoop, he caught a whiff of shampoo, and heard the rustle of soft fabric as Cori closed the door behind her and stood on the highest step. She was wearing cutoffs that probably belonged to Allison, and a shirt in the palest blue he'd ever seen. Her hair was pulled back in a loose ponytail and tied with a narrow ribbon. She looked about eighteen, which was just was about how old she made him feel.

Despite the long hours he'd put in and the lateness of the hour, it wasn't fatigue that whispered through his veins. It was something else, something much, much stronger, and infinitely more pleasant.

He settled his hands on his hips and gave her a casual shrug. "I don't really have anything against the kid, aside from the fact that he's seventeen. But if he calls me *Mister* Delaney one more time, things could get ugly.''

A smile stole across Cori's face, followed by laughter. The sound was marvelous, catching. It had a powerful effect on his body.

''Oh, Travis,'' she said. ''You're a long, long way from being old.''

''That's what I keep telling everyone,'' he answered.

Cori went down to the next step, suddenly feeling very lighthearted. Travis might claim he wasn't experiencing the beginning twinges of a mid-life crisis, but she didn't know how he explained away the traces of irritation she heard in his voice every time the topic of his age came up.

Keeping her voice low, she said, ''Mornings and evenings, this place tends to be a madhouse. Out here, after darkness has fallen, everything turns quiet and peaceful. It's my favorite time of the day. It looks as if you've put in a long day, too. Would you like to relax and enjoy the quiet with me for a few minutes?''

She lowered to a sitting position on the top step. He followed, a few seconds behind. His belt creaked slightly, the denim of his jeans brushing her arm on his way down. She moved to the right to give him a little room, and took a deep breath. He smelled faintly of sunshine and sawdust, and largely of man.

Since there wasn't a porch, Cori had never thought it necessary to put up an outside light all the way back here. Consequently, the only illumination came from the elongated shapes the living room lamp was throwing onto the grass through the front window and screen door. She could hear the low drone of the television program she'd been trying to watch, not to mention the deep breath Travis took.

''So this is your favorite time of the day,'' he said quietly, his voice a low rumble in the still night.

She made a sound that meant yes, adding, "It's a good thing I enjoy the night, because I sure spend a lot of them waiting up for Allison these days."

"I suppose that's one of the many trials of parenthood, isn't it?" he asked.

Cori contemplated his question, thinking it was just the opening she needed if she wanted to ask him how he'd feel about spending a little quality time with Allison. His earlier references to his mid-life crisis made her proceed very carefully. Running one finger over the hem of her shorts, she asked, "Have you ever spent much time with kids, Travis?"

"Not really."

His reply hadn't exactly left her with a good lead-in. "I mean," she said, trying again. "You seemed to enjoy tossing that Frisbee to Ross and Allison this morning."

"I guess," he replied.

Cori wanted to nudge him for his vague answers, but she didn't see how she could fault him for telling her the truth. Letting her gaze stray across her tiny yard, she decided to try one last time. "Since Allison seems to think a lot of you, I thought you probably had a soft spot in your heart for kids in general, maybe teenagers in particular, that's all."

She chanced a glance at him from the corner of her eye, then slowly turned her head so she could see him more clearly. He hadn't said anything, and now she knew why. He was watching her. There were stars overhead, but they couldn't hold a candle to the glimmer deep in his brown eyes. He was looking at her face, the expression in his eyes sending her emotions so low in her body she was sure she could feel them brushing against her bare toes.

"In all honesty, Cori," he finally said, "I haven't really thought a lot about kids. But I have been spending a lot of time these past few weeks thinking about how they're made. Believe me, there hasn't been anything soft about my thoughts, or what they've been doing to my body.''

Mesmerized, she watched his lips move over every syllable, his words sculpting an erotic image in her mind. There might not have been anything soft about Travis, but everything went soft inside her. Her blood seemed to turn to molasses, her heart to mush, and lower, she felt a gentle stirring once again, like a rosebud slowly uncurling another petal.

She'd had no intention of leaning the tiniest bit closer, but he was looking at her so intently, and her nose picked up the faint scent of his skin, a dark, musky scent that made her eyes flutter down and her lungs draw in a deep, dewy breath. By the time she realized what had happened, her face was very close to his, and her thoughts had slowed to match her heartbeat.

Travis saw the effect his words and nearness were having on Cori. Her lips parted and her eyes took on a sensuous glimmer. When he'd pulled into the driveway to pick up his tools, he hadn't expected this. He'd hoped for a glimpse of her, and maybe a few words with her. Sitting this close to her, the desire that had been building inside him since he'd kissed her for the first time here in this very garden took hold of him, guiding his chin down, his lips apart, and the air from his lungs.

He touched his mouth to hers, and it happened again. Need exploded between them. Each time he saw her, his need grew stronger, his desire more intense. She seemed as surprised by the joining of their mouths as he was, and just as responsive. Her lips parted under his, her breathing coming in deep drafts. Her hand found its way to his chest, her fingers spreading wide over his heart. He flexed the muscle beneath her palm, and was awarded with her deep-throated moan.

Suddenly, he had to touch her in return. He slipped the ribbon from her hair, spreading his fingers through its long, silky strands, steadily drawing her closer, closer, until she was practically lying across his lap where his desire was straining for release.

Her hands were working their own magic on him, kneading his shoulders, stroking down his arms, and back up again, around to his back, and all the way down to his hips. All the while, the kiss went on and on, their sighs becoming stronger, their mouths and hands seeking but not quite finding.

"Travis, we have to stop."

Her voice was little more than a rasp, her lips touching his as she spoke. He answered the way she had, in a voice as dusky as the night, on a breath they drew together.

"I never want to stop, Cori."

"Someone might see us."

He took her breast in his hand, loving the way it swelled against his palm, loving the onrush of desire surging through him at the same time. Cori's head fell backward, and her eyes fluttered closed.

"No one can see us, Cori," he whispered on a husky voice. "It's dark out here, but if you're worried, invite me inside."

Cori heard the thin edge of control in his voice, and realized that when Travis had kissed her last night, he'd been careful to mind his p's and q's. He wasn't being careful now. His lips had worked magic on her mouth; his hands were working magic nearly everyplace else. Every single muscle in his body was straining toward hers, and his hands were everywhere, stroking her breasts until she was yearning to be free of her bra, then smoothing higher and lower. When they glided around to her back, they slipped into her back pockets.

"Oh, Travis, what are you doing to me?"

"I want to do more—so, so, much more. But not out here. I want to go someplace where there's just you and me, someplace quiet and dark. Take me inside."

He nuzzled her neck with his warm mouth, tickling and arousing at the same time. She smiled without meaning to, and opened her eyes. With her head tipped way back, the first thing she saw was starlight. Gazing at all those far-away glimmers of light, all the things she'd dreamed about last night filtered into her mind, all the murmurs and sighs, and bare skin against bare skin. It had been so long since she'd felt this way, so long since a man had touched her, and set her on fire.

This is what Allison had been talking about when she came to me about protection.

Thoughts of her daughter finally brought back a semblance of rationality. "We can't do this, Travis."

"I know, I know," he whispered against her jaw. "We really can't do this out here, in front of anyone who might happen by."

Straightening slightly, she said, "No, that isn't what I meant."

"Hmm," he murmured, his lips skimming the sensitive little hollow beneath her ear.

She moaned softly, but she still managed to say, "We can't do this. I can't do this."

As if he was coming up out of a deep fog, he asked, "What do you mean?"

"I promised Allison I wouldn't. We have a pact."

Travis pulled away from her far enough to look into her eyes. Her explanation was coursing through him, but it couldn't quite keep up with his desire.

"A pact?" he asked dazedly.

"Yes. A pact," she said, sitting up a little more with every word.

This wasn't the first time he'd heard her mention something about a pact, but in his condition, he wasn't thinking clearly and couldn't remember what she'd said the other times. Her shoulders stiffened, and if he wasn't mistaken, a soft blush tinged her cheeks. It was enough to make him leery, and to force his thoughts to clear a little more.

"You and Allison have a pact." This time it wasn't a question.

"Yes."

He took a deep, steadying breath, but it failed to calm him. Trying to keep his voice quiet in the still summer night, he opened his mouth to speak, and ended up grinding out a question on one sharp breath.

"What the hell kind of a pact?"

Chapter Eight

What the hell kind of a pact?

Cori heard the deep rumble in Travis's voice. It reminded her of thunder, which was fitting since he'd bolted to the ground like lightning.

She found her feet more slowly. Standing on the bottom step, her face was nearly level with his. She remembered thinking that his eyes were the warmest brown she'd ever seen. They were warm right now, all right, but this was the kind of heat that was the result of anger and shock.

His lips were thinned, his jaw clenched. His chest expanded with the deep breath he took, and his hands were clasped tightly on his hips. She knew what she'd find if she let her gaze continue down the length of him, but she didn't think that would be wise. It would remind her of the desire that had pulsed with a life of its own mere moments ago. And she had to put an end to that desire, and explain about her pact with her daughter.

A mosquito buzzed in her ear and a moth fluttered against her front window. The only other sound in the garden was the deep breath Travis slowly drew to the bottom of his lungs.

She saw a light go out in the Morning Glory room. The lilac hedge hid her cottage from view of most of the inn's windows, but not from that corner room on the third floor. Travis deserved an explanation after the way she'd kissed him moments ago. She wanted to give it to him, but she wanted to do it in private.

He slapped his palm against his neck the same time she whisked a bloodthirsty little insect from her bare arm. "I guess there are a few drawbacks to sitting outside in the dark," she said quietly. "Let's go into the house before these mosquitoes eat us alive."

Travis knew he was staring, but he couldn't help it. He didn't know what to make of this pact Cori supposedly had with Allison, and he sure as hell didn't know what to make of her invitation to follow her inside.

By the time he'd taken the three short steps and strode through her front door, he'd managed to get his breathing under control, and for the most part, the rest of his body, too. He'd wondered what the inside of her home was like that first time she'd shown him her gardens. He was finally in her front room, but all except the haziest of impressions were lost on him tonight.

"I could get you something to drink."

Her voice had been only slightly louder than those coming from the portable television in the corner. Still feeling groggy, he turned slowly and regarded the woman who had spoken.

Cori was standing behind a wicker chair near an archway on the other side of the narrow room. He'd never seen her eyes quite so dark, or her face quite so pale. Her hands were clasped around the back of the chair, her white-knuckled grip a dead giveaway to her elevated case of nerves.

He wasn't too far gone to realize that her nervousness was his fault. Aw, hell. Guilt was something he enjoyed almost as much as unspent desire.

Running his hand through his hair, he said, "I don't need anything to drink, Cori. I'm fine."

"Good. I mean, if you're sure. Well, um, in that case, I suppose you're waiting for an explanation."

The woman was something. Her lips were still swollen from his kisses, her hair and clothes slightly disheveled from his hands. She'd been completely uninhibited mere minutes ago, her kisses unrestrained, the touch of her hands nothing less than amazing. And here she was trying to stammer through an explanation she thought he deserved to hear.

Desire, slower this time, but no less intense, wound its way through him all over again. Giving her a look he hoped would put her at ease, he shortened the distance between them, settled his hands to his hips, and finally said, "What just happened between us was pretty damned powerful, Cori, and I'd be lying if I told you I'm not experiencing some equally powerful aftereffects. But you don't owe me anything."

Cori felt her lips part on a hastily drawn breath. That quickly, her tension drained out of her. In its place, she felt an odd sense of awe.

She hadn't dated much these past several years, but she'd had enough experience with men to know that most of them didn't appreciate being lured to the point of no return only to be stopped cold. In her experience, men in Travis's predicament had a tendency to be rude and nasty. More often than not they demanded an explanation, if not the opportunity to finish what they'd started.

Travis wasn't demanding anything at all.

He really is a nice man.

The realization shouldn't have started that liquid warmth flowing through her again, but it did. Loosening the grip she had on the rocking chair, she took a deep breath and said, "When you came to my rescue that day in front of the dry cleaner's, I thought you were special. Now I know I was right."

Travis felt his eyes widen. Hell, why wouldn't they? Cori had said the last thing he'd expected. When was he going to learn not to be surprised by this unpredictable woman?

She thought he was special.

He liked the sound of that, but that wasn't all he liked. He liked the way his heart sped up and the way his breathing slowed. He liked the way his blood pounded through him, rolling and pulsing its way into the part of him that was still throbbing with need. That wasn't all he liked, either. He liked the way Cori was looking at him, too, as if she'd found something pretty damned unique. In fact, he liked that the best of all.

Now that his self-confidence was back, he sauntered a little closer. In a voice that was low and purposefully seductive, he said, "I never argue with someone who says I'm right."

She shook her head at him the way she had every other time he'd given her some cocky line. Blood pounded in his ears, and nearly everywhere else. Shadows stretched from the edges of the room. He was more interested in the desire stretching between him and Cori.

"I'm so relieved that you're not terribly upset about this pact Allison and I have concerning sex."

If there was any part of him that wasn't alert before, it was now that she'd mentioned sex. He took a step closer and let his hands slide from his hips. What he wanted to do was slip them around her back until she was completely wrapped in his arms. Instead, he stood perfectly still and waited for her to continue.

"It's ironic, isn't it?" she asked.

"What's ironic?" he asked, his gaze homing in on her mouth.

"The fact that until now, *not* having sex hasn't been much of a sacrifice for me. I mean, I know women supposedly peak in their thirties, but it's been so long, I almost forgot what I was missing. No wonder Allison's having the devil of a time keeping her end of our bargain."

Something jarred inside his head. "I beg your pardon?"

She wet her lips and tipped her head the tiniest bit to the left. "I know you don't expect an explanation, but it would probably help you understand if you had one. You see, about a year ago Allison and I made a pact. Neither of us will, um, sleep with, you know, anybody."

Every word she said sent a bigger sense of dread through him. He didn't like the anxious expression on her face, and he sure as hell didn't like what he was hearing.

"What I'm trying to say is that Allison and I have promised each other that we aren't going to consummate any relationship we might have with a man."

Suddenly, Travis knew what the jarring sound had been inside his head. It was the bottom dropping out of his night, and quite possibly his lower jaw hitting the floor.

"Ever?"

He was aware that his voice had risen. Evidently, so was Cori, because her eyes darted over his entire face before she said, "Well, someday. After a wedding ceremony. On the honeymoon."

His misgivings didn't take the time to increase by the second. They blew right through the roof.

"The *honeymoon?*" he bellowed.

"Believe me," she said, hurrying so fast she tripped over her words. "This in no way means I'm trying to force anyone to marry me. I stopped looking for a husband a long time ago. I'm just trying to explain that I can't, that you and I can't, that I won't . . ."

She'd stammered through this part of the explanation when she'd been in his arms on her front stoop. At the time he hadn't been able to think straight because her hands had been everywhere, and so had his. He preferred then to now, but no matter how much she hemmed and hawed, a few things were becoming clear. She wasn't telling him that this wasn't the right time in their relationship to make love. She wasn't talking about a matter of a few days or weeks or even months. She was talking about . . .

He clamped his mouth shut, hoping to clamp off that thought at the same time. Blood pounded inside his head. He tried to offset it by taking a deep, steadying breath. He opened his mouth to speak. And out gushed a string of cusswords that would have cost him more Hail Marys than he wanted to think about if Braden's mother had heard.

Good God. Cori was talking about celibacy.

In his condition, celibacy wasn't a word he wanted to *think* about, let alone say out loud. He paced to the couch and back again, did an about-face and repeated the process. A muscle worked in his jaw, which was clenched so tight he could feel his teeth grinding.

This was turning out to be one helluva weekend. A *surprise* thirty-ninth birthday party on Sunday, and *this* honest-to-God kicker tonight.

But celibacy?

Him?

He clenched his teeth even harder, pain shooting through his jaw where that bruise had been a few weeks ago. Forcing his jaw to relax, he noticed the flicker of headlights on the far wall. He glanced out the window and saw an old Camaro slowly coming up the driveway.

Travis had no idea what to say following Cori's explanation. All he knew was that he had to get out of there.

Now. Running a hand over the whisker stubble on his chin, he said, "The kids are back. I've gotta go."

She said something, but the way his thoughts were screaming, he barely heard. He glanced at her, and wished he hadn't. She was still standing next to that wicker rocking chair, watching him as if she thought he was a bomb that might just go off any second.

The fact that she was right forced him to get a hold of himself. He took another deep breath, mumbled something he hoped passed for a goodbye, and pushed through the door.

Even though she knew it was coming, Cori blinked when the screen door sprang back to its closed position. She hurried to the door and peered out, but she already knew what she'd see. Sure enough, Travis was striding away as fast as his feet would take him.

Ross and Allison were standing next to the car. Drawing apart slightly, Allison said, "Oh, hi, Travis!"

"Hey, Mister Delaney."

Travis answered without slowing down, his voice a deep rumble in the otherwise quiet night. Allison and Ross stared after him as if they'd never seen a man so hell-bent on leaving.

"What's wrong with him?" Allison called when she noticed her mother in the doorway.

Cori floundered, at a loss for something to say.

"Mom, have you had a date with Travis two nights in a row?"

Before Cori could answer, she heard Ross say, "She probably just told him about that stupid pact."

Allison cozied up to Ross, smiling at him with all the sass and charm she'd been born with. "Do you guys ever think about anything else?" she asked coyly.

Ross gave Allison a reluctant grin, which turned into a grudging smile, which won him a quick kiss on his young cheek and a whisper in his ear.

"Travis and I haven't been out," Cori answered. "He just stopped in a few minutes ago to pick up his tools. Are you two ready to come in?"

"We thought we'd take a stroll through the garden first," Allison said, sliding her hand into Ross's.

"Okay. Don't stay out too long, though. The mosquitoes are hungry tonight."

"We won't."

Watching the kids stroll away, Cori couldn't help noticing how their arms slid around each other's backs. Their steps slowed, their voices dropping to hushed whispers the instant they rounded to the other side of the lilac hedge.

Peering out into the darkness, Cori felt inordinately sad. She saw a pale object lying on the bottom step. Slipping through the door without making a sound, she scooped up a narrow blue ribbon. Smoothing it between her fingers, she remembered how Travis's fingers had felt in her hair. She remembered the way the moon had reflected in his eyes, too, and the way being near him had made her feel.

The garden had grown silent once again, and she imagined that somewhere, Allison and Ross were kissing— probably the way she and Travis had kissed tonight. She closed her eyes against the thought, but when she opened them again, she knew she'd done the right thing. No matter how difficult it had been to put a stop to the passion that had a way of erupting between her and Travis, it was something she'd had to do, for Allison's sake.

Cori hoped that Travis would come to understand, because, although she doubted he'd appreciate the description, he really was a nice man. The clank of a tailgate interrupted her thoughts. She could barely make out Travis's shape near the other end of the driveway, but she heard the truck's door creak open, then slam shut. Within seconds, the engine chugged to life; taillights flickered and gears ground impatiently.

Listening as the engine faded away into the distance, she supposed that even *nice* men had their limits. She turned away from the door and closed her eyes. Swallowing the lump that had risen to her throat, she wondered why it was that doing the right thing always seemed to be so hard.

"Smile!"

Travis couldn't fake more than a passing grimace.

"Come on, Travis, you've gotta smile for the pictures," Great-Aunt Maude cajoled.

If one more person told him he had to smile, he wasn't going to be responsible for his actions.

"I think our Travis has reached his limit," Maude's twin sister, Mavis, said, peering at him over the top of her trifocals.

Travis looked around at the group of Calhouns and Simmons that was gathered around him. Good old Mavis had hit the nail on the head that time. He'd reached his limit, all right, fifty-nine minutes ago, right after he'd stepped into Sam and Ginny's backyard and *pretended* to be surprised.

Pretending to be happy was beyond him. Way beyond.

"You're as young as you feel," Mavis spouted, smoothing her plump hand down her flowered dress.

"My, yes," Maude agreed.

"Thirty-nine, you say?" Mavis's husband, Henry, asked.

"Doesn't seem possible, does it, Henry?"

"I should say not. How time flies."

"If I were thirty years younger," Mavis said.

"My, yes, if we were thirty years younger," Maude agreed.

If Mavis and Maude were thirty years younger, they would still be fifty-three. *Which is only fourteen years older than I'm about to be.*

"Does Travis suddenly look a little peaked to you, Mavis?"

"As a matter of fact, Maude, I believe he does."

"Lean down here, dear, and let me feel your forehead."

Travis accepted the attention with about as much enthusiasm as he accepted the fact that he had to kiss both old ladies' lined cheeks and endure being pressed against yet another ample bosom. The only woman he wanted to be pressed against was Cori.

Damn. Where had that thought come from?

He'd driven around for a long time after leaving her place Friday night. Time and distance had cleared his mind, but they hadn't done much to relieve his desire or his disappointment. The cold shower he took later hadn't helped, either. Neither did all the hours of hard work he'd put in these past two days.

All around him, the Calhouns were talking, or arguing, depending upon a person's perspective. Someone shrieked, and two giggling young boys waving water pistols scurried around the side of the house, their mothers close on their heels. There were thirty-five people present. So far, seventeen of them had spouted some sage words of wisdom concerning his upcoming birthday. Travis was doing his best to steer clear of the other eighteen.

He spotted Braden's mousy cousin Lester approaching, and ducked around a small group of stoop-shouldered uncles. But Travis was too late. Lester changed directions and met him on the other side, spoiling his getaway.

Of all Braden's cousins, Lester reminded Travis the most of Uncle Artie. He was already starting to dress like him, right down to his baggy plaid shorts and the black socks he wore with his lily-white tennis shoes. The man was annoying, but he was family. Sort of. That was why Travis did his best to put up with him and be nice. Not that it was easy.

"Hi, there, Travis."

"Lester."

"Nice party, hmm?"

"Yeah, swell."

"How does it feel to be thirty-nine, hmm?" Lester asked.

"I wouldn't know. I'm only thirty-eight."

There was twittering all around, a few hearty guffaws, and, of course, Lester's nasal snort. It required all Travis's willpower to keep from groaning out loud.

Everyone was having a marvelous time. Everyone except him.

He caught a movement out of the corner of his eye. The blur of a blue and red striped T-shirt and dirty sneakers sped into his line of vision. Travis ducked, and Lester yelped as ice-cold water hit him in the side of the head via a water pistol. Travis almost smiled for the first time all day. Almost.

The little gunslingers screeched with glee. Lester swore out loud, which earned him a reprimand from Ginny, then moved on to bother someone else.

Travis scanned the yard, hoping to spot a tree to hide behind or a patch of shade that was unoccupied. The yard had never been large, and today, there weren't many places that were hidden from the view of well-wishing Calhouns. There were no rose trellises or shaded walkways, no flowery vines trailing up picket fences, no antique mailboxes or secluded places where a blanket could be spread on a soft patch of grass and a woman could be thoroughly kissed.

He pushed himself away from the deck's wood railing with so much force that several guests drew their eyebrows down in consternation. He did his best to look natural, then strode down the steps and on to the back of the property and the relative privacy of the back fence.

He leaned his forearms on the shoulder-high fence and heaved a huge sigh. Yesterday, he and Braden had spent fourteen hours going back and forth between the job site out on Lake Waubesa and their office downtown. After another eight hours of head-scratching today, the problem was on the verge of being solved.

Somehow, two sets of blueprints had turned up—the one the subcontractor had used to dig the basement, and the one the owners had turned in to the office at Northwood Builders. Unfortunately, the prints were as different as night and day. So far, neither the subcontractor nor the homeowners were owning up to the mistake, but now that he and Braden had gotten to the bottom of it, the problem, like most problems, could be corrected. He couldn't say the same for the problem he was having getting Corinna Cassidy out of his mind.

Her name had popped into his head at least a hundred times these past two days. Unfortunately, the word "celibacy" popped in right along with it. Against his better judgment, he'd driven past her house last night. His heart had sped up when he'd glimpsed the light in her window. He'd started to slow down when he remembered the pact she had with Allison. Instead of pulling into her driveway, he'd pressed his foot to the gas pedal and drove on home to his quiet apartment on the other side of town.

He caught a movement out of the corner of his eye, bringing him back to the present. Turning his head, he saw that he wasn't really alone. Braden's younger sister, Annie, was leaning against the fence a dozen feet away.

"What's the matter?" he asked, striding a little closer. "Did the family get to be too much for you?"

"What?" Annie asked, as if she was coming out of some deep thoughts of her own. "Oh, no, I'm used to them. How about you?"

Staring out across a neighbor's backyard, Travis shook his head and said, "Nah. I've learned to handle most of them, but if one more person slaps me on the back and refers to a mid-life crisis or asks me about my cholesterol levels, I'm going to have to hit something."

"I know what you mean. Rachel is convinced that there's something worrying me, and you know how the family is. If one person so much as *thinks* something, everyone knows it."

Leaning one hip against a sturdy post where several black balloons bobbed in the breeze, Travis studied Braden's little sister. Annie Calhoun had stuck her tongue out at him the first time he met her. By the time he came to live here, she'd been a pudgy seven-year-old who'd inherited her mother's tendency toward bossiness and her father's dark hair. She'd grown up since then, and in the process, she'd grown thin. Was it his imagination, or had she also grown pale?

"Where's Rachel now?" he asked, referring to Braden's other sister.

"I don't know. I saw my chance to escape and took it, but I'm sure I'll be discovered soon enough."

"There you two are!"

Travis and Annie both turned in time to see Ginny hurrying toward them. "See what I mean?" Annie whispered under her breath.

"What's this I hear about the two of you? Annie, aren't you feeling well?" Ginny asked her daughter. "And Travis, what's this about a mid-life crisis?"

Travis and Annie took turns shrugging and shaking their heads. "Come on," Annie said. "If we can't beat 'em, we might as well join 'em."

"That's what I always say," Ginny declared. Sliding an arm around each of their backs, she steered them into the center of the yard where a group of first cousins swallowed them whole.

An hour and a half later, the backyard was nearly empty. The party was officially over, and Travis was unofficially relieved. Ginny and Rachel had poor Annie cornered on the deck, and Sam and Uncle Artie were talking nearby. The argument that broke out between Ginny's husband and her only brother was almost as predictable as the setting sun.

"I'll bet you ten bucks that these black tablecloths and balloons were Uncle Artie's idea," Braden said. "See? They match his socks."

Travis reached for a stack of used paper plates.

"For crying out loud, Travis," Braden sputtered. "You must really have it bad if jokes about Uncle Artie don't make you laugh."

He had it bad, all right. But he didn't see what he could do about it.

"What's the latest count?" Braden asked, changing the subject.

Wadding up a black tablecloth, Travis said, "Thirty-one."

"Only thirty-one members of my family said something stupid about your birthday? We usually do better than that. But it looks like you survived."

"Maybe. But if one more person tells me I'm as young as I feel, or asks if I've found any gray hair, I swear you won't be able to hold me back."

Stuffing the last two paper tablecloths into a trash can, Braden asked, "What do you want to do now?"

"I think I'll go on home."

"Alone?"

Travis didn't want to answer, but Braden's silence and piercing gaze finally forced him to say, "What?"

"I was just wondering," Braden said, "if your bad mood is the result of the fact that your birthday is tomorrow, or that blonde you mentioned a few weeks ago, the one Mom fixed that picnic lunch for."

Travis wasn't really surprised that Ginny had mentioned that lunch to Braden, but he sure as hell wished Braden hadn't brought it up right now. "Who says I'm in a bad mood?"

Braden's snort reminded Travis of Ivy. It made him scowl all the more.

"I'm pretty sure Veronica's friend is still interested in meeting you. According to Veronica, that woman could take your mind off your troubles and make you feel ten years younger in no time at all."

Travis already knew a woman who could take his mind off his troubles, a woman who made him feel about seventeen, a woman whose long blond hair smelled faintly of jasmine and whose sighs filled his dreams, a woman who'd made a pact with her sixteen-year-old daughter, a woman who...

"Hi ya, Travis old boy."

He turned around, and came face-to-face with Ginny's sixty-five-year-old bachelor brother. "What is it, Artie?"

"I believe I've spied a gray hair."

Braden vaulted over the picnic table and placed himself between the man grinning from ear to ear and one who was clenching his fingers into fists at his side. Placing an arm on Travis's shoulder, he steered him toward the front yard.

"Whoa," Braden said. "You and I both know my mother would forgive us for just about anything, but she'd never forgive you for flattening her only brother's nose. Why don't I give Veronica a call and see if her redheaded friend is busy tonight?"

These past weeks of frustration converged inside Travis like a giant throbbing headache. "I'd rather pound Uncle Artie."

"Come on, Travis. What do you say?"

"I don't know, Braden. I don't think I'd be very good company."

"Why not let Jessica be the judge of that?"

"Jessica?"

"Yeah. You just leave everything to me."

"Mom, were you in love with my father, really and truly in love?"

Cori straightened so suddenly, the freshly laundered pillowcase fell out of her hands. Caught completely off guard, she glanced across the Buttercup Room where Allison was leaning against an antique dresser.

"I really and truly thought I was in love with him, kiddo. Why?"

Allison switched her weight to one foot and gave her mother an unconvincing shrug. Cori had been as open and honest with her daughter as she could possibly be. Allison knew the circumstances surrounding her birth. She knew her teenaged mother had loved her long before she was born, and that the boy who had fathered her hadn't known the first thing about taking responsibility. She knew he'd been cocky and rebellious and had had sandy blond hair and gray eyes, and a childhood that was troubled with a capital T. She even knew that his name was Johnny, but until today, she'd never asked for any more information about him.

"I don't just think I love Ross. I know I do."

Cori could have argued with that statement, telling Allison that she was too young to know what real love was, but she thought better of it. Going back to her task, she smoothed the wrinkles from the clean sheets, slipped the pillowcase over the fluffy pillow, and pulled the butter yellow comforter up to the white headboard.

"Did he ever pressure you, Mom?"

Sitting on the edge of the newly made bed, Cori took her time answering. Sometimes that period in her life seemed so long ago, and other times the memories were so vivid it could have happened yesterday. Johnny Smith had been on the wild side, but he'd made Cori feel special at a time in her life when she'd felt ugly and uncoordinated and stupid. She'd been so hungry for affection, for acceptance, she'd mistaken his attention for love.

Looking at her daughter's slender back, she said, "He pressured me, but he didn't force me. Is Ross pressuring you?"

Allison's head jerked around, the rest of her following more slowly. "No, not at all. Well, maybe a little. Sometimes."

"I suppose that's natural, Allison, but that doesn't mean you have to give in."

"Is it natural for a boy to, you know, start looking at other girls—girls who might be willing to give him what he wants?"

"If he loves you, really loves you, he'll wait."

"Do you honestly think so?"

Cori glanced around the room, her gaze straying out the window where a slight breeze was stirring the leaves on the maple tree. She and Travis had shared a picnic lunch beneath the shade of that tree. They'd nearly shared a lot more.

She pushed herself to her feet and wandered around the room. How many times had she thought of him since he'd bounded out of her house Friday night? How many times had she relived every word they'd said, analyzing every expression that had crossed his face?

It was shortly after ten o'clock in the morning and all the guests had left for the day. Travis hadn't shown up for work. She wondered how his surprise party had gone last night. She also wondered if he still preferred blond hair to red.

"Oh, Allison, I do think so. Men have the same responsibility to remain true to a relationship as women do. Wouldn't life be simpler if this whole sex thing didn't exist?"

Allison stuck her hands on her hips and cocked her head at a lofty angle. "It might be simpler, Mom, but it sure wouldn't be as much fun."

Cori threw a pillow at her precocious daughter. Laughing, Allison tossed it back again. She left the room moments later, complaining about the geometry class she had to attend in half an hour.

Cori went about readying the room for the next guests who were due to arrive late tomorrow. Since the Buttercup Room was next to the back stairway and the door was wide open, she heard Allison descend the stairs. Seconds later, the back door banged shut.

She went about her work, dusting furniture and vacuuming the floor. When she finished cleaning the tiny yellow bathroom, she thought she heard the door open again downstairs. Footsteps scudded on the kitchen floor below. They sounded too heavy to belong to Allison, and Ivy had gone to the store. Wondering if her friend could have forgotten something, Cori went to the top of the stairs and called, "Ivy, is that you?"

For a moment, there was only silence. Just when she was almost convinced that she'd imagined the footsteps, a deep voice carried to her ears.

"No, Cori. It's me."

Chapter Nine

Travis settled himself more comfortably against the counter and watched Cori descend the back stairs. Her head was high, her shoulders stiff, her eyes wary. It reminded him of the way a person might approach a rattlesnake, or an ornery S.O.B. After the way he'd stormed out of her house Friday night, he could hardly blame her.

He waited to say anything until she reached the bottom landing. Holding up a steaming mug, he said, "I hope you don't mind that I helped myself, because I really need this cup of coffee."

"No, no. Of course I don't mind. That's what it's there for."

Someone who didn't know her as well as he did might not have heard the forced brightness in her voice, or seen the hesitation in her movements as she turned and took the remaining two steps. He knew she was watching him, which meant she'd probably noticed how bleary-eyed he looked this morning. There had to be at least a hundred questions zinging through her mind this very minute. If she wasn't so damned proud, she'd come right out and ask.

But Corinna Cassidy was proud. He'd sensed it the first time he met her. It was one of the things that made her so infuriatingly special. He'd thought about her for a long time last night, and sometime in the wee hours of the morning, he'd finally realized why her pride was so important to her.

He'd been sitting right across from her in that truck stop when she'd told him about her parents. Although he didn't fully understand why she wanted to hear from them after all these years, he'd seen her fingers shake several times when she'd checked the mail. Her parents had turned their backs on her when she'd needed them the most. As a result of their high standards and cold hearts, she'd been forced to face the world with nothing. Nothing except her pride.

Since he wasn't moving very fast this morning, he took his time crossing his ankles, then raised his cup of coffee to his lips for another sip. He wasn't exactly sure what the heaviness in his chest meant, but he knew it was his turn to try to explain.

After giving the caffeine a second or two to kick in, he finally said, "That snowball Braden called about last Friday has turned into an avalanche. Even though we haven't be able to prove it, we're sure it was the owner's mistake. He's threatening to sue unless we issue a written apology and put his house on the top of our list of priorities. So, I'm afraid my vacation is over."

"Oh. I see. If you'll submit an invoice for the work you've done, I'll make sure you're paid," she said quietly.

"I'm not finished."

"But I thought you just said you have to go back to work at your own company."

"I did. I do. But I still plan to finish what I've started."

He had to give her credit. The only indication she gave that she'd caught the double meaning behind his words was the slight raising of her eyebrows.

"It shouldn't take me more than a day or two to finish laying the flagstones and build your gazebo, but I'll either have to do it in the evening or on a weekend."

"Okay," she said, striding to the counter where she emptied the remaining coffee into a light blue mug and slowly took a sip.

"Hits the spot, doesn't it?" he asked.

"Is it helping with your hangover?"

He moved his head so fast cannons went off inside his skull. Waiting for the din of the explosion to recede, he studied her over the rim of his cup. "I can think of something that would help me a lot more."

She turned and gave him a snort that was huffier than Ivy's and Braden's put together. For the first time in as long as he could remember, it was all he could do to hold on to his serious expression.

"What would you say if I told you I've joined the Navy and will be shipping out tomorrow?"

She stared at him silently, but he noticed the way one corner of her mouth rose fractionally.

"That's what I thought you'd say."

He watched her take another sip of coffee. Her skin looked smooth and creamy. Her cheekbones were high, her nose turned up just enough to be considered pert. This close, he could see the faint freckles across her nose and the shadows her eyelashes cast on her cheeks when she blinked. He didn't know how she'd managed to get all that hair of hers fastened on top of her head, but he sure liked the effect. It was a regal hairstyle for a regal woman. The wispy tendrils framing her face and neck made her appear fragile. The glint in her eyes was another story.

"What if my doctor told you I'll go blind unless I make love immediately?"

She raised her haughty little chin another notch and said, "I'd probably ask your doctor if redheads could cure this condition."

The lack of sleep and the last two beers he'd had at Bruno's last night had left him feeling sluggish. In comparison, Cori seemed amazingly sharp-witted. In her own roundabout way, she was asking a very important question. Travis didn't know what to tell her. Braden's description of Veronica's friend had been pretty accurate. Her hair was red, her legs were long, and her bra size must have been in the second half of the alphabet. She wasn't desperate, but the way she'd moved her hips beneath her skintight jeans and touched him at every opportunity had let him know she was willing.

He took another sip of coffee and tried to put his thoughts in order. It wasn't easy. He hadn't had an orderly thought in two and a half days.

"I spent a lot of time thinking last night, Cori, about a lot of things. This condition of mine has nothing to do with hair color. It has to do with you."

She looked up at him, her eyes searching his. Holding her gaze, he continued. "I played a couple of games of pool with Braden, Veronica and Jessica down at Bruno's. We all had a few laughs and more than a few beers. But I went home alone."

"You did?"

He nodded. "Aren't you going to ask me why?"

He wasn't surprised she remained silent. Undeterred, he placed his cup on the counter and moved a little closer. "I went home alone because she wasn't you."

"Oh, Travis."

He took her cup from her fingers and placed it on the counter next to his. His arms went around her, trapping her hands between their bodies. Their lips met in a lingering kiss that made him want so much more. When their lips parted, he touched his forehead to hers and opened his eyes.

"Has anyone ever told you that you're a contrary, difficult woman?"

She pulled her head back and looked into his eyes. "Do you want the list in alphabetical order?"

The sudden burst of his own laughter made his head pound. He winced, but as far as he was concerned, her subtle humor had been worth the pain. She freed her hands, placing both palms on his chest. Looking up into his eyes, she said, "There's something I think you should know, Travis."

"What's that?"

"I'm not going to change my mind about that pact. I can't."

Along with being contrary and difficult, she was also so steadfast and serene it left him in awe. This time, it didn't take him long to reply. "I understand, Cori. I don't like it. But I do understand."

"What does this mean?" she whispered.

"This means I agree to your terms. I want you in my bed, but if I can't have you there, I'll settle for the chance to be with you in other ways. It also means that my complexion will never clear up."

Cori felt her lips slide into a grin. Travis Delaney had the complexion of a god, and the smile of a devilishly honorable man.

"What do we do now?" she asked.

"I don't know. I've never gone in for one-night stands, but I've rarely been completely celi—"

She couldn't help noticing the way he practically choked on the end of his statement. "Is 'celibate' the word you're looking for?" she asked.

"Believe me, that's the last word I'd go looking for. I'm not going to pretend that this is going to be easy, but I guess we're just going to have to take it one day at a time."

He took a backward step and glanced at his watch. Running his hand over his bloodshot eyes, he said, "There's one more thing. After my blind date last night, Braden's more convinced than ever that I'm going through a mid-life crisis. I'd appreciate it if you kept this pact to yourself. After all, I do have a reputation to protect."

"Oh, Travis."

"You can *Oh, Travis* me later. Now I have to get back out to Lake Waubesa and see how much progress Braden and Pete and the rest of guys on the crew have made."

One more quick kiss, and he was striding toward the door.

"Travis?"

He glanced over his shoulder.

Slanting him a warm look and a tender smile, she said, "Happy birthday."

His eyes took on the glimmer of summer lightning. They crinkled at the corners, smiling a full five seconds before his lips did. She'd seen him smile before, but nothing prepared her for the softening and swelling sensation that worked its way into her heart.

"I'd like to come back after work," he said. "I know evenings are busy here in the inn, but maybe we could sneak away for a little while and go for a drive."

"I'd like that."

"All right, then. I'll see you later."

"All right, but Travis? There's one more thing I'd like you to know."

"What's that?"

In a voice that was so tender it was almost a murmur, she said, "You don't have to worry about your reputation. It's safe with me."

Travis parked his Jeep at the curb and looked around. It was shortly after seven in the evening. The small parking lot near the street was full, and Ivy's Garden was bustling with activity. One family was playing cards around an ornate wrought-iron table on the front porch. Two little girls giggled as they skipped along the curving garden path. An old man was smoking a pipe while his wife sputtered at him about his health. The man stared directly at Travis and, without saying a word, blew a perfect smoke ring over his wife's head.

Travis had an uncustomary urge to grin. Similar urges had come over him at the oddest times all day. The guys in the crew had taken to looking at him even more strangely than usual. Since he had no idea how to explain what was happening to him, he'd thrown all his energy into his work and counted the hours until he'd see Cori again.

When she'd told him his reputation was safe with her, he'd nearly staggered and had all but forgotten to breathe. He'd never felt exactly that way, and he wasn't sure he liked it. Something had shifted deep inside his body, sending desire surging through him. It was happening again right now. He didn't know what it meant. He only knew he had to see Cori. Now.

He wasn't sure where she'd be this time of the day, in her cottage with Allison, or in the inn. Deciding to try her house first, he strode that way, nodding at a middle-aged couple he met on the path. A movement beneath the rose arbor caught his attention. His steps slowed, and he tried to throttle the dizzying current racing through him.

Since Cori's back was to him, he took advantage of the opportunity to watch her from this angle. She was wearing pale yellow slacks that showed off her waist and the curve of her hips to perfection. The matching blouse had sleeves that stopped just above her elbows. The material rippled and fluttered with every movement she made as she clipped rosebuds and placed them in a shallow basket.

Travis didn't have any idea what he was going to do about the desire deep inside him. Considering the pact she had with her daughter, what could he do? He only knew he had to get closer to her. Being careful to stay out of her line of vision, he ducked around to the back of the arbor and slipped through the curved archway. She let out a little yelp when he pulled her to him, but the moment she saw it was him, she smiled, her body going pliant, her eyes warm as she swayed toward him.

"Travis, you surprised me."

She might have tried to make it sound like a reprimand, but her voice was too husky to hold much censure. It was doing crazy, erotic, fanciful things to his senses. Running a hand up her arm, he said, "I told you I was coming back."

She shook her head the way she always did when he developed a cocky attitude. Unable to keep from touching her, he inched back a few steps, pulling her with him to an area that was more thickly covered with leafy vines and deep pink roses, awarding them a little more privacy.

As if she sensed the need to whisper, she said, "You're definitely moving faster than you were this morning."

"I've had an incredible amount of energy ever since I left here this morning."

He let his hand trail down her back, reveling in the way she automatically arched her spine. "Aren't you going to ask me why I have so much energy?" he asked.

"I don't think that would be a very good idea."

"Spoilsport."

She rolled her eyes, then continued. "Besides, Ivy has a little surprise waiting for you in the inn and I have strict instructions to take you inside as soon as you arrive."

"Don't tell me she made me a birthday cake."

"And ruin the surprise?"

Travis felt his heart speed up and his breathing deepen. God, he loved it when she raised her chin in that haughty manner, and when her smile became ever so smug. Bringing his face to within inches of hers, he whispered, "I was hoping for another kind of surprise, Cori."

Her eyes lowered to his mouth, and her pulse sped up where his fingers encircled her wrist. Travis knew she wouldn't break her pact with Allison. That didn't mean they couldn't partake in a tantalizing fantasy or two. He didn't really expect her to ask him what he was hoping for, but he wasn't about to let such an opportunity slip away. Lowering his mouth close to her, he whispered in her ear.

She drew in a quick breath, her eyes darkening a shade at a time. "Oh, Travis, what am I going to do with you?"

He had a few suggestions, but before he could voice any of them, Ivy called, "Cori. Travis. Come on inside so Ross and Allison and our guests can join in the celebration."

Half under his breath, he asked, "What makes her think I'm celebrating?"

One by one the guests began to make their way toward the inn. Glancing through the white lattice, Travis grumbled, "Now do you see why I hate birthdays?"

Cori looked at him, her eyes bright. As they strolled toward the back door, she reached for his hand and gave it a squeeze. And he had to force himself to breathe all over again.

"Now tell me the truth. Turning thirty-nine didn't hurt so bad, did it?" Ivy asked, wiping cake crumbs off the counter in her old kitchen.

Travis made some noncommittal reply, then glanced up the stairway where Cori had disappeared a few minutes ago. He knew evenings were busy times in the inn, but he was impatient to have her to himself, if only for a short time.

"You might as well make yourself comfortable," Ivy insisted. "Corinna's liable to be a while."

"What's she doing?"

"Since I don't hear any more raised voices, she's probably smoothing ruffled feathers. It's this way every summer. The Taylors and the Stuarts take their vacations together each June. They're best friends the rest of the year, but halfway through their first week here, they're always at one another's throats.''

"So this could take Cori a while?"

"I'm afraid so."

Reluctantly, he sat down on a painted stool on the other side of the counter. "Does Cori spend a lot of her time smoothing ruffled feathers?"

"A fair amount. She does it well, doesn't she? Look how she calmed you down when Ross happened to mention that a man your age probably wouldn't have enough wind to blow out thirty-nine candles."

Travis saw Ivy hide a smile to herself, and caught himself before falling into her trap and sputtering that Ross didn't *happen* to mention anything. That kid had known exactly what he was doing.

"What's the matter? Cat got your tongue?"

There was something in the older woman's voice that made him understand why Cori said she was her dearest and sometimes darnedest friend. Ivy Pennington was shrewd, and if the twinkle in her eyes was an accurate indication, she was also enjoying this conversation.

Suddenly feeling too fidgety to sit still, he slid to his feet and paced to the windows. Staring out, he said, "I think I handled things pretty well, considering. I lived through three verses of that stupid birthday song that was sung, for the most part, by people I've never seen before, I blew out every last candle on the cake and I never laid a hand on the kid. Now, would you like some help with those dishes?"

"*Tcht*. Lisa says you have a bad-boy smile, but underneath, you really are a gentleman, aren't you? Maybe that's why I've never seen so much sparkle in Corinna's eyes."

"Never?"

She huffed slightly, but when he strode to the sink, she handed him a towel. "I always knew there was something about you that reminded me of my Baxter. Now I know what it is. He used to fish for compliments, too.''

''What do you mean, *too?*''

''I'd hate to have to repeat myself, but I'd hate to see Corinna get hurt a lot more.''

Travis heard the warning in Ivy Pennington's simple statement. Reaching for a dripping plate, he said, ''I'm not planning to hurt her, Ivy.''

She arched her eyebrows and said, ''I'm glad to hear you say that. Just what *do* you plan to do?''

He dried the plate, feeling slightly uncomfortable with the question. The truth was, he *wanted* to whisk Cori away from the inn and kiss her the way he had that afternoon in the garden and again a few nights ago on her front stoop.

Glancing toward the stairway, he knew that wasn't all he wanted to do. Since he couldn't very well tell Ivy any of the specifics, he said, ''I'll tell you one thing I'd like to do. I'd like to pay a little visit to Cori's parents and tell them exactly what I think of them.''

''I think you'd be surprised at what you'd find.''

Travis jerked his head around to look at Ivy. ''What do you mean?''

''Her parents aren't monsters. According to Corinna, they were model citizens, and probably still are. They go to church and don't cheat on their taxes. They cry at funerals and donate to worthy charities. Part of the reason Corinna became the woman she is today is due to their influence.''

''Then you don't think they were coldhearted for kicking her out when she needed them the most?''

Ivy shrugged slowly. ''All I'm saying is that, sometimes, people do the wrong things for the right reasons. Sometimes, they can't see the forest for the trees.''

''You sound as if you're speaking from experience.''

''That I am, Travis. That I am. Like Cori's parents, I had high ideals. You see, a long time ago, I nearly pushed

Baxter out of my life. That man and I were married for nearly thirty-seven years. If he were here today, he'd tell you they were the happiest *twenty*-seven years of his life. And he wouldn't be completely kidding. We had some hard years. We stuck together and made it through. Too many people give up too soon nowadays."

She reached for another stack of plates and said, "You're probably wondering what this has to do with the price of beans. But I'm getting to that. You see, I wasn't born knowing the meaning of practically everybody's name. I learned them from studying books filled with names for babies. I wanted a child so bad I ached. As the years passed, the ache grew to an empty kind of pain. I didn't accept being childless. I couldn't. It got to the point where it was easier for Baxter to go to the corner bar than to come home to me. I'm glad I finally saw the light, finally realized that Baxter was all the family I needed. When he died, I didn't know what I was going to do to survive living without him."

Travis stopped drying dishes and stood perfectly still, listening to every word Ivy Pennington said. There were lines in her face, and gray all through her hair. He thought she was an incredibly beautiful woman, inside and out.

"The Lord works in mysterious ways, Travis. That He does. A year after my Baxter went to be with the Lord, I met Corinna. She and Allison became the children I never had, and I became the folks they needed. As far as I'm concerned, it was Corinna's parents' loss."

Slowly reaching for another plate, he said, "Do you think there's a chance she'll hear from them this summer?"

"I hope she does, but I just don't know."

"Do you know why this letter is so important to her?"

Ivy nodded. "I think she wants their love. And she wants their forgiveness."

"Forgiveness for what? Making a mistake?"

"For not being the kind of child they wanted her to be."

Travis swallowed, hard. He had to clear his throat in order to speak. Even then, his voice was lower than usual. "I'd still like to tell them exactly what I think of them. Do you know what else I think?"

"Something tells me I'm about to," she answered.

Without missing a beat, he said, "I think Cori was lucky to have found someone like you to take her in."

Ivy Pennington did her best to disguise a sniffle, but Travis saw through her like a picture window. Washing a plate she'd already washed twice, she said, "I've always thought I was the lucky one."

As if she finally realized what she was doing, she rinsed the plate and placed it in the drainer. Looking out the window where the setting sun was streaking the sky with pink and gold and blue, she said, "That girl was already strong and proud and beautiful when I met her. Now that she's a woman, those traits are even more evident. Wouldn't it be wonderful if someone could make her see herself that way?"

"Make who see herself that way?"

Ivy and Travis both jumped, their gazes swinging to the stairs Cori was silently descending.

"Merciful heavens, child!" Ivy declared. "You startled me."

Cori was all set to repeat her question, but she glanced at Travis, and her thoughts scrambled. The heated expression in his eyes should have been outlawed, but she was awfully glad it wasn't. He'd looked at her this way earlier today, right after she'd wished him a happy birthday and told him his reputation was safe with her. A similar expression had crept across his face when they were underneath the rose trellis a little over an hour ago. It was the kind of look only a man could give a woman, the kind of look that said he could hardly wait to get her alone. It made her heart speed up and her body feel so warm she wondered if it showed.

"Are you all done unruffling feathers?" Ivy asked.

Cori nodded then cast a glance up the stairs. Lowering her voice to a whisper, she said, "Both couples have retreated to their separate rooms for the night. They're still sulking, but I have a feeling they'll be best friends again by morning."

She looked back in time to see Travis place a wet plate on the counter and toss his towel over his shoulder. Without waiting to see where it landed, he strode straight to her and said, "Now, about that drive."

Late-evening air streamed in through the open windows, cooling Cori's face, fluttering the wisps of hair that had escaped the knot at her nape. She could have closed the window, but she didn't want to. The cool breeze somehow added to the giddy sense of excitement of driving through the dusky night on unfamiliar roads with a man who wanted her but had agreed to see her on her terms.

They'd driven west for a time, then north and east and west again, until she was thoroughly turned around. Travis seemed to know where he was going. Strangely, she trusted him to get them there, although so far he hadn't told her where *there* was.

They talked about his day, and hers, oldies songs playing low on the radio. Spotting a sign that said Wisconsin Dells, 65 Miles, she said, "When I was little I had a friend whose mother taught us to sing 'The Farmer in the Dell.' Since my father grew up in Wisconsin Dells, I thought the song would mean a lot to him. One day when I was about six, I surprised my parents and sang every verse for them."

"Were they proud?" he asked quietly.

She glanced out the side window, where closely built houses had given way to gently rolling fields. "I don't think so. They shared a look over the top of my head. My father said it was very nice, and my mother said I had a fine voice, then proceeded to teach me songs befitting her daughter.''

"What kinds of songs?"

"Oh, church and Bible songs, mostly, and a few songs from some of the old musicals."

"Did you like to sing?" he asked.

"Not as much after that."

Travis squeezed the steering wheel a little tighter. Every time he learned more about Cori's parents, he liked them less.

Turning onto a back road he'd discovered years and years ago, he said, "I always hated to sing. Of course, it might have had something to do with the fact that I couldn't carry a tune in a basket. My mother never could, either, not that that stopped her. She really used to get the alley cats going in the summer."

"Travis Delaney! I do believe you just had a pleasant memory from your childhood."

"I slipped," he said, shrugging one shoulder.

She smiled into the darkening countryside skimming past her open window. "What would you do," she asked, "if your mother and father showed up at your place tomorrow?"

Travis thought long and hard for a minute or two. "Honestly?" he asked.

She nodded, and he said, "I don't know what I'd do. Probably nothing. Outside of a strange kind of curiosity, whatever I felt for my parents is long gone."

"You wouldn't want to show them anything if you saw them today?" she asked.

"Oh, I suppose I'd like them to know I'm okay, no thanks to them."

"No offense, Travis, but I can't imagine feeling that way. If my parents showed up on my doorstep, I'd welcome them with open arms."

Travis didn't really want to talk about Cori's parents. He'd been thinking about something Ivy had said in the kitchen before Cori came downstairs. *Wouldn't it be wonderful if someone found a way to prove to Cori how strong and good she really is?*

Her parents had done a number on her. As far as he was concerned, she didn't owe them a thing. They sure as hell didn't deserve to be welcomed with open arms. Why she'd want to prove anything to them after the way they'd treated her as a child was beyond him.

"Do you know what I'd like to show them more than anything else?" she asked.

"You'd like to show them Allison."

She nodded then said, "Yes. I'd like them to see what a wonderful granddaughter they have. Then I'd take them through Ivy's Garden. I'd tell them they were right about some things. I'd admit that I made some mistakes. And then I'd tell them that one of those mistakes, having a baby so young, was the best thing I've ever done. Maybe this year they'll answer my letter. Maybe I'll finally be a member of my own family again."

He turned another corner, the Jeep slowly creeping over the bumpy road. "Do you think you'll hear from them?" he asked.

"I was hoping to receive a reply sooner, but it's just like my father to wait, to contemplate every angle, to weigh his decision with utmost care. He and my mother are both very methodical, thinking everything through before acting upon it. That's why it was so difficult for them to understand why I decided to go against their wishes."

"What wishes were those?"

"Well, they were more like decrees than wishes. I was to dress a certain way and behave a certain way. And they absolutely forbade me to see Allison's father. Of course, telling me I can't do something is like waving a red flag in front of my face.''

Travis took his foot from the accelerator and his eyes from the lane in front of him. He was on the verge of making an important discovery.

"Travis, where are we?"

It was nearly impossible to see her in the gathering darkness, but he saw the angle of her chin as she looked from him, out her window, and back again.

"I don't know if this place has a name anymore, but it used to be called Parkers' Point."

"We're going parking?"

His instinctive response to the incredulity in her voice was similar to every other response he'd had where Cori was concerned. Desire sank into his body, spreading through his veins, tunneling to the very center of him.

He pulled to one side of the secluded meadow, turned off the Jeep's engine and reached for her hand. Just like that, something clicked in his mind, and he knew exactly what he was going to do.

In a whisper-husky voice that might as well have been red flags waving in the breeze, he said, "Yup. We're going parking. But you *can't* kiss me, Cori. And you *can't* smooth your hand across my chest, and you *can't* press your lips to my neck, and you *can't* . . ."

He heard her slowly drawn breath, and then her blouse was sliding like a whisper along the back of her seat as she slowly moved closer. "You, Travis Delaney, are as transparent as glass."

Her hand found its way to his chest, and her mouth to the side of his neck where she pressed a smile-shaped kiss to his rapidly heating flesh. His hands went to her waist, his elbow banging against the steering wheel, his knee bumping the gearshift lever. He groaned and she laughed. The sound of her laughter alone would have been worth his discomfort, but he had the added bonus of discovering one way to help Cori win back her self-respect.

He pulled her out of her bucket seat, fitting her across his lap between his chest and the blasted steering wheel. One hand trailed up her shoulder to the side of her face, guiding his mouth to hers.

Her lips parted beneath his, her mouth giving and taking with incredible feeling. When the kiss ended, he turned his head, pressing another kiss to the hollow below her ear. ''I'd forgotten just how much fun parking is.''

''I can't believe we're actually doing this. What if someone sees us?''

His lips moved on to the base of her throat, his fingers deftly unfastening the button there. ''I doubt that anyone knows about Parkers' Point anymore,'' he murmured as another button slipped from its slot.

''Travis,'' she whispered, covering his hand with hers. ''I don't want to make this any more difficult for you, so you'd better not unfasten any more of my buttons.''

Another button popped from its hole.

''What are you doing?''

His palm slipped inside her open blouse, covering one perfectly shaped breast. She sighed, automatically arching, straining toward his hand.

''I'm touching you, and kissing you, and holding you. If I have my way, I'm going to give you dozens of opportunities to practice your newly acquired skill.''

As his fingers pushed her bra out of the way and his hand came into contact with warm, soft flesh, he drew in a ragged breath. ''You do remember your newly acquired skill, don't you, Cori? The one in which you tell me no and mean it.''

''Do you mean you're not going to get angry if I stop us from going too far and breaking my pact with Allison?''

''I have a feeling I'm going to be plenty frustrated, but I won't get mad. I promise.''

"Really?"

"Why don't you make me prove it?"

She shifted away from him slightly, a moonbeam illuminating one side of her face as she studied him. When she accepted his challenge, he felt at least a hundred feet tall. She raised her mouth to his for a dreamy kiss. Her hand trailed down his chest to the center of his stomach, spreading wide over his midsection, slipping lower to the buckle on his belt. And lower.

Oh, yes, Cori, yes. His desire surged beneath her hand, aching for release. He held on to his control and groaned without taking his mouth from hers. He planned to give her many more opportunities to take him to the brink of control, then stop them from doing what they both wanted.

He only hoped it didn't kill him.

"Oh, Travis."

"I've been waiting all day to hear you say that."

Cori smiled against his mouth, then moved to whisper a kiss on his left shoulder. His breathing was as labored as hers, and she was drowning in sensation. Her heart was taking turns speeding up and slowing down, and her body was so responsive it seemed to have turned to liquid. Travis seemed to know where to touch her to bring her the most pleasure.

She was certain she'd never been touched by a more virile man. She was also certain he wanted to do more than touch. But he was allowing her to set the pace, to enjoy the moment. He was giving her the power to stop them from going too far.

She pulled away slightly, testing his reaction. He took another ragged breath, but he let her go. Tears filled her eyes, making her glad for the cover of darkness. It required every last ounce of strength she possessed to move farther away from him. Yet in doing so, she'd never been filled with so much joy.

She could hear the rustle of his clothes as he tucked his shirt in. Back on her side of the Jeep, she took her time straightening her own clothes. There were so many things she wanted to say to him, but the feelings in her heart were too new, so all she said was, "Whew."

Headlights flickered from behind them, illuminating the inside of the Jeep enough to see Travis's expression. His lips, which were still swollen from her kisses, were set in a straight line. His face was all hollows and angles, a muscle working in his clenched jaw. He was a man in the throes of a strong passion, yet he seemed to be doing everything in his power to pull himself together.

As the headlights came closer, he raised his eyebrows and managed half a smile. She returned his grin, then cast a glance out her window. The other car turned, slowly heading for a secluded spot at the other end of the grassy field. She glanced away, then did a double take.

"Look, Travis. That looks like Ross's car."

"It sure does. That's got to be Ross with his hat on backwards."

"And I'd recognize the outline of Allison's wavy hair anywhere."

"I guess kids still come to Parkers' Point, after all," Travis said.

Casting him a sidelong glance, she whispered, "Kids aren't the only ones."

His groan was all male as he said, "Why in the world do kids put themselves through this?"

"Why did you?"

"Believe me, Cori, what we just did was worth the discomfort."

Cori smiled into the darkness, her eyes trailing back to the black Camaro whose lights were now off. "I wonder what the kids are doing."

Staring out the window, she thought it was very gentlemanly of Travis to refrain from stating the obvious.

Chapter Ten

"Isn't that Mr. Delaney's Jeep?" Ross asked.

"Omigosh!" Allison said, sliding down in her seat. "Mom must be with him."

"No kidding!"

"This is so weird."

"Aren't they a little old to be parking?" Ross asked.

"I don't know, but we have to get out of here."

She glanced over her shoulder, but she could hardly believe what she saw. Moonlight glinted off the dark roof of Travis's Jeep. Inside, the outlines of two people's heads were clearly visible. It was her mother and Travis, all right. And they were parked in the most romantic meadow near Madison.

"Do you think they saw us?" she asked.

"People who come here aren't usually all that interested in their surroundings. Maybe Mr. Delaney isn't so old after all."

"Ross! You're talking about a man who's with my mother. Now come on, let's go."

"This really is weird, but let's just wait a minute and see what they do."

"I don't want to see what they do!" Allison exclaimed.

"I don't mean that. I mean let's see how long they stay."

"Oh. I hope she hasn't seen us."

"If your mom is anything like you, Mr. Delaney probably hasn't been able to take his eyes off her long enough to look around."

"Oh, Ross."

"Why don't you come a little closer and say that again?"

Ross's voice had taken on that low, husky rasp that turned her heart to goose down and her knees to melting wax. She had a hard time resisting him when he let his voice dip that low, his words coming slow and smooth and dreamy.

"What do you say?"

"Oh, Ross."

"That's what I was hoping you'd say. C'mere."

"I can't come there with my mother parked a few hundred feet away."

"You sit close to me on your living room sofa when she's in the next room. Besides, Allison, are you always going to do everything your mother tells you to do?"

She gave his words a moment's consideration, then stiffly moved a little closer. When she fit her shoulder underneath his arm, he kissed her hair, then moved it aside to brush his lips against her ear. Every time he did that, the strangest thing happened. His lips were as warm as a caress against her soft skin, but the warmth didn't stop there. It glided to a place much, much lower, a place that was physically unconnected, yet stole her breath away.

Her eyelids always grew so heavy when that happened that she couldn't possibly hold them open. She couldn't possibly hold back the sigh that floated up from her throat, either.

An engine rumbled to a start and lights flickered through her closed eyelids. At first, she thought she was seeing stars, but when she opened her eyes, she saw that it was headlights bouncing off the rearview mirror.

Keeping her head low, Allison watched Travis's Jeep slowly turn around and drive down the curving lane toward the country road. Ross took her chin in his hand and lowered his face to hers. "Alone at last," he whispered.

The next thing she knew he was kissing her and she was giving herself up to the headiness of his touch, and the unfamiliar, exciting yearning in her young body.

It was a few minutes past eleven. Cori knew, because she'd been watching the clock ever since Travis had kissed her goodbye at the door forty-five minutes ago. Allison wasn't home yet, and Cori couldn't get the image of Ross's car parked in that secluded meadow out of her mind.

Ah, that secluded moonlit meadow.

She closed her eyes and smiled into the stillness of her own quiet kitchen. She didn't know whether this dreamy sense of intimacy was from the memory of the way Travis had kissed her, or the lingering effects of the kisses themselves.

For years, she'd ignored the sexual aspect of her life. Since meeting Travis, old and forgotten feelings had been rekindled, and her senses had been brought to life. She crossed her arms at her waist and closed her eyes, remembering how his hands had felt on her body. He'd started a smoldering passion deep within her. His kisses had been lusty, his breathing ragged, his body taut and ready. He'd given her hands free rein on his body, and then, before they'd reached the point of no return, she'd pulled away. It had cost him, but he'd let her go.

She'd never met a man like him. She'd also never been parking in the same meadow as her daughter.

Headlights flickered on the wall. Cori swung around, paced to the window, intent upon greeting Allison. Just like that, she was back in the kitchen again. What in the world was she going to say?

A door slammed. Moments later, a car's engine faded as it backed from the driveway. Cori took her hands from her cheeks and forced herself to take a deep breath. She heard the distinctive click as the screen door's handle was depressed. By the time Allison had pulled the door open, Cori was standing in the middle of the living room.

"Allison!"

"Mom!"

They'd spoken at the same time, their feet frozen to the floor. Their gazes met, held, then darted away, as if neither of them knew where to look or what to say next. Cori was the first to find her voice. "I don't know whether you noticed it or not, but . . ."

"I noticed."

"You did? Then you saw me at . . ."

"Parkers' Point?" Allison asked. "Yeah. I saw you."

"Oh. Do you go there often?"

"Do you?"

Cori snapped her mouth shut and took a quick breath. Allison's question had caught her off guard, but it shouldn't have. That girl of hers had always been able to think on her feet.

"Actually," Cori said, "this was the first time I've been there. And just so you know, our pact still stands."

"For me, too."

"Really? Oh, Allison, I'm so glad."

They both looked around the room, feigning an interest in furnishings they'd seen a thousand times. Allison stretched her hands over her head and faked the worst yawn in history. "Well," she said, "It's getting kinda late. I think I'll go to bed."

Cori nodded and said, "That sounds like a good idea. I think I'll turn in, too."

She turned off the kitchen light and locked the door. Neither of them said a word as they strode through the narrow front room and on into the short hall. Opening facing doors, they ducked into their respective bedrooms and slowly turned around.

"Good night, Allison."

Cocking her head to one side, Allison said, "'Night, Mom. I still think this is weird. I mean, how many other kids have mothers who go parking?"

"I think you might be surprised, kiddo."

"I already am."

They stared at each other for a long moment. And then they both started to laugh.

Before her laughter trailed away, Allison darted to the bathroom down the hall and quietly closed the door. Cori stood there in her open doorway, her heart nearly bursting with love for this winsome, willowy creature who was her daughter. Listening to the night sounds in her little house, she wished her parents could see how bright and beautiful her little girl was, and what a beautiful young woman she would undoubtedly become.

She closed her door and strode to the window where she peered through the thin slats of her blinds. The moon was a silver half circle in the clear black sky, and the stars were bright and plentiful. Gazing at all those twinkling white lights, an age-old nursery rhyme played through her thoughts.

Star light, star bright... When the last line had whispered through her mind, she placed her hand over her heart and said a silent prayer.

"Okay. Let me see if I've got this straight," Cori said, rolling down the window on the passenger side of Travis's

Jeep. "Rachel and Annie look enough alike to be twins, but Rachel is two years older. Uncle Artie looks nothing like Ginny, but they're brother and sister. Ginny and Rachel are convinced that there's something bothering Annie, so they're calling in the troops and have arranged a special family gathering."

Travis took his eyes from the road and fixed her with a helpless look. "I'd planned to introduce you to them in small doses, but I'm afraid the Calhouns don't do anything in a small way. Every event is a major production."

Cori laughed at his wry expression, and settled herself more comfortably in her seat. It was Wednesday evening. He'd stopped into the inn again last night. Unfortunately, she'd been so busy with the needs of the guests that, except for a kiss that had practically curled her toes, and a whisper in her ear that had made her eyes widen and her heart rate soar, she and Travis hadn't had a moment alone together.

She could never repeat what he'd revealed in that whisper, at least not out loud, but her cheeks colored at the memory alone. Ivy and Allison had both been watching her strangely ever since. They'd taken turns asking about the perpetual glint in her eyes. Since she'd promised Travis she'd guard his reputation, she'd only smiled and shrugged. She hadn't told them that her feelings felt as new and fragile as rose blossoms, or that she thought she might be falling in love.

The rumble of Travis's deep voice brought her back to the present. "As busy as the inn was the last time I was there, I'm a little surprised you managed to get away on such short notice tonight."

"You can thank Allison for that. She offered to fill in for me for a few hours. She has a big heart, but sometimes I swear that girl is too smart for her own good. Did you hear what she said to me as I went out the door?"

Travis shook his head, and Cori remembered how flushed Allison's cheeks had been from all her trips up and down two flights of stairs. Her fatigue hadn't kept her from holding the door for her mother. It hadn't kept her from smiling broadly and winking badly, either.

"She told me not to do anything she wouldn't do."

Travis glanced at her and said, "I can see what you mean about that kid."

Although his words had been teasing, Cori recognized the warmth in his eyes for what it was. He wanted to be alone with her. A familiar shiver of awareness tap-danced across her shoulders and down her spine because she knew that wasn't all he wanted. She knew, because she wanted the same thing. Even though part of her was disappointed because she couldn't allow herself to be that intimate with him, a bigger part of her was in awe of her strength, and of his. It took an incredibly big man to make this kind of sacrifice, especially in this day and age.

Watching the scenery go by, she thought about some of the things Travis had told her about his childhood. He hadn't exactly had a model upbringing. His father had taken up with other women before finally deserting him completely and his mother had been an alcoholic. He'd gotten into more than his share of trouble in school, and yet he'd become a wonderful man.

She wondered how many kids would have gone the other way, ending up on the wrong side of the law as a result of a childhood like his. Sitting there in the quiet intimacy of the car, she realized that she wanted to learn more about the people who had taken him in and made him a part of their family.

"Tell me about some of the things the Calhouns have done in a big way."

He used his right-turn signal, then cut through the traffic and took the Old Saulk Road exit. "All right," he said, "But go ahead and stop me if you get bored."

"I don't see how you could ever bore me."

Travis kept the Jeep under control, but not his breathing. He cleared his throat, but he didn't even try to pretend not to be affected by her statement. A jolt of sexual desire shot through him with so much force he almost blurted his need for her out loud. There was really nothing about their conversation that should have been lust-arousing, yet his desire for this woman had never been stronger. The closer he came to knowing her, the more certain he was that he had to make her his.

"Travis? Is everything all right?"

"What?" Then, coming to his senses, he said, "Sure. Everything's fine."

He told himself to get a grip. After all, he wasn't some rutting buck or overzealous teenager. He was a man, and he was old enough to control his own lust. He hoped.

Clearing his throat, he said, "What do you want to know about Ginny and Sam?"

"Anything. Anything at all."

"Okay. But I warned you."

He told her about all the birthday parties that had taken place in the Calhouns' backyard, about the hoopla there had been when Rachel and Annie had made their First Communions. He even told her about the high school graduation open house they threw in his and Braden's honor, and how it would probably go down in history for its sheer size alone.

Peering at the stretch of highway in front of her, she said, "I finished my high school education in night school after Allison was born."

"Then you never had a party?"

"My parents probably would have taken me out to dinner in a nice restaurant if things had been different. As it was, I was just thrilled to have my diploma."

Travis took his eyes off the road to look at her. She seemed to be watching all the neat white houses with their postage-stamp yards go by, so she didn't notice his measuring stare. He doubted she even realized what she'd said, but to him, it was another testimony to the childhood she'd sacrificed to keep her baby.

Dragging his gaze back to the street, he said, "You'd better not let Ginny get wind of that information, or you'll likely find yourself surrounded by strangers wishing you luck upon your belated graduation."

She looked at him, her eyes round with surprise. Within seconds, she started to laugh. "Oh, Travis, surely you must be exaggerating."

"You'll see," he said, turning into Ginny and Sam's driveway at the end of the block.

"They can't be as noisy and nosey as you say."

A loud harrumph was his only answer.

An hour later, Cori could have eaten her words. If she'd had any room left in her stomach, that is. Enough food had been set out to feed a small army. Every time someone made a dent in it, Ginny bustled to the refrigerator and whisked out more. Cori was beginning to wonder if some unseen person was slipping food in through a secret door in the back. The only thing that made her question the notion was the fact that none of the Calhouns she'd met so far would have been content to remain unseen or unheard.

As unbelievable as it was, the Calhouns really were just as Travis had described them. The noise level had fluctuated between a dizzying buzz and a deafening roar since the moment she and Travis had stepped foot inside the house. Right now, Artie Simmon and Sam Calhoun were arguing tersely, Ginny and Rachel were discussing something or other in heated whispers, and Braden and Travis were talking business in serious undertones.

The entire family was incredible, every one of them charming in their own way. She'd liked Braden Calhoun instantly, although he was a little too cocky for her taste. Still, his grin was genuine and knowing, his attitude laid-back and fun-loving. He was the same height as Travis, but his hair was blond and his body was broader, thicker, more like his father's. Annie and Rachel were friendly, too. Except for their hair color, they resembled their mother, although, tonight at least, Annie was much more subdued than the rest of the family.

To hear Travis tell it, Arthur Simmon was from another planet. Seeing him in the midst of the rest of the family, Cori realized that, although they seemed to love to tease him, he also held an important place in the family. Artie was of average height and build, with thinning gray hair and serious blue eyes. It wasn't often that you came across a man who'd been a bachelor for sixty-five years, and Cori couldn't help wondering why he'd never married.

Yes, all the Calhouns were fascinating, but the person who truly captivated her attention wasn't blood-related to the others. Travis didn't look anything like the Calhouns, who were noisy and boisterous, raising their voices and gesturing with their hands, yet he seemed as much a part of the family as any of them.

Since everyone else's attention was elsewhere, Cori had a few minutes to herself to study the only man she'd met in years who tugged at her heartstrings and stirred her longings. Travis's skin was tanned from the hours he spent in the sun. His dark hair was a little shaggier than it had been when she'd first met him. Here inside, she couldn't see the bronze and rust highlights in those tresses, but she knew they were there. She liked the way his khaki slacks fit his narrow hips, and the way he'd pushed the sleeves of his navy knit shirt up to his elbows. She was discovering that she liked a lot of things about this man.

She liked his broad mouth and straight eyebrows, his strong chin and his nose that was just crooked enough to make her think it had been broken a long, long time ago. He happened to glance her way. And caught her looking at him. Voices rose all around them, but as his gaze held hers, the noise faded. He tipped his head toward a few of the Calhouns, his expression seeming to say, I told you so. She started to smile, but was interrupted by a commotion on the other side of the room, where Ginny and Rachel were interrogating Annie.

"No. For the hundredth time, no. I'm not sick. I'm not dying."

"But you're pale, dear," Ginny insisted.

"And you've lost weight."

"So?"

"So, have you seen a doctor?"

"Yes, sis, you really should see a doctor. Who knows what you might have? Why, someone at work just found out she has a rare blood disorder, and just the other day I heard on the news that . . ."

"I do not have a rare blood disorder."

"Then have a piece of chocolate cake, dear."

"I don't want a piece of cake, Mother," Annie sputtered.

"Are you upset about something? Is that it?"

"I am not upset."

"You sound upset," Ginny insisted.

"And I am not sick."

"But you are pale," Rachel pointed out.

"Of course I'm pale. I'm pregnant!"

There was one, huge, unanimous gasp as everyone in the room sucked in a deep breath and stared at Annie. With both hands covering her mouth, Annie looked the most surprised of all.

Ginny got a pained look on her face. It took a lot to get Sam Calhoun worked up, but tonight his neck turned red and he began making a grunting sound men make when their tempers were about to go straight through the roof.

"Now, Sam, take it easy," Artie said.

"Take it easy? *Take it easy?*"

And then holy hell broke loose.

"What do you mean you're pregnant?"

"Are you sure?"

"How in the hell did this happen?"

"There's no need to swear, Sam."

"I'll swear if I want to, dammit."

"What in the hell were you thinking?"

"She couldn't have been thinking."

"Is it Joe's?"

"Of course it's Joe's. It is Joe's, isn't it?"

"I knew that man couldn't be trusted."

"Just wait until I get my hands on him."

Other than the fact that she never heard Travis's voice, Cori had no idea who said what. She only knew that every person who spoke did so in a louder voice than the person who had spoken before. Poor Annie grew more pale with every passing second.

Cori moved without thinking, propelled by instinct more than anything else. She whisked around the people who were barking questions, and stopped before Braden Calhoun's little sister. In a low, soothing voice, she said, "Congratulations, Ann. When is your baby due?"

In place of the deafening roar, the room became eerily silent. Annie Calhoun's eyes widened, her mouth opening around a silent *Oh.* Her features softened by degrees, and so did her voice as she said, "In the beginning of January."

"How lovely. My daughter was born in March."

"You have a daughter?" Annie asked, sinking onto a kitchen chair.

Before Cori could do more than nod, Rachel cut in. "You mean you're nearly three months along and you didn't tell me? Why in the world not?"

Annie cast her sister a sardonic look that spoke volumes. Rachel snapped her mouth shut, looking duly chagrined.

"What are you hoping for?" Cori asked. "A little boy or girl?"

"A little girl, I think. Although with the first baby, it doesn't really matter, does it?"

"It never really matters," Ginny said with a sigh. "You love them regardless."

Annie and Ginny shared a long look. From Cori's angle, it looked as if Ginny's eyes were glazed with unshed tears. A smile trembled on her mouth, and she opened her arms wide. Annie was in them in a second.

And holy hell broke loose all over again.

Arms became tangled in what looked like a group hug. Although there was still worry and shock, this time the voices resounding from one corner of the room to the other were excited and, for the most part, happy.

"Are you sure you're all right?" Sam asked.

"Yes, Dad. I'm sure. I know it's a terrible shock to all of you. It was to me, too. But I want this baby. Joe and I both do."

"I hope it's a boy," Braden said.

"A girl would be nice, too."

"I still can't believe this."

"Our first grandchild, Ginny."

"January, huh? Might even be a tax write-off, if the little bugger cooperates and comes a little early."

"No wonder you didn't want any cake."

Annie took turns nodding and shrugging at every other statement.

"You may look a little pale," Braden declared, "but honestly, sis, you've never looked better."

"A baby. But Annie, you're not married."

"I know, Uncle Artie."

Travis stayed on one side of the room, watching the rest of the family make fools of themselves over Annie's news. He would congratulate Annie, but later, after some of the commotion died down. Right now, he was too in awe of Cori to move.

She stood in the center of the room, silently watching the scene unfold. As usual, the Calhouns had come on like gangbusters. And as usual, Cori's innate gentleness and inborn charm had gone straight to the heart of the issue. A baby was going to be born, and she was happy for Annie, a woman she barely knew.

Travis had to force himself to swallow, to breathe. Lust was roused within him, stronger than ever before. He'd thought he was old enough to control his own lust. Problem was, he was feeling more than lust. And he didn't know how in the hell he was going to control that.

Suddenly, he realized something he should have known all along. When it came to Corinna Cassidy, he was in over his head.

Travis stood at the screen door, looking out. He and Cori had spent the first fifteen minutes back from Sam and Ginny's strolling through the dimly lit garden. Now, she was in the kitchen making a pot of coffee, and he was trying to make sense of everything that had happened tonight.

He turned his back to the door and moved about the narrow room. He'd been inside Cori's house before. Tonight, he took the time to notice his surroundings. The inn was decorated with antique furniture and flowered wallpaper, with lacy curtains, straw flowers and frilly doilies. The furnishings in Cori's house were different. The walls were painted, not papered, the carpet a plain light beige. This room was uncluttered, subdued, homey. He glanced at the cover of a teen magazine and leaned over the coffee table to study the geometry book opened to page 118.

His heart hammered in his chest, and his desire was still thick and heavy. Neither had anything to do with geometry problems. It had to do with Cori.

They'd stayed at Sam and Ginny's longer than he'd planned, mostly because no one would let him take Cori away. Before the night was through, Annie told her parents that she and Joe Fortino, who was in the army, planned to be married before a justice of the peace the following week when he came home on leave.

Ginny and Sam were aghast at the thought of such a setting and suggested having a big church wedding instead. Annie assured her mother that she and Joe didn't want any fuss. Sam and Ginny insisted that a big wedding wouldn't be any fuss. Annie crossed her arms and stood her ground. So did Sam and Ginny. Voices had risen so high Travis wouldn't have been surprised if the roof had been palpitating.

Once again, Cori's voice had been the epitome of rationality as she'd said, "You could compromise. Maybe have a *small*, informal wedding with just family, and maybe your parish priest. You could even have it outside in Ivy's Garden, if you'd like."

By the time he and Cori had finally left, a date had been set for the following Wednesday evening. Ginny had a call in to Father Griffith. Cori had made a few phone calls, too, and her friend Lisa had been hired to cater a small, simple buffet. Travis didn't know why he should have been surprised. But he still felt thunderstruck.

These new feelings were eating away at his composure, swelling to the point of bursting until he didn't know what to do with any of them, least of all his desire. He knew of only one way to alleviate his pent-up need. Unfortunately, he'd promised Cori he'd let her set the pace, that he wouldn't push her or rush her or sweep her off her feet straight into bed.

Maybe he should take up running. Better yet, maybe he should start working twenty-four hours a day instead of fourteen. He knew he had to do something, or he was going to explode.

There was a rustle of soft fabric behind him, and the quiet shuffle of footsteps. He turned and found Cori walking toward him, a mug of steaming coffee in each hand.

Raising one eyebrow, he said, "Now that I've thought about it, caffeine probably wouldn't be a very good idea right now."

"It's decaffeinated," she said, placing both mugs on the low table in front of the blue-and-yellow plaid sofa. Taking a seat at one end of the sofa, she blew into her coffee and sighed. "What a night."

"This was an unusually hectic night, even for the Calhouns," Travis explained.

"Do you mean their emotions aren't always this close to the surface?"

Her subtle humor worked some of the tension out of him. Striding toward her, he took his hands from his pockets and settled himself on the sofa.

Glancing sideways at him, she said, "I think the Calhouns are a lovely family, and they're certainly protective of you. You should have seen some of the looks I got from Rachel and Ginny."

"Rachel and Ginny look at everyone that way."

"I doubt that. Oh, and another thing. I thought Artie was charming."

"Do me a favor and never let him hear you say that. If you do, there will be no living with him."

She grinned at him then said, "Under the circumstances, I think they all reacted quite well to Annie's little bombshell."

"Yeah. They certainly have their moments, but they're not bad. Was this anything like the way your parents reacted to your news?"

She stopped blowing into her coffee and looked straight ahead. "My parents didn't say a word. For two days."

Travis clenched his jaw.

"Of course, this is a little different. Annie is twenty-seven. I was sixteen. Being unmarried and pregnant doesn't have the negative social ramifications it once did."

Excuses. She always made excuses for her parents' behavior. As far as he was concerned, the situation was traumatic, no matter how old the single mother was and what the year. Since he was hardly in a position to lecture about social graces, he changed the subject.

"Your offer to let Ginny have the wedding here was brilliant."

"Sometimes an uninvolved third party can see things others can't. Besides, I never pass up an opportunity to show off Ivy's Garden. It's the perfect setting for a summer wedding. We might have to invite some of the guests, and I'll want to spend extra time weeding and watering my flowers, but the hollyhocks, daylilies, daisies and irises will still be blooming then. All my annuals will be gorgeous, and the rose trellis and arbors will be covered with blooms."

He listened as she chatted on, letting her excitement over her garden and the upcoming wedding work over him, too. Dropping her voice to a whisper, she said, "I have an ulterior motive for wanting to have the wedding here, a slightly sneaky one. I want Allison to see what can happen when two people's passion gets out of control."

"Are you still worried about her and Ross?" he asked.

Nodding, she said, "I noticed another red mark on her neck the other day, and every once in a while she practically snaps someone's head off. I think she's wrestling with her conscience. And she as much as told me that Ross is starting to pressure her."

While Cori went back to talking about the wedding, Travis thought about the pressure that was building inside him right now. If Ross was experiencing anything like it, he wasn't surprised that the kid was starting to work on Allison.

"You know," he said quietly, "I think I might have a temporary solution to this problem. You'd like to have your gazebo completed in time for Annie's wedding, right?"

At her nod, he continued. "Then I think I'll ask Ross to help me build it and finish laying those paving stones. You'll have to pay the punk, of course, but when I'm finished with him, he'll be too tired to even *think* about anything else."

"You'd do that for me?"

His *harrumph* echoed through the entire house.

"But why?" she asked.

He held her gaze, then finally said, "Maybe with a little luck, it'll have the same effect on me."

The low, sultry vibrancy in his voice caught Cori off guard. It had been an eventful evening, an eventful week, an eventful month. Actually, ever since she'd met Travis, everything around her had taken on a new intensity.

Suddenly feeling utterly feminine, she lowered her chin, arched her eyebrows and said, "Do you really think you need luck, Travis?"

He studied her through narrowed eyes. "Do you really want to know what I think?"

She nodded coyly, a mischievous light coming into her eyes.

"I *think* I'm creating a monster. Now, come here, so I can kiss you properly."

Cori set her cup on the table and practically floated into Travis's arms. His mouth covered hers a heartbeat later, his lips warm and persuasive. Just before giving herself up completely to the swooning harmony between them, she vowed to tell him that there was nothing proper about his kiss, nothing whatsoever.

His hand worked its way between their bodies, covering her breast. A shudder passed through her, heat following close behind. Her eyes closed and his hand inched to her other breast.

On second thought, maybe she'd tell him later.

Chapter Eleven

Travis hiked one shoe onto the top step and tiredly knocked on Cori's screen door. Her voice carried to his ears, seeming to come from far away. He walked inside, closing both doors behind him. A lamp was lit in the corner of the living room, and light spilled from the kitchen doorway. Cori wasn't in either room.

"I'll be right out, Travis," she called. "Make yourself at home."

This time he pinpointed the direction her voice was coming from, and was tempted to follow it down the short hall. Instead, he strode to the sofa and sank into the soft cushions.

His head fell forward and his eyes closed, his hand automatically kneading the muscles at the back of his neck. He'd just come back from his place, where he'd taken a quick shower and grabbed a bite to eat. Before that, he'd spent thirteen hours building Cori's gazebo and laying flagstones.

He and Ross had shoveled dirt, leveled the ground and extended the curving path to the building site for the new gazebo. They'd unloaded the truck and carried heavy boards, which they'd proceeded to cut and nail into place. Bit by bit, lumber and nails had been transformed into a hexagon-shaped gazebo complete with comfortable benches and a black shingled roof.

Ross possessed the cockiness of youth, but he was also a hard worker. Together, they'd finished the project in record time. Travis was pleased with a job well done, but he felt the results of all that hard physical labor in every muscle. It couldn't be helped. Cori, Ginny, Rachel and Annie wanted to have the wedding ceremony inside the new gazebo, and when his women wanted something, he made sure they got it.

He stopped massaging his neck and stared straight ahead, wondering when he'd started to think of Cori in those terms. No matter how many times she'd filled his dreams, she wasn't his woman, not in the real sense of the word. That was part of the problem, part of the reason for his fatigue. Night after night he left her, only to crawl into his own bed alone, so worked up he couldn't sleep for wanting her.

He'd always thought celibacy was for monks, and he was no monk. All jokes aside, he didn't think it was wise to force a man who used to be called Lightning Delaney to go without sex for an indefinite period of time. Wise or not, he came back here every evening when his work was done. The reason was simple. He couldn't stay away.

A cool hand covered his, and Cori's soft voice whispered in his ear. "Let me."

Those two little words started an ache inside him, an ache that had nothing to do with overworked muscles or the lack of sleep. Her hands were magic, and so was her touch. Oh, no, he was definitely no monk.

She cupped the back of his neck, gently kneading the kinks out of his muscles with the pads of her fingertips and the palms of her hands. He let loose a low groan, which earned him the melodious sound of her laughter. He breathed in the scent of garden flowers, and caught himself smiling.

"Does this feel better?"

Images shimmered through his mind, images of a few things she could do if she really wanted him to feel better. His thoughts turned hazy, his body drew taut. He groaned an answer, and her hands moved down his neck, across the bunched muscles in his right shoulder. By the time she'd worked a particularly tight knot from between his shoulder blades, he was practically purring like a mountain lion.

"I can't believe you finished the gazebo," she whispered. "After the way you worked today, I'm a little surprised you wanted to come over tonight."

He'd wanted to come over tonight, all right, but that wasn't all he wanted. He wanted Corinna Cassidy on him like a new coat of paint. He wanted her everywhere, in every way, with everything she had.

"Travis?"

"Hmm?"

"Oh, nothing. I was just checking to see if you were awake."

He smiled again. God, it was becoming a habit.

Rotating his neck and shoulders, he said, "I'm awake, Cori. Believe me, I'm awake." After a few moments of silence, he said, "I practically worked Ross into the ground today, but I don't think our plan worked."

"Really?"

He shook his head.

"Then he isn't too exhausted to even *think* about his rampaging hormones, after all?"

He shook his head again.

''How can you be sure?'' she asked, pressing her lips to the back of his neck.

He reached behind him and gave her hand a tug. She rounded the end of the sofa and landed on his lap with a startled little ''oh!'' He wrapped his arms around her, settling her against him the way he'd wanted to all day. Her ''oh'' changed to ''ah,'' and it was her turn to smile.

''Now do you know why I'm sure?''

Cori felt the hard ridge of him against her hip, and nearly sighed out loud. The knowledge that *she'd* done this to him filled her with so much excitement she couldn't speak. She looked into his eyes, and her heart turned over. There was passion in the depths of those brown eyes, but there was heartrending tenderness, too.

He seemed to be waiting for her to make the next move. The way his jaw was clenched tight let her know exactly what his restraint was costing him. She wanted to tell him what he did to her, what he meant to her, but she couldn't seem to find the words.

His eyes, though half-shut, filled with a deep, curious longing, and suddenly, words weren't necessary. She smoothed her hand along his cheek, then let her fingers trail over his ear and into his shower-damp hair. She inhaled the scent of soap, after-shave and man, then brought her lips to his.

Every time she kissed him felt like the first time. Her pulse sped up, her breathing became shallow, and her thoughts turned as hazy as a long-forgotten dream. She'd kissed other men, but no one had ever made her feel the way Travis did.

He didn't try to hide his need. He simply wrapped his arms around her and buried the fingers of one hand in her hair, tipping her head back so he could kiss her more thoroughly. When their mouths broke apart on a gasp for air, he moved on to kiss her cheek, her chin, the hollow at the base of her neck.

"How long before Allison comes back?" he asked, his voice a husky rasp against her skin.

"An hour, at least."

"That should give us almost enough time," he said, bringing his head up so he could look at her.

Cori saw the masculine glimmer in his eyes, and the intense expression on his face. She let her hand trail up his arm and whispered, "Enough time for what?"

The next thing she knew, she was lying on her back on the sofa, staring up into Travis's ruggedly handsome face.

"Enough time for anything you want, Cori, anything at all."

He stretched himself out next to her, most of his weight levered on his right knee, hip and elbow. His left leg was bent across her knees, and his hand, well, his hand seemed to be everywhere. It skimmed her shoulders, then trailed down the center of her chest, smoothing along the sensitive skin at her waist. His palm glided down to her hips then on up to the bodice of her blouse, where he began to work the button at her throat free.

She watched his face through half-closed lids, wondering how long it would take for him to notice her little surprise. Within moments, his eyebrows rose fractionally and his lips lifted into a smile that was filled with so much masculine appreciation it stole her breath away. His gaze roved, lazily appraising her, his surprise at discovering that she wasn't wearing a bra quickly turning to raw need. His hand covered her breast, caressing and massaging until she made a sound deep in her throat. When he lowered his mouth to each peak, the sound turned into a sigh.

His breath was hot and moist on her bare flesh, his lips sending an incredible sensation through her. Her back arched, her breasts swelled beneath his lips, and her hips moved in a rhythm as old as time itself.

"You did this for me?" he whispered.

"I didn't want to tease you, Travis. But it was so warm today, and bras are so uncomfortable, and since I can't give you everything you want, I wanted to do something special for you, only you."

"You, Corinna Cassidy," he whispered huskily, "are an incredible woman."

His fingers slowly but steadily inched lower. She covered them with her hand, stilling their progress. "Everything you do to me is incredible. We can't. For Allison's sake, and for your sake, too."

He let his hand rest beneath hers for a moment, bringing his mouth to hers for another kiss. And then he was reaching down, skimming her hip and moving on down past her thigh, his hand inching its way beneath the hem of her skirt, his fingers smoothing over her soft flesh, then slipping beneath the satin-and-lace edge of her panties. Her gasp ended the kiss, but his exploration had just begun.

"Travis," she whispered some time later, "what are you doing to me?"

He didn't answer for a long time, but when he did, it was in the voice of a man in the throes of a powerful passion. "You promised Allison you wouldn't let things go too far. Sweetheart, you never said I couldn't touch you and pleasure you in a hundred different ways."

"But what about you?" she whispered.

"I'm here, Cori. I'm right here."

With that, he brought his mouth back to hers, dragging his body over hers until she cradled his hardness exactly where he'd stroked moments before. Heat pulsed through her, the hot length of him pressing against her where she was soft and moist and ready.

Their kisses were openmouthed, their breathing was ragged. She loved the feel of him, the weight of him pressing her into the cushions at her back. Everything about him went singing through her veins until she could think of nothing except the need that had built inside her, and the one thing that she craved.

She'd never know how she found the strength to drag her mouth from his, just as she'd never know where she found the self-control to straighten slightly. She turned her head to one side, and took a shuddering breath. Reaching for his hand, she stilled his roaming fingers, then wrapped her arms around his back and hugged him with everything she had.

He surfaced more slowly, his heart beating an erratic rhythm against hers. After interminable moments when she wasn't sure what he would do, he rolled heavily to his side.

His mouth was set in a straight line, a muscle working in his jaw. His gaze raked over her exposed flesh, and if she lived to be a hundred and ten, she'd never forget the open admiration in his eyes. She started to cover herself, but he stilled her movements with his hand.

"Let me," he whispered.

Smoothing one rough palm over her naked thigh, he painstakingly replaced her skirt all the way to her knees. and brought both edges of her blouse together to cover her breasts. When he was finished, he kissed her on the chin, and gulped in several deep breaths of air.

"Oh, Travis, I never meant to let things go so far."

Placing a large hand on her waist, he drew her closer and said, "I didn't do anything I didn't want to do."

"I know, but I feel guilty about what this does to you."

"Don't," he said. "I want this as much as you do. But Cori? I'd say you've pretty much perfected your ability to say no and mean it, wouldn't you?"

His expression was filled with amusement and regret. She sat up, and deftly began refastening the pearly buttons on her cream-colored blouse, saying, "It's all the practice you give me. Not that it's easy to stop after the things you do to me, with me, for me."

He encircled her wrist with his fingers and leaned up on one elbow so his face was close to hers. "It isn't easy for me to stop, either, but I'm the one who wanted to feel eighteen again. Lately it's all been coming back to me as if it were yesterday."

"I bet you were a devil when you were eighteen," she said, smoothing a fingertip across his clenched jaw.

"That's what a girl named Linda once told me from the inside of my old Chevy."

Cori hit him with a pillow.

The pillow fell to the floor, and his voice turned serious again. "I thought I had it bad for her, but she wasn't half the woman you are, Cori, not by a long shot."

He kissed her again, and then he was on his feet and was striding toward the door.

"Are you going to take another long walk through the garden?" she asked.

She was growing accustomed to his gravelly *har-rumph*s.

"I think I'll go straight home and take a long cold shower. Not that it'll do much good."

She smiled at his exasperated tone. "If it's any consolation, cold showers haven't brought much relief to me, either."

He turned slightly. "What you're trying to tell me is that I'm not suffering alone," he said in a tone of voice that didn't sound very consoled.

She nodded and felt her smile broaden.

Running a hand through his hair, he said, "I'm planning to paint your gazebo tomorrow afternoon, but do you think we could steal away for a little while in the morning?"

Cori finished fastening the last button, then swung her legs off the sofa and rose to her feet. "As long as all the guests have had their breakfasts, I should be able to get away. What did you have in mind?"

"I don't know yet, but it's going to have to be something perfectly safe, something where there are other people, lots of other people, so that I can't touch you, and..."

"All right," she said before he could continue. "I think doing something perfectly safe sounds like a good idea. It will certainly be a new experience for us, don't you think?"

He turned around and reached for the door, but not before she glimpsed the smile lurking on his face. She called good-night, and he closed the door. She plucked the throw pillow from the floor and lay down on the couch, the smile he'd tried to hide lingering around the edges of her mind.

Annie Calhoun's wedding was only a matter of days away, and Cori had a million and one things to do to prepare the inn and garden for the event. Instead of seeing to any of them, she stretched out on her side, letting everything that had happened tonight replay through her mind.

Wrapped in the warm aftermath of Travis's caresses and barely-there smiles, her body grew warm and languid. She was immensely proud of the example she was setting for Allison, but something else was happening to her, too, something incredible, something she swore she'd never let happen to her, but was powerless to fight. She was falling in love.

Travis climbed down from the six-foot stepladder and swiped a hand across his brow. He reached for the can of paint with one hand, and dipped his brush in with the other.

A long sigh carried to his ears on the sultry midday breeze. Being careful not to let the paint drip onto the ground, he glanced over his shoulder. Allison was sitting on a white bench twenty feet away, her hair blowing freely about her face and shoulders. She was wearing a pair of denim shorts and a knit shirt that hugged her young curves and probably drove her boyfriend crazy. It was no wonder Cori didn't like letting that kid out of her sight. A book was opened on her lap, but her eyes were on something in the distance.

With even strokes, he spread the paint over the bare wood and called, "That's the fourth time you've sighed in the last five minutes."

She turned her gray eyes to his and shrugged, but she wasn't fooling him.

Balancing the paintbrush on the edge of the can, he strode closer and asked, "What are you studying?"

"Geometry. It's stupid. I mean, why should I care about the Pythagorean Theorem? I'm absolutely never going to use this stuff."

"Pretty boring, huh?"

"I'll say. I absolutely, positively hate math, don't you?"

Lowering himself to sit next to Cori's daughter on the wrought-iron bench, he shrugged and said, "My favorite subject in school was recess."

"Oh, Travis. You're so lucky you're grown-up."

Travis rested his shoulders against the back of the bench, thinking that it sounded as if there was more behind Allison's statement than a dislike for geometry. Since he knew next to nothing about kids, and even less about the female variety, he didn't think it would be wise to comment.

Allison continued to stare out over the garden. He wasn't sure what she was looking at, but when her voice came again, it was softer, shakier. "Everything is so confusing, ya know? Things were a lot easier when I was a kid."

"What kinds of things?"

"Everything. "

"Boys?"

"I suppose."

"Does this have to do with any boy in particular?"

"No. Yes. I don't know. Maybe."

"There's nothing like a decisive woman."

She glanced at him in surprise, and then her lips lifted into a smile so much like Cori's it made him pause.

"I tried to talk to Lisa and Jillian about this, but they think I'm still a kid. I talked to Mom, but there are just some things a girl can't tell her mother, ya know? What do you think, Travis?"

Travis thought he should have left well enough alone and finished painting the gazebo. Unfortunately, it was too late for that now.

"Do you think I'm just a kid?"

Although Allison seemed like little more than a girl to him, he realized that she was actually in that precarious stage Ginny used to refer to as woman-child. He looked at her, and found her staring at him with rounded eyes. Choosing his words carefully, he said, "Don't be offended, Allison, but I think you're smack-dab in between being a kid and being an adult."

"Great. Does this in-between age have a name?" she asked.

"The experts call these your teenage years, but don't worry. As far as I know, they only last seven years or so."

She gave him a haughty little huff. He realized that there was a lot of that going around around here.

"You haven't told me what you think of the new gazebo Ross and I built."

She dropped her chin into her hand and said, "I don't know what I think anymore. Maybe that's why this is so hard."

"What's so hard?"

After a moment, she quietly said, "Life."

He stretched his legs out in front of him and folded his arms at his chest. Slanting her a sideways glance, he said, "Do you think you could be a little more specific?"

She sighed again and said, "It's just that Ross wants…"

Her voice trailed away, but Travis knew what she'd meant. After a long silence, he asked, "What about you, Allison? What do you want?"

Her eyes glazed with uncertainty, and for a moment he thought she might burst into tears. Then, she bit her lip and let her gaze trail back down to the book on her lap. With that innate sense of conviction that was part of her character, she said, "For one thing, I want to pass the stupid final exam in geometry on Thursday. And then I never want to have to think about obtuse angles, isosceles triangles, or any kind of theorems for as long as I live."

Travis leaned a little closer and studied the diagrams in the open book on Allison's lap. Peering at the gibberish in small print, he said, "I don't know much about theorems, but I do know my way around angles and triangles. Bring your book over to the gazebo, and I'll show you what I mean."

"Don't tell me you actually use the stuff in this book!"

"That's the strange thing about life, kid. You never know when you're going to use what you learn."

"Puh-lease."

Travis didn't know what was more endearing, the way she emphasized that one word, or the way she rolled her eyes. While he fought the urge to ruffle her hair, he realized how old he probably sounded. Suddenly, it didn't matter, because what he'd told Allison might just be the most profound words of wisdom he'd ever uttered in his life.

A person really didn't know when he was going to use what he learned. He certainly never would have believed he'd have this much need for the patience he'd garnered from Sam Calhoun. Sticking to Cori's terms had required more self-control than he'd thought he possessed. He'd done it to prove to her how strong she really was. In the process, he was learning a few things about himself, and what he was learning, he liked. Except for a passing physical resemblance, he really was nothing like his old man, at least not in any way that counted.

Allison turned the page and sighed again. Looking at her, Travis did something else he thought he'd never do. He silently recited one of Ginny's prayers. For once in his life it wasn't for penance. It was for fortitude, so that he might know what to say to this sixteen-year-old girl who wasn't nearly as sure of herself as she pretended to be.

Cori pushed through the laundry room door and headed for the back stairs, her arms stacked high with three sets of fresh sheets for the Apple Blossom Room, the Rose Petal Room, and the Daisy Room.

Ivy looked up from the table where she, Lisa and Jillian were taking a break, and said, "Corinna, you've been running on high speed ever since you got back from your date with Travis. The work will wait a few minutes. Come. Sit."

Before Cori could argue, Jillian looked up from her Sunday newspaper and said, "Listen to this."

"You'd better not be planning to read me my horoscope, Jillian," Lisa sputtered.

"This isn't the horoscope page. It's an article about a small town in South Dakota that's advertising for women."

Something in Jillian's voice made Cori stop and slowly turn around. She placed the freshly laundered sheets on the table and reached into the refrigerator for the pitcher of pink lemonade.

"Let me see that," Lisa said, reaching for the newspaper.

While Lisa scanned the article, Cori settled herself against the edge of the counter and took a long sip from her frosty glass. The temperature outside was soaring again, and so was the humidity. In all honesty, she couldn't really blame the warm flush of her skin on the weather.

She'd felt overheated ever since she'd gotten back from her "safe" date with Travis. It was truly amazing just how incredibly erotic safe outings with that man could be.

"It says here," Lisa said, pointing to the article, "that the town's name is Jasper Gulch, but the press is calling it Bachelor Gulch."

"Then they're really advertising for women?" Cori asked.

"Do you mean like mail-order brides?" Ivy added.

Without giving Jillian a chance to answer, Cori asked, "Are you thinking of going there?"

"That's a wonderful idea," Lisa declared, jumping to her feet. "Oh, Jillian, it might be fun..."

"Of course I'm not thinking of going there," Jillian stated emphatically. "I'm not looking for a man, remember?"

"It says here that they just need women to come to their town, that's all," Lisa argued. "Let's drive over there this weekend and check it out."

Cori wasn't surprised that Lisa ignored Jillian's protests, but she was a little surprised to see color rise to Jillian's cheeks. Even though Cori's heart went out to her friend, she thought that maybe that flash of color was a good sign. Maybe it meant that Jillian was ready to take another chance on love.

Evidently, Lisa thought so, too, because she said, "According to this article, Jasper Gulch is a nice little town with less than seven hundred people. There are five marriageable women, and sixty-two eligible bachelors."

"Sixty-two?" Cori asked.

"And there's probably something wrong with each and every one of them, or there wouldn't be five marriageable women," Jillian said softly.

"What if there isn't anything wrong with them? What if they're all just waiting to meet a person who's right for them?" Lisa asked.

"Forget I mentioned it." Jillian slapped the paper together and pushed it aside. "Now, do you want me to help you with this list or don't you?"

"Oh, all right," Lisa retorted. "We might as well plan this wedding supper, since it's unlikely that we'll ever have the opportunity to plan our own."

"Oh, Lisa, we'll probably plan yours someday soon, but we'll never plan mine. Now, what are these initials next to number four?"

Cori looked at Lisa, who didn't appear at all ready to drop the subject of Bachelor Gulch. Letting out a deep breath, she finally said, "That's G.A.M. Those letters stand for the bride's Great-Aunt Mavis. She's bringing the groom's cake."

"And the relish tray?"

"It's being supplied by someone named Maude."

"The seven-layer salad?"

"Would you believe it's one of the bride's cousin's specialties?" Lisa sputtered.

Cori swallowed another sip of her lemonade and said, "Lisa, I thought Ginny hired *you* to cater the buffet supper."

Lisa waved three sheets of paper in the air and shook her head. "As far as I can tell, the only thing I'm in charge of is supplying the crusty rolls, and the weather."

Cori smiled to herself. That certainly sounded like Ginny Calhoun.

"Oh, my," Ivy said. "What in the world are we going to do if it rains?"

One by one, four pairs of eyes looked to the long row of windows on the other side of the room. It didn't take their gazes long to shift from the clear blue sky to the two people who were standing underneath it, one a man and the other a teenaged girl.

Cori stepped around the table and slowly strode to the screen door. Her hand somehow found its way to her throat and her head automatically tipped to one side. Travis and Allison were standing beside the gazebo in the side yard, their heads close together. Instead of looking at the open book in her hand or the angle Travis was pointing to near the roof of the gazebo, Allison peered up at him, the open look of admiration in her eyes evident all the way from the kitchen.

"Now there's a sight for sore eyes," Ivy said softly.

"Didn't I tell you that all Allison needed was a little adult male attention?" Jillian asked in a gentle voice.

"That wouldn't hurt any of us," Lisa grumbled.

Cori smiled, but her heart swelled with a feeling she didn't wholly recognize. Tears stung the backs of her eyes, and her throat felt thick and tight.

For a moment, she was too caught up in her own emotions to speak. She'd known there was something special about Travis from the moment she'd met him. She hadn't told Lisa or Jillian or even Ivy, for that matter, about the way he made her feel. They knew about her pact with Allison and probably automatically assumed she wouldn't break it for any man. Part of the reason she hadn't confided in them was because she'd promised Travis that she'd guard his reputation, but there was more to it than that. Her feelings were so new and so fragile that she wasn't ready to share them, not even with her best friends.

Travis's kisses could make her feel like singing, and she hadn't felt like singing since she was a little girl. But what truly amazed her was the flickering sense of peace she felt each time she straightened, each time she called a halt to their lovemaking. Bit by bit, that flickering sense of peace was turning into a fledgling inner strength she hadn't known she possessed.

He hadn't spoken of love, but she knew he cared. A man didn't go to such lengths to please a woman unless he cared. Each time she saw him, her feelings deepened. It was as if she'd been sleeping for a long time and was slowly awakening. Even though she knew that what she was experiencing with Travis was real, she felt as if she was floating in limbo. She didn't fully understand it, but this sense of weightlessness had something to do with the part of her life she'd left behind seventeen years ago, and the letter she longed to receive.

"Aren't you glad you asked Travis to spend some quality time with Allison?" Lisa asked.

When Cori finally found her voice, she had to squeeze it past the wonder that was lodged next to her vocal chords. "That's just it," she whispered. "I never got around to asking him."

"You mean?" Jillian asked.

Cori nodded. "He must be spending time with Allison because he wants to."

Ivy sniffled, and Lisa said, "A bad-boy smile and a heart of gold. What a combination."

Yes, what a combination, indeed, Cori thought to herself.

"You see, Jillian?" Lisa taunted. "There might be a man just like Travis out there somewhere, but you won't even look."

"I don't know," Cori said softly. "You can look if you want to. In fact, you probably should, but I don't think you'll find any exactly like Travis."

"Why is that?" Lisa asked.

"Because I'm beginning to realize that Travis Delaney is one of a kind."

Chapter Twelve

"Such a beautiful bride."

"And Joe certainly looks handsome in his dress uniform."

"Doesn't he, though?"

"My, yes."

Travis stood on the freshly cut grass in Ivy's Garden, listening to bits and pieces of the same conversations he'd already heard at least a dozen times. All around him men who wore blue collars five days a week stood in small groups pulling at their starched shirts and ties while women wearing gauzy flowered dresses flitted from one group to the next.

The food table was nearly empty, the wedding cake half-gone. Although the wedding reception was winding down, no one had actually left. Travis was beginning to wonder if they ever would.

He and Braden were standing near the punch table. Not far away, a few of the uncles were still whispering about the way Cousin Lester had stood up during the ceremony, ready to speak his mind about the fact that Annie was wearing white when everyone present knew she was going to have a baby. While the guests had held their breath, Sam and Artie had both risen to their feet and turned around. With eyes narrowed in warning, they'd given Lester a quelling glare, which had sent him sinking into his chair as if his knees had turned to jelly.

Braden ladled more punch into his cup and stared across the garden without lifting it to his lips. "It's hard to believe my baby sister is really married."

Following the course of Braden's stare, Travis started to say something, but he picked Cori out of the crowd near the rose trellis, and ended up nodding instead. He would have been the first to admit that Annie looked truly beautiful in her mother's lace, yet he couldn't seem to keep his eyes off Cori. The breeze pulled wispy tendrils of her hair from the intricate twist on top of her head. He would have liked nothing better than to unwind the rest of those golden tresses and watch them fall around her shoulders.

He and Cori hadn't taken any more outings, safe or otherwise, since Sunday. The construction business had been booming, and there had been an endless list of things for Cori to do to prepare the garden for today's wedding. Travis had still come over every night. One night he'd talked to her while she worked. Another evening he'd helped her weed her flowers. But no matter how busy they were, they were never too busy to want and need something they couldn't have.

"Did you hear that Uncle Artie threatened to throw Lester into the nearest bubbler if he so much as breathed a negative word to either Annie or Joe?" Braden asked.

Travis cleared his throat, trying to clear his mind at the same time. "That's only one of the versions I've heard," he replied.

Sam and Artie's united front would undoubtedly be brought up at family gatherings for years to come, but as far as Travis was concerned, it hadn't been the most memorable moment of the day. The instant he would never forget had occurred halfway through the ceremony.

Annie and Joe had been exchanging their most sacred vows when Travis's gaze was inexplicably drawn across the flagstone aisle. Cori, who had been seeing to a last-minute detail moments before the wedding began, was standing to one side. He doubted she was aware that she'd steepled her fingers over her lips, or that her eyes had glazed with unshed tears, but he'd never forget the way her expression had brimmed with tenderness. He'd also never forget the jolt of sexual desire that had shot through him in that moment, or the deep, abiding emotion that had followed.

That same emotion had been wreaking havoc with his senses for weeks, but until that instant, he hadn't known what it was. Now that he knew, the anticipation that had been churning inside him throbbed with new meaning. For the first time in his life, Travis Delaney was in love. He wanted to yell it, sing it, shout it. More than anything, he wanted to whisper it to Cori and hear her whisper it in return, which was what he planned to do, if everyone would just leave.

Clouds were starting to darken overhead, and all around him conversation turned to the weather. Maybe if it started to rain the Calhouns and Fortinos would get the hint. He'd go down on bended knee if he had to, but he was going to tell the woman he loved how he felt. As soon as they were alone.

"I don't know how you do it."

Travis dragged his gaze to Braden. Feeling dazed, he asked, "You don't know how I do what?"

Braden gestured toward Cori and lowered his voice even more. "I don't know how in the hell you, you know, refrain."

Travis had been a little surprised when he'd casually mentioned that particular fact to Braden last night. What surprised him even more was the realization that he wasn't ashamed or embarrassed. In fact, he was pretty damned proud.

Squeezing the cup in his hand, he said, "You should try it sometime, Braden."

"Oh, no. Not me."

Travis almost laughed at the alarm in Braden's blue eyes. "You might be surprised at what you'd discover about yourself," he added.

"Are you saying that it gets easier?"

Travis's *harrumph* drew several stares. Keeping his voice as low as Braden's had been, he said, "If anything, it gets harder."

"Then why do you do it?"

In that instant, Cori tipped her head back and laughed at something Mavis and Maude were saying. Travis's eyes narrowed, and he finally replied, "Because I happen to know one woman who's worth the wait."

"Does this mean you're over your mid-life crisis?"

He didn't know what Braden was expecting, but he doubted it was his sudden burst of laughter.

"What's so funny?" Braden asked.

Travis only shrugged.

"What's with you?" Braden insisted. "I've never known you to be so tight-lipped about a woman."

What could he say? He'd been thirty-nine years old for less than two weeks, but he was beginning to think he'd found his fountain of youth. Of course, Artie would call it the bubbler of youth, but the terminology didn't matter. Travis Delaney had never felt anything so incredible in his life. The shock of it ran through his body and sent his blood pounding in his brain. With his patience growing thin and his need growing strong, he placed his cup on the table and started to walk away.

"Where are you going?" Braden called to his back.

The wind pulled at his tie and blew through his hair as he glanced over his shoulder and slowly turned around. Normally, he wasn't an easy man to read, but evidently Braden didn't have any trouble deciphering his expression tonight.

"Never mind," Braden said, that old Calhoun grin sliding across his face. "I think I already know. Good luck."

Suddenly, Travis felt the way had more than twenty years ago when Braden had loftily asked him why he didn't just move in with his family. Then, as now, he'd masked his sincerity with a male swagger and a knowing grin. Travis hadn't been fooled either time. His mind filled with limitless possibilities, the notion making him bold. Feeling as if the sky was the limit, he turned around again and strode straight to Cori.

Not caring who saw, he placed his hands on her waist and whispered in her ear. Mavis and Maude twittered like schoolgirls, and Cori turned slightly, holding his gaze. Instead of blushing, her lips softened knowingly, the look in her eyes everything he'd hoped it would be.

Man, he loved it when she turned smug.

"It was a beautiful wedding, wasn't it, Travis?"

He answered without tearing his gaze away from Cori's. "Beautiful, Aunt Maude. What time do you think everyone will leave?"

Mavis and Maude twittered all over again. Cori's smile broadened, and Travis knew he was in for a long, long night.

Allison hurried through the door and dumped the mail on the table. She dashed down the hall to her room, and was back again mere minutes later. A quick glance at the living room clock had her shaking her head. Rats. She was ready early.

She looked at the clock again then perched on the edge of a chair. Within seconds she was on her feet again, pacing from one end of the room to the other. The unfamiliar voices of the wedding guests carried to her ears from the other side of the lilac hedge. The sounds covered the quiet, but they didn't quiet her thoughts.

A door creaked. With her heart in her throat, she spun around, her hand flying to her heart as Ross ducked through the seldom-used back door.

"Ross! I thought you were going to drive by and wait for me around the corner."

"I couldn't wait."

Her heart hammered in her chest, but the heat in his gaze still managed to make her senses reel. For once, he wasn't wearing his baseball cap, and Allison was sure he'd never looked more rugged. His shoulders appeared broader, his eyes darker, his expression more serious than she'd ever seen it.

"Are you ready?" he asked.

"I don't know about this, Ross."

He strode closer, his gaze holding hers. "Do you love me, Allison?" he asked in that tone of voice that always turned her heart to mush.

"You know I do."

"I love you, too. That's why this is going to be so special."

"Do you really think so?" She hated the way her voice shook, but didn't know what to do about it.

He nodded and walked ever closer. "What could be more special than the first time for us both?"

"Oh, Ross."

He smiled, and smoothed her hair away from her cheek. "I have, you know, everything we need in the glove compartment of my car. My parents are going to be gone until tomorrow afternoon, so we'll have the entire house to ourselves. Once we get there, we can take this as slow and easy as you want.''

''Promise?'' she asked.

He took another step, the expression on his face enough to take her breath away. ''I promise, Allison.''

Without giving herself a chance to think, she reached behind the sofa and pulled out her overnight case and followed Ross through the back door. The wind blew her hair in her eyes, seeming to suck the air out of her lungs. She slipped through a gap in the lilac hedge, then glanced over her shoulder.

''What's wrong?'' Ross asked.

''I don't know,'' she whispered. ''I feel like I'm being watched.''

''Do you think someone saw us?''

She looked again. It was after nine o'clock. The sun was probably still up, but the thick clouds made it seem later. She heard voices coming from the wedding reception, but didn't see anything out of the ordinary. She shrugged, thinking it was probably only her own unease.

Ross didn't push her or force her. He simply reached out and offered her his hand. With tears stinging her eyes and love filling her chest, she placed her fingers in his.

Together, they skirted the edge of a neighbor's yard and cut through a side alley where his car was parked. She slid across the seat without letting go of his hand. And then he was starting his car, and they were speeding away, her heart beating an erratic rhythm all the while.

''Goodbye!''
'''Bye!''
''Good luck!''
''Drive safely.''

Cori stood next to Travis near the front of the crowd that had gathered to send Annie and Joe on their way. The newlyweds ran through the deluge of birdseed raining down on them. With hands clasped, they turned at their car's door. Annie waved to everyone, then tossed her bouquet straight into her brother's hands.

While the guests laughed uproariously, Cori happened to glance at Ginny, who was dabbing at her eyes with a tissue, literally laughing and crying at the same time. Joe opened the door for his new bride, and Annie started to get inside. Before everyone's eyes, she spun around again, her long dress and veil flying behind her as she bounded into her parents' arms for one last hug.

A lump formed in Cori's throat, a tear spilling onto her eyelashes as she tried to imagine her own parents' embrace. When Travis pulled her closer, she glanced up at him, and found him watching her with an expression she'd never seen before.

Joe and Annie drove away, balloons and streamers fluttering behind them. All around Cori, people were calling to one another. She was so carried away by her response to the fire in Travis's eyes she barely noticed anything else.

Travis had always been intense, but there was something different about him tonight. There was a new sense of urgency in his eyes, in the touch of his fingers, and in the words he whispered in her ear. It was almost as if there was a tangible bond between them.

The clouds began churning overhead, and the late-evening breeze began to smell like rain. Cori managed to tear herself away from Travis's side to speak with Ivy, who hurried inside to see to the inn's guests, and to help Jillian and Lisa take care of the leftover food, punch and cake. The Calhouns began leaving, and once the tasks were done, Lisa and Jillian soon did the same.

Finally, Cori and Travis were alone.

"I thought they'd never leave."

Cori's pulse quickened at the depth of feeling in Travis's voice. "Travis," she whispered. "What's come over you?"

He turned her into his arms and kissed her in the middle of the garden where anyone could have seen. But Cori didn't care if anyone saw. She gave herself up to the delightful shiver that ran through her. The wind tore through her hair and whipped at the hem of her dress. Travis wrapped his arms around her, and she was warm.

"Cori, I..."

The first pattering of raindrops kept him from finishing whatever he'd been about to say. He cast a quick look at the sky, then grasped her hand in his. "The sky is going to open up any second. Come on. We'd better make a run for it."

They made it into her house only moments before the downpour came. Winded and laughing, he turned her into his arms all over again. Rain bounced off the roof and ran down the windowpanes, the deluge adding to the headiness of the moment. His mouth covered hers, urgent, exploratory, drugging.

She didn't realize she'd made any sound until he made it back to her. Something banged and thumped from the direction of the kitchen. "That must be the back door," she whispered.

When the sound came again, she added, "That's strange. We never use that door."

She took a backward step, letting her hand trail down his arm. Before heading for the kitchen to close the door, she said, "I could make some coffee."

He caught her hand in his, then slowly let it go. "All right. While we wait for it to brew, there's something I want to tell you."

It wasn't easy to turn away from the husky emotion in his voice. She strode into the kitchen, her heels clicking over the linoleum. Feeling as if she were floating, she latched the screen and closed the inside door.

Travis was leaning in the doorway when she turned around. For a long moment, he stood motionless, and so did she. Mesmerized, she watched him push himself away from the doorway and slowly stride closer.

"What time will Allison be home?"

"She's spending the night with Heather."

She'd answered without conscious thought, and she strode to the table the same way. She placed her palm on the smooth surface, her fingers coming into contact with the day's mail. She looked down automatically, her gaze straying to an envelope with a postmark from Green Bay.

A suffocating sensation tightened her throat, and her mind went blank. She hadn't been aware that Travis had walked closer, but suddenly, he was next to her. He picked up the envelope, and placed it in her hand.

"It's from Green Bay," she said inanely.

"I know. Maybe you should open it."

She knew he was right, but suddenly, she was afraid of what she might find. It took her shaking fingers three tries to open the flap. Staring at the envelope, she took a deep breath for courage then reached inside, unfolding a sheet of stationery bearing her mother's and father's names. Her heart beat heavily, fear and hope warring in her chest as she began to read the words written in her father's precise scrawl.

We are writing in regard to the letter we received from you over a month ago. We've given the matter careful consideration, just as we do each year when your letter arrives. We find a certain amount of peace in the fact that you are well, but it dredges up old disappointments, too. Rest assured that we've put a portion of our estate in a trust for you and your child. The remainder will go to our charities. Our attorney will contact you when it's time. Until then, please do not distress us with more letters. You made your choice seventeen years ago, and we must all live with that choice.

Edmund and Drucilla Cassidy.

For a long moment, Cori's sense of loss was beyond tears. Her throat ached. Her head ached. More than anything, her heart ached.

A teardrop rolled off her eyelashes and fell to the page. With that one tear, her last spark of hope was extinguished. *They don't want me. They don't love me.*

She took a shuddering breath, then handed the letter to Travis. Without taking the time to scan the words, he opened his arms to her the way she'd longed for her parents to do. She went into them and turned her face into his neck, all in one motion.

"They don't want me. They never wanted me."

Her voice was as soft as tears, so full of dashed hopes and broken dreams that Travis wanted to cry out. He wanted to tear the letter to shreds, and then he wanted to do the same to her parents. Instead, he wrapped his arms around Cori, wishing there was something he could say to ease her pain.

"They're blind, Cori. And so wrong."

Her sigh seemed to come from the bottom of her soul. She gulped, trying so desperately not to cry. He'd never known anyone as strong as she was, and had never felt so close to another person's anguish.

"You're beautiful, Cori," he murmured, molding her closer, "the most beautiful woman I've ever known."

She started to shake her head, but he plunged on, keeping his voice low, his mouth close to her ear. "Yes, you are, but not just on the outside. You're beautiful on the inside, too, so beautiful it takes my breath away. *You* take my breath away. You have since the moment I met you."

Tears welled in her eyes, and he continued to rock her back and forth, his hands skimming over her back, his lips nuzzling her neck. Bit by bit, her body grew warm, her shivers less frequent. He whispered a kiss into the hollow beneath her ear, and nearly groaned out loud when she pressed her face into his touch.

Her hands began to move across his back, her lips seeking their own brand of comfort on his neck and chin. Gradually, her breathing deepened, and her shudders turned to sighs.

He inhaled the scent of garden flowers, his heart hammering in his chest. Desire poured through him until his body was pounding with need. She looked up at him, the tear-glazed expression in her eyes driving all but the need to kiss her from his mind. He lowered his mouth to hers, longing stretching over him, drawing him ever closer to the edge.

Thunder rumbled; rain pelted the windowpanes. Darkness had fallen outside, the storm somehow adding to the warm intimacy of the dimly lit kitchen. Travis's hands worked their way down her back, pulling her against the part of him that was hard with need. He moved against her, knowing he shouldn't, couldn't, wouldn't.

She wrapped her arms around him, fitting her body so close to his it was as if she were trying to make them one. Her high-heeled shoes brought her closer to his height, her heart beating wildly against his. Her legs straddled his, their mouths melding until he could barely think of anything except making her his.

"Cori, honey," he rasped, dredging up willpower he hadn't known he possessed. "We'd better..."

As if she hadn't heard, she nuzzled his neck with her lips. Her hands roamed about his back, spreading lower. And lower.

"Cori," he whispered, trying again.

He opened his eyes, the tears glistening on her lashes sending his thoughts to the other side of the moon. He made a valiant effort to rein in the desire pounding through his body, trying not to think about how bad he wanted her, and how good she felt.

"Cori, we have to stop."

He took a shuddering breath and forced himself to go very still. She moved against him as if she needed his warmth more than she needed air to breathe.

"Hold me, Travis."

Every warm emotion Travis had ever felt rushed to the very heart of him. He brought both his hands to her face and kissed her again, a long, slow, drugging kiss. When the kiss ended, she implored him with her eyes, her lips, her very soul.

He shook with need, his desire warring with his integrity.

"Please, Travis, don't let me go."

"But . . ."

"Please."

Her softly whispered plea worked into his thoughts, melting over his senses. He gazed down into her eyes, and he was lost. She was already hurting; a woman like her shouldn't have to hurt, and she sure as hell shouldn't have to beg.

Thunder rumbled again, closer this time. Without another moment's hesitation, he scooped her into his arms and strode into her narrow living room, and on through the short hall.

Chapter Thirteen

Cori wrapped her arms around Travis's neck, drawing toward his warmth. She was vaguely aware that they were passing through shadowy rooms, but her surroundings barely registered. Somewhere in the deep recesses of her mind were hazy images of weeks' worth of wanting, of long, tiring days spent working, of worries, and of disappointment. She felt sad, but with every step Travis took, that sadness faded farther and farther away.

He shouldered his way into her bedroom, then stood for a long moment holding her in his arms. The next thing she knew she was slowly sliding down his long, rugged body. She felt the carpet beneath her shoes, her dress swishing into place around her legs. Light from the hall spilled into the room, accentuating the expression on his face. His lips were swollen from her kisses. His eyes, though half-closed, were literally brimming with tenderness and with passion. He wanted her, only her.

Emotion welled up in her until she wanted to cry out. She stepped out of her heels without thinking, because at the moment, she was beyond conscious thought. Her hands glided up his chest, around his neck, the action bringing more of her body into contact with his.

"You feel so good," she whispered.

His jaw was clenched tight, a muscle working in one cheek. She'd never seen a man more ravaged by need. His innermost emotions played across his face, and she knew his feelings for her were genuine. Longing stretched over her, and she raised her face to his.

She closed her eyes a heartbeat before his lips touched hers, the kiss like the soldering heat that permanently joins metal. Suddenly, there was no disappointment, no worries, no weariness. There was nothing except this man, this moment, in this room.

"Travis, I want..." Her voice trailed away because she wanted so many things she didn't know how to finish.

"I'll give you anything you want, Cori, anything you need, anything you wish for."

His voice had dipped so low, she was sure she could feel it brushing along her sensitized skin. Her emotions followed its trail, sweeping along her body, stirring up goose bumps that somehow circled her heart, then slowly seeped inside.

She worked the knot of his tie loose, and he slowly lowered her back zipper. Driven by instinct alone, she lowered her arms, letting her dress fall to the floor with a quiet swish. She stepped out of it, then deftly pulled his tie from his collar. The top button on his white shirt came next. When she'd unfastened the last one, she pushed the shirt off his shoulders, baring his chest for her exploration.

Travis bore her soft touches and fleeting kisses as long as he could. He'd spent night after night imagining this moment, but nothing had prepared him for the wanton woman in his arms, or the need that had taken on an

identity of its own within him, and within her. He'd
planned to take this slow, to make it last all night. Cori
seemed to have no such plans of her own. His shirt was already on the floor, his belt unfastened. When she lowered
his zipper, any thoughts he'd had of going slow disappeared.

He grasped her by her hips and pulled her hard against
him. She made a sound deep in her throat. He gave it back
to her in a searing kiss. Her satiny slip bunched in his
hands. In one smooth motion, he whisked it over her head.
With each item of clothing they removed, their lips met
again, every kiss more frenzied than the last. And then she
was standing naked before him, her skin soft and supple,
glowing white in the semidarkness.

In his imagination, he'd been a skilled lover with nerves
of steel, planning every move, every caress in order to
bring her more pleasure than she'd ever thought possible.
But his imagination hadn't prepared him for the reality of
Corinna Cassidy in the flesh. He couldn't think, let alone
plan. He could only react, could only tangle his arms and
legs with hers, moving, moving, drawing them both closer
to the bed.

He'd never know how he had the presence of mind to
remove the foil package from his wallet. He tossed it to the
bed, then eased her down to the mattress, following her
inch by inch. Neither of them said a word, but then, words
weren't necessary. The only thing that was necessary was
her touch, and his, their kisses, and the need pounding
through him, growing stronger with every passing second.

Her body was pliant and soft, yet strong in a way that
filled him with wonder. She shifted beneath him, stretching her legs out, wrapping them around him. He kissed her
shoulder, the soft slope of each breast. She surged beneath his mouth and slid her fingers through his hair.

And then she was reaching down, her fingertips working their own brand of magic on his body. When she took

him in her hands, it was all he could do to hold on to the last shred of his control. Need drove him on, and suddenly, all the hours, all the days, all the weeks and months of waiting came together with a driving force that literally pounded through him with the need to make her his.

He tore the foil package open with his teeth. Seconds later, he rose up before her and guided her legs apart. She wrapped her legs around him, and pressed a kiss to his shoulder as he found his way to her.

Cori felt her body give in places she hadn't felt in a long, long time. Her own gasp filled her ears, but it was Travis who filled her senses. Her eyes drifted shut and a throaty sound drifted from her lips. It had been so long since she'd known the security of her parents' love. Now she knew she'd never have it again. But she loved the man in her arms, and felt loved by him in return. Her senses reeled with that knowledge, her body quaking with sensation.

Travis started to move, and everything changed. Her breasts tingled against his hair-roughened chest, and of its own will, her body began to writhe. As he increased the tempo, her hips rose up to meet him. A long time ago she'd made love, but she'd never experienced anything like this. This pleasure was pure, explosive. She whispered his name; he answered with hers. Her passion grew stronger, and so did his. Tremors began low in her body, ebbing and flowing, until they consumed her.

Travis felt his control slipping. He increased the tempo, Cori's cries of release all it took to send him with her beyond the point of no return and into a place that seemed to be made for them alone.

Thunder rumbled outside, the sound matching the blood pounding in his ears. His movements gradually slowed, then stilled. He opened his eyes, and found himself gazing into hers. He rolled to his side and pulled her close, waiting for his heart rate to return to normal.

She rested her cheek on his chest, his hand softly stroking her smooth arm. After several minutes, she asked, "What are you thinking?"

How many times had a woman asked him that question? How many times had his mind scrambled for an answer? For the first time in his life, the question didn't make him flounder. For the first time in his life, he knew the answer.

"I was thinking that you're incredible."

Lightning flashed, momentarily illuminating the room. She raised her head to look at him, tender thoughts shaping her smile. It nearly took his breath away, and made him smile in return.

He skimmed a finger over the pearly earring dangling from her ear. In a voice that was oddly soft and reverent, he said, "When I was watching the breeze flutter through the strands of your hair earlier, I wanted to untwist the rest and watch it fall around your shoulders. I just realized that I never quite got around to doing it."

She raised up on one elbow, winsomely reaching a hand to her hair. There was a quiet click as she removed a large barrette. A few shakes of her head sent her hair cascading down around her shoulders, just as it had in his imagination. However, his imagination hadn't prepared him for the slow, thickening sensation that was starting low in his body all over again.

"Ah, Cori?" he asked.

"Hmm?" she replied, slowly moving so that her hair brushed along his chest and shoulder.

"Do you have any idea what you're doing to me?"

She arched her eyebrows and slanted him a purely feminine look. He sucked in a quick breath and laughed out loud. Corinna Cassidy knew exactly what she was doing. Oh, yes indeed.

Before things got out of control, he slid from the bed and disposed of the condom, reaching for his wallet for another. She lithely shimmied under the covers, a knowing smile pulling at the corners of her mouth.

"Do you always carry two, Travis?"

He crawled into bed beside her and slid his fingers into her hair. Looking directly into her eyes, he said, "Sometime I'll tell you just how long it's been since I've needed one of these, let alone two."

"Then it's been a long time for you, too?" she asked in a whisper-soft voice.

"I thought it was because I was in a slump. Now I know I was just waiting for you."

She stroked him, the butterfly touch of her fingertips sending a different rhythm through his body. His gaze made a slow climb up her lush curves to the softness of her gaze. Feeling himself surge beneath her hand, he pressed a kiss to her lips, and he could wait no longer. His desire kicked like a jackhammer, anticipation racing through his bloodstream all over again. He lowered her back to the mattress, and began to make love to her a second time.

She kissed his neck, his chin, the sensitive spot beneath his ear. On a laugh that was as melodious as a song, she said, "You're definitely over your mid-life slump."

He was growing accustomed to grinning at the drop of a hat, but he doubted he'd ever get used to the love that filled his chest to the point of bursting. Capturing her hand in his, he said, "That's what I've been trying to tell you."

She laughed again, and Travis knew it was one sound he'd never grow tired of. His thoughts became hazy and languid, his body warm and sure. He would have liked to give her moonbeams and starlight. Since he couldn't give her those things, he'd give her everything else, everything that made him whole.

Suddenly, the night felt infinitely young, and so did he.

Cori came awake gradually, as if she were drifting back to earth in layers. She became aware of a delicious smell, and slowly opened her eyes. Before she knew why she was smiling, she stretched her leg toward the other side of the bed and rolled over.

In the time it took her to realize that that side of the bed was empty, she recognized the aroma wafting to her nose. Her smile broadened, and she flung back the covers and slid her feet to the floor.

Someone was frying bacon, and she knew who that someone was.

She took her robe from the closet and made a quick stop in the bathroom. Excitement lengthened her stride as she hurried toward the kitchen, her robe flying out behind her. She paused in the doorway, a wondrous grin pulling at her lips.

Travis was moving about her kitchen, opening and closing cupboard doors and clinking silverware, generally making the noise of ten men. His slacks were slung low on his hips, clinging to the delectable curve of his backside that she now knew intimately well. His shirt was tucked in but unbuttoned, the tiny glimpse she had of bare pectoral muscles sending memories cascading through her mind.

He turned, and found her watching him. His eyes swept over her approvingly, his chin coming down at a lofty angle. "I hope you like your bacon crispy."

Matching his lofty expression, she strode into the room and said, "I think you know exactly what I like."

Travis still wasn't quite accustomed to that touch of haughtiness lurking in Cori's voice and eyes. That didn't mean he didn't like it. Oh, how he liked it. He'd known they shared an intense physical awareness of each other from the first moment they met. Now he knew they had a great deal more in common than physical desire, although that in itself was pretty damned amazing.

He'd awakened early, staring at the ceiling as the room slowly grew lighter with the dawn of a new day. He'd been concerned about how Cori would react to him in the morning. He'd never intended to make love last night and was worried about how she'd feel when she realized she'd broken her pact with Allison. He could see no evidence of self-recriminations of any kind in her eyes this morning. Either she wasn't upset about what had happened between them last night, or she had forgotten the pact.

He removed the pan from the burner, trying to decide how to broach the subject. Striding ever closer, she beat him to a different topic. "I knew you were a genius with a hammer and saw, but I never pictured you with a spatula in your hand. That bacon smells wonderful, so you must know your way around a frying pan."

He slapped a blue kitchen towel over his shoulder and said, "I woke up starving and since we both have to work this morning, I decided to fix you breakfast. I didn't find any eggs or pancake mix, so bacon and toast is going to have to do."

"I make pancakes from scratch, but if you'd like, I could get dressed and go borrow a few eggs from Ivy."

"To tell you the truth, Cori, I'd rather you never got dressed again."

"Never?" she asked, her eyes turning three shades darker than her long, blue robe.

The sun was shining this morning, filtering through the window over the sink. In the light of day, the freckles on her nose were visible. Her face looked clean-scrubbed, her hair freshly brushed. He had a sudden hankering to run his fingers through it the way he had last night.

Taking the few remaining steps separating them, he said, "If I had more of those little contraptions in my wallet, I'd prove it to you."

She blushed, and then she laughed. The next thing he knew, she was in his arms, turning her face into his neck, smoothing her hands around his back. He closed his eyes and breathed in her fresh scent.

"You smell like a garden of flowers in a morning mist," he whispered huskily.

"It's my shampoo," she answered, smiling.

Inhaling deeply, he said, "Uh-uh. This scent couldn't come from any bottle. This is all you."

"I told Allison the same thing a few weeks ago."

Allison.

Cori felt herself straighten. In the blink of an eye, the sequence of events that had brought her to this moment flashed through her mind. The door opened behind her. Turning at the sound, she watched as Allison stepped into the kitchen.

Her daughter cast a fleeting glance from Travis to Cori. Her hair was mussed, her eyes puffy.

"Honey, what is it?" Cori asked in that mother-soft voice she used when she knew Allison was hurting.

Allison's face crumbled, and she made a beeline straight into Cori's arms.

Chapter Fourteen

Cori wrapped her arms around her daughter the way she had when Allison was small and her feelings had been hurt or her knees scraped. She didn't know what was wrong this time. She only knew that Allison's heart seemed to be breaking.

Smoothing her hand over her little girl's wavy hair, she whispered unintelligible words of comfort. "Shh, it's all right. I'm here."

"I'm so sorry, Mom."

"What is it, Allison? What happened last night at Heather's?"

Allison seemed to be trying to slow down her flow of tears. She straightened her shoulders and took a shuddering breath. Raising her head, she whispered, "Promise you won't hate me?"

Cori's misgivings were growing by the second. After casting a quick glance at Travis, she turned her attention back to Allison. Keeping her eyes level and her voice steady, she said, "There's nothing you could ever do to make me hate you, kiddo. Nothing, do you understand?"

Allison finally looked at her, her bloodshot eyes brimming with emotion. "I lied to you."

Holding her daughter's gaze, Cori quietly said, "The sooner you tell me what it is, the sooner we can deal with it."

Allison glanced shyly at Travis, then down at the toe of her shoe. "I told you I was spending the night at Heather's house. But I didn't. I went home with Ross."

Cori felt an instant squeezing hurt. "Were his parents home?"

Allison shook her head without looking up.

"Are you all right?" Cori finally whispered.

Allison's eyes flew to hers. Within seconds, tears were running unchecked down her young face again. "I don't know if I'm all right. I don't know if I'm ever going to be all right again."

Cori had never felt so ill-equipped to deal with any situation in her life. With thoughts spinning through her mind, she opened her mouth to speak, but her throat had closed up and she had to try again. "Do you want to talk about it?" she whispered.

"Ross broke up with me."

For a moment, Cori wasn't sure she'd heard correctly. It certainly wasn't what she'd expected Allison to say.

"He what?" she asked.

"He broke up with me."

"But why?"

"Because I didn't want...because I wouldn't...I just couldn't, you know? I just couldn't."

Relief swept through Cori with so much force it nearly buckled her knees. "Oh, Allison. Do you mean you didn't make love, didn't..." This time it was Cori's voice that trailed away.

Allison shook her head. Swiping at her tears with the back of her hand, she said, "I wasn't ready. I guess our pact still stands, huh?"

Cori felt the blood drain out of her face. Realization dawned, and with it came such pain, such a sense of failure it was all she could do to hold her head up.

You're weak of the flesh, Corinna. Weak. You've made your bed, now lie in it. The memory of her mother's voice had never been more clear, or so cutting.

Travis had stood as still as possible, trying to blend in with the background so that mother and daughter could talk. He'd heard every word they said, and he knew the exact instant Cori's worry turned to guilt. Her eyes flew open and her face became pale.

On a shuddering breath, Allison quietly asked, "Will you ever be able to forgive me for lying to you?"

Travis knew he should leave so Cori and Allison could talk in private, but he was afraid that if he did, Cori would be lost to him forever. She'd convince herself that what they had was over, or worse, that it never should have happened.

"I'm proud of you for being so strong, for using such good judgment, and for standing up for what you believe in. I don't deserve a daughter like you."

Cori's voice sounded hollow, as if she'd searched her soul and didn't like what she found. Allison's face nearly crumbled all over again. Travis didn't know how either one of them managed to hold on to their composure.

Allison glanced at her watch and said, "I have to wash my face and change my clothes and then I have to go to school. My final exam is today."

"Are you sure you're up to it?" Cori asked.

Allison shrugged, then met Travis's gaze.

He stepped forward, speaking for the first time since the girl had arrived home. "Allison only thinks she isn't good at math. She knows angles and triangles inside and out, don't you, kid?''

With a sense of conviction he was coming to recognize as part of her personality, she gave him a wavering smile, then turned her attention back to her mother. ''Ross dropped me off at Heather's house around two, and I finally fell asleep a little after four, so I got a little rest. If I miss this exam I'll have to retake the entire class, and I really, really don't want to do that.''

After a long moment of silence, she added, ''I thought Ross loved me.''

''Maybe he does, in his own way,'' Cori answered.

''Not enough to wait for me.''

''Oh, honey, I'm sorry you're hurting.''

''Am I going to be grounded forever?''

Travis thought Cori was going to break down then and there. Instead, she folded her arms at her ribs and somehow found her voice. ''I don't want you to worry about that now. Try to concentrate on geometry for the rest of the morning, okay?''

Allison spun away to the other side of the room. At the doorway, she turned around again, saying, ''Mom? You really are the greatest.'' Moments later, a door clicked shut down the hall.

Travis saw Cori's eyes close. He wanted to take her into his arms, but she didn't look ready for that. He shortened the distance between them. Stopping little more than one step away from her he quietly said, ''She's quite a girl, isn't she?''

Cori's head came up slowly, and he didn't like what he saw in her eyes. She strode to the table where she picked up the letter from her parents. ''I broke my pact, my promise to her. My parents are right about me. They've always been right.''

Travis felt his blood begin to do a slow boil. He paced to the table where she was standing, tried to speak, then paced to the other side of the room. "How can you say that?"

"Actions have a way of speaking for themselves."

"Cori, look at me, talk to me."

That stubborn expression came over her. Her chin came up and her shoulders went back. "I think you should leave."

Before he could argue, the phone jangled. No sooner had Cori replaced the receiver when it rang again. The first time was Ivy checking to make sure Cori was all right, and the second was Braden, who was doing everything in his power to hold down the fort, so to speak, but was reaching the end of his rope.

By the time Travis hung up the phone, Allison was back in the kitchen. Since it was obvious that she and Cori had more to say to each other, he took a fortifying breath and headed for the door. With one hand on the doorknob, he turned, and found both Cassidy women watching him.

"I have to get down to the office. Good luck on your geometry exam, Allison. I know you can do it."

"Thanks, Travis."

His gaze homed in on Cori and he said, "I'll be back later this morning. We'll talk then."

"I'm going to have a busy day and really don't know where I'll be later this morning."

He felt his eyes narrow, but he didn't care. "Don't worry," he said ominously. "I'll find you."

Without another word, he strode through the door.

Travis pulled into the small lot and quickly came to a stop. His Jeep was sitting at a cockeyed angle, but he was in too big a hurry to care. He couldn't remember the last time a morning had gone so awry. It should have been the best day of his life. After all, he'd fallen asleep last night with the woman he loved in his arms. That particular woman happened to be as stubborn as the day was long.

Earlier, Ross had shown up at the Northwood office downtown to collect his pay for building the gazebo. He'd hemmed and hawed for a few minutes, and then he'd said, "Allison and I broke up."

Travis had planned to give the kid a piece of his mind, but the boy looked haggard, upset. "I love her, man. But I'm seventeen. What am I supposed to do, wait until I'm thirty?" he'd said, his voice cracking on the last word.

Travis had handed the boy his money and shrugged. He wouldn't want to be a kid again for anything in the world.

After Ross left, Travis and Braden had straightened out a problem with an order, calmed an irate customer, and hired another carpenter. Then he'd climbed into his dusty Jeep and drove straight to Ivy's Garden.

He happened to love Corinna Cassidy. And if she thought he was going to let the best thing that had ever happened to him slip right through his fingers, she could think again.

If he knew Cori, she'd be doing everything in her power to keep herself so busy she wouldn't have time to think. Unless he missed his guess, she'd be doing it inside the inn. He marched straight to the back step and yanked on the door.

The sounds of women's laughter carried to his ears, followed by a hearty guffaw that sounded familiar. By the time his eyes had adjusted to the dim interior, he found four pairs of eyes on him like glue—Ivy's, Jillian's, Lisa's, and Braden's uncle.

"Artie?" he asked incredulously.

"Hi, Travis, ol' boy," Artie replied. "I'm probably the last person you expected to see here, huh?"

Travis glanced at Lisa and Jillian, who wore matching smiles, and at Ivy, whose eyes sparkled with a new light. "It's all right, Travis," she said with quiet dignity. "I invited Arthur over for brunch this morning."

"Ivy here is a fine cook, a fine woman," Artie declared.

Ivy grinned like a schoolgirl and said, "His name means 'noble hero,' you know," as if that explained everything.

"That's nice," he said distractedly. "Where's Cori?"

"She's cleaning the Morning Glory Room on the third floor. You can go ahead and go on up if you'd like. It's the first room on the..."

By the time Ivy finished, Travis had cleared the top landing. He strode down the second-story hall and continued on to the stairway that led up to the top floor. From there, he followed the whir of a vacuum cleaner.

Without waiting for her to notice his presence, he yanked out the plug and faced her, all in one motion. Striding ominously closer, he said firmly, "You listen here, Corinna Cassidy. You are the most stubborn woman I've ever met, but you're also everything I thought I'd never find. You're funny and warm and beautiful and bright and passionate."

"Travis, I..."

"Yes. Passionate," he cut in. "And for your information, you're the best mother that girl of yours could ever ask for. And another..."

"That's what Allison said this morning."

"...thing, I happen to love you... What did you say?"

She raised her haughty little chin and skirted the edge of the bed. For some reason, Travis's mouth went dry.

"Allison said the same thing a little while ago when she got back from summer school. I told her everything, and she..."

"You told her everything?" he cut in. "Even..."

"The part about us making love?" she asked before he could finish. "I didn't go into detail, but yes, I even told her about that."

Cori walked toward him, her steps purposefully slow, her eyes never leaving his face. It was so like Travis to come bursting into the room and proclaim his love for her as if he wanted her to make something of it. Well, she planned to make something of it, all right.

She'd poured all her energy into the tasks in the inn this morning. No matter how hard she'd worked, she couldn't get one incredibly rugged carpenter out of her mind. Nearly every conversation she'd ever had with him had replayed through her mind. Nearly every touch of his hand, fleeting and otherwise, had played over her senses.

She wasn't proud of the fact that she hadn't kept up her end of her pact with her daughter, but she was learning to forgive herself. She'd shown the letter she'd received from Green Bay to Allison. Her little girl shook her head and said, "You're a better parent than they could ever dream of being."

Ivy had sniffled when she read it. Lisa and Jillian weren't nearly so kind. They'd sputtered up a blue streak, calling her parents every name in the book. And then they'd accepted her exactly as she was, just as they always had. In that instant, Cori had realized that she'd been chasing a pipe dream. She'd wanted to be a part of her family, when her real family had been right here all along.

It had taken Travis Delaney's steadfastness and stubbornness to open her eyes. He'd swept her off her feet the first time she met him. It was about time she returned the favor.

"Er, what did Allison say when you told her?" he asked, looking decidedly ill at ease.

Walking ever closer, she replied, "She wrinkled up her nose and said, 'Eeew,' and then she asked when I'm going to make an honest man out of you."

Late-morning sunlight filtered through the lacy curtains behind Cori, seeming to cast the entire room in a warm glow. Nothing she said should have been lust arousing, yet Travis's desire for this woman had never been stronger. Now that he knew her intimately, he wanted her all the more.

She seemed to know what she was doing to him. Rather than looking embarrassed, she raised her chin and met his gaze, proudly serene, infinitely feminine. It wasn't easy to think clearly when she turned all that intensity on him, so he let his instincts rule. His hands settled to his hips and a grin befitting the most arrogant of men settled to his mouth.

"And just how do you plan to do that?" he asked, his voice dipping low.

"I thought I'd marry you."

She was in his arms in a heartbeat. Her head tipped back as he swung her off her feet, her laughter stealing his breath away.

"Does that mean yes?" she asked.

"Oh, yes," he answered, lowering his face to hers. "That definitely means yes."

"I love you, Travis," she whispered when the kiss ended.

"And I love you, Corinna. I meant to tell you last night, but I ended up showing you, instead. From now on, I intend to do both."

With her face only inches from his, she stared into his eyes. She recognized the haughtiness in his expression, but she was coming to recognize the sincerity as well.

He'd given her something important last night. But he'd been giving her something even more incredible for weeks. Every time he'd kissed her, every time he'd laughed with her, every time he'd touched her, allowing her to set the pace, he'd given her back a part of herself she'd lost a long time ago. Her self-esteem, her self-worth, and the realization that she *wasn't* weak in the flesh. Ivy had been telling her that for years. It had taken Travis to make her believe.

Smiling, she whispered. "I think Ivy's sweet on your Uncle Artie. Allison's growing up, and Lisa and Jillian are talking about moving to South Dakota."

"That's only a few states away," he said softly.

"I know. There's something else that's changed this summer. I found you, Travis, and that's the best change of all."

With her words sending a pulsing sensation through his body, he set her on her feet and slowly looked around. Pale blue morning glories were stenciled near the ceiling all around the room. The curtains and bedspread were made of a fabric in muted shades of cream and blue, so that the air itself appeared to take on a similar hue.

"So this is the Morning Glory Room," he said.

"My favorite room in the inn," she answered.

Travis remembered the first time she'd told him that. She'd been showing him the inn that Sunday nearly a month and a half ago. A strange longing to see this room had come over him that day. Today the longing was much, much stronger, but it had nothing to do with the room.

"When were you thinking of marrying me?" he asked, pressing his forehead to hers.

"I'd like it to be soon."

"Good. Now, why don't you show me exactly what it is you find so fascinating about this particular room."

"I'd love to."

He reached for her top button.

"Right after the wedding," she whispered, stilling his fingers.

"After the wedding?"

When she nodded, he groaned out loud.

"I guess if I'm going to be a father to Allison, I might as well start setting a good example."

"I think you're going to be a wonderful father," she murmured.

"It isn't going to be easy," he insisted. "Because every time you kiss me I feel eighteen."

She pulled away from him slightly, and looked into his eyes. "If you think you feel young now, just wait until your fortieth birthday. By then, there very well could be a little Delaney in the family."

Travis's mouth dropped open. "A little Delaney?"

"I've always wanted another baby, but this time, I'd like to have the man I love at my side."

"I like the sound of that," he declared.

"Travis, I think there's something you should know."

"What's that?"

"When I was a little girl, I always dreamed of having four children."

He growled deep in his throat and fitted her more tightly to his body. "Now I know I've created a monster."

"So have I," she murmured. "So have I."

When she started to laugh, he lowered his mouth to hers, capturing her lips, her laughter and her love.

* * * * *

COMING NEXT MONTH

HONEYMOON HOTLINE
Christine Rimmer

That Special Woman!

Talk-show host Nevada Jones was good at dispensing advice
to the lovelorn—only now she needs guidance herself, because
masterful Chase McQuaid is used to getting what he
wants—and now that includes Nevada!

MAKING MEMORIES
Ann Howard White

The sudden amnesia chilled her blood...she found herself
dressed as a prostitute, lying in a disreputable alley and
straddled by a devastating, leather-clad stranger. Who was
she? Who was he—a saviour or a threat?

AFTER THAT NIGHT...
Helen R. Myers

In the rearview mirror Jordan Mills watched the man behind her.
He drew down his sunglasses just enough to see her...and for her
to see him. Would she ever forget that shocking night in
Memphis with *him*...Stone Demarest?

COMING NEXT MONTH

MARRIAGE MINDED
Kayla Daniels

Rugged bad boy Ryder Sloan was back—with only one thing on his mind for Sara Monahan: *marriage*! But Sara was no longer the innocent girl who'd once fallen so foolishly in love. She was a single mother, with two little ones to protect...

THE CASE OF THE ACCIDENTAL HEIRESS
Victoria Pade

Strummel Investigations

Virile Logan Strummel thought his new client Maggie Morgan was simply nuts—or about to pull off an incredible scam! How could Maggie Morgan expect him to believe that she had been switched—heart and soul—into another woman's body?

MACKENZIE'S BABY
Anne McAllister

Nothing in Carter MacKenzie's life was going according to plan—certainly not his involvement with Annabel Archer's kids nor his sudden acquisition of a baby! But Carter could cope with anything—apart from kissing Annabel!

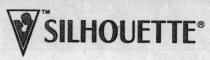

Bestselling author of *Romancing the Stone*
and *Jewel of the Nile*

CATHERINE LANIGAN

DANGEROUS LOVE

ONE MAN, THREE WOMEN

Richard Bartlow was a man people noticed. He
was ruthless when he needed to be and sincere
when he wanted. He was sexy, ambitious and
charming. And he was dangerous. Three women
knew only too well *how* dangerous.

*"Lanigan succeeds in spinning a highly suspenseful,
romantic tale."*

—Publisher's Weekly

**AVAILABLE IN PAPERBACK
FROM JANUARY 1997**

LINDA HOWARD

New York Times **bestselling author**

Against the Rules

An intoxicating love story full of passion and humour

At seventeen, Cathryn Ashe has fought Rule Jackson and lost. If she lost this time Rule would take more than her innocence...

"You can't read just one Linda Howard!"
—bestselling author Catherine Coulter

"Howard's writing is compelling."
—Publishers Weekly

AVAILABLE IN PAPERBACK FROM JANUARY 1997

"Mortimer has a special magic."
—Romantic Times

CAROLE MORTIMER

*Their tempestuous night held a
magic all its own...and only she
could mend his shattered dreams*

Merlyn's Magic

**AVAILABLE IN PAPERBACK
FROM FEBRUARY 1997**

New York Times **bestselling author**

JAYNE ANN KRENTZ

Legacy

A story of two unlikely lovers

Honor Mayfield thought that her chance
meeting with Conn Landry was a stroke of
luck. Too late she realised she was falling for
someone who was seeking to avenge a legacy
of murder and betrayal.

"A master of the genre...nobody does it better!"
—Romantic Times

**AVAILABLE IN PAPERBACK
FROM FEBRUARY 1997**

LAURA VAN WORMER

✦

JURY DUTY

Dubbed the 'Poor Little Rich Boy' case,
this notorious trial will change forever the
lives of the twelve New York City
residents called to the jury.

*"A legal three-ring circus with brains and
wit, populated with colorful New Yorkers of
every stripe and class"*
—Kirkus Reviews

**AVAILABLE IN PAPERBACK
FROM FEBRUARY 1997**

FREE!

FOUR FREE
specially selected
Special Edition™ novels
__PLUS__ a Mystery Gift
when you return this card...

Return this coupon and we'll send you 4 Silhouette Special Edition® novels and a mystery gift absolutely FREE! We'll even pay the postage and packing for you.

We're making you this offer to introduce you to the benefits of the Reader Service™– FREE home delivery of brand-new Silhouette novels, at least a month before they are available in the shops, FREE gifts and a monthly Newsletter packed with information, competitions, author pages and lots more...

Accepting these FREE books and gift places you under no obligation to buy, you may cancel at any time, even after receiving just your free shipment. Simply complete the coupon below and send it to:

THE READER SERVICE, FREEPOST, CROYDON, SURREY, CR9 3WZ.

EIRE READERS PLEASE SEND COUPON TO: P.O. BOX 4546, DUBLIN 24.

NO STAMP NEEDED

Yes, please send me 4 free Special Edition novels and a mystery gift. I understand that unless you hear from me, I will receive 6 superb new titles every month for just £2.40* each, postage and packing free. I am under no obligation to purchase any books and I may cancel or suspend my subscription at any time, but the free books and gift will be mine to keep in any case. (I am over 18 years of age)

E7XE

Ms/Mrs/Miss/Mr _____
BLOCK CAPS PLEASE

Address _____

_____

_____ Postcode _____

RACHEL LEE

◆

A FATEFUL CHOICE

**She arranged her own death—
then changed her mind**

*"Ms Lee's talents as a writer are
dazzling. Put this author's name on
your list of favourites right now!"*
—Romantic Times

MIRA®

AVAILABLE IN PAPERBACK
FROM MARCH 1997